She'd never gott that before

She'd never touched any that.

She never thought she could.

Fingertips tracing the angles and dipping into the contours of his rugged face. Julia's palms receiving a jillion little jolts of electricity as she rubbed them along his beard.

Nothing in her limited experience had ever made her so aware of a man.

In last night's brief, charged moments with Mac, something inside her had awakened. All her school-girl dreams of what it might be like to be truly intimate with a man had escaped the little Pandora's box she kept tightly locked deep inside her heart. That little locked box had saved her from humiliation more times than she cared to remember.

I'm thinking of you as a woman, he'd said.

Well, she was certainly thinking of him as a man....

Dear Harlequin Intrigue Reader,

Cupid's bow is loaded at Harlequin Intrigue with four fabulous stories of breathtaking romantic suspense—starting with the continuation of Cassie Miles's COLORADO SEARCH AND RESCUE miniseries. In *Wedding Captives*, lovers reunite on a mountaintop… unfortunately they're also snowbound with a madman!

And there's no better month to launch our new modern gothic continuity series MORIAH'S LANDING. Amanda Stevens emerges from the New England fog with *Secret Sanctuary*, the first of four titles coming out over the next several months. You can expect all of the classic themes you love in these stories, plus more of the contemporary edge you've come to expect from our brand of romantic suspense.

You know what can happen *In the Blink of an Eye*…? Julie Miller does! And you can find out, too, in the next installment of her TAYLOR CLAN series.

Finally, Jean Barrett takes you to New Orleans for some *Private Investigations* with battling P.I.'s. It's a regular showdown in the French Quarter—where absolutely anything goes.

So celebrate Valentine's Day with the most confounding mystery of all…that of the heart.

Deep, rich chocolate wishes,

Denise O'Sullivan
Associate Senior Editor
Harlequin Intrigue

IN THE BLINK
OF AN EYE
JULIE MILLER

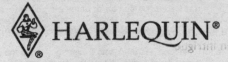

HARLEQUIN®

TORONTO • NEW YORK • LONDON
AMSTERDAM • PARIS • SYDNEY • HAMBURG
STOCKHOLM • ATHENS • TOKYO • MILAN • MADRID
PRAGUE • WARSAW • BUDAPEST • AUCKLAND

ISBN 0-373-22651-9

IN THE BLINK OF AN EYE

Copyright © 2002 by Julie Miller

This edition published by arrangement with Harlequin Books S.A.

® and TM are trademarks of the publisher. Trademarks indicated with ® are registered in the United States Patent and Trademark Office, the Canadian Trade Marks Office and in other countries.

Visit us at www.eHarlequin.com

Printed in U.S.A.

ABOUT THE AUTHOR

Julie Miller attributes her passion for writing romance to all those fairy tales she read growing up, and shyness. Encouragement from her family to write down all those feelings she couldn't express became a love for the written word. She gets continued support from her fellow members of the Prairieland Romance Writers, where she serves as the resident "grammar goddess." This award-winning author and teacher has published several paranormal romances. Inspired by the likes of Agatha Christie and Encyclopedia Brown, Ms. Miller believes the only thing better than a good mystery is a good romance.

Born and raised in Missouri, she now lives in Nebraska with her husband, son and smiling guard dog, Maxie. Write to Julie at P.O. Box 5162, Grand Island, NE 68802-5162.

Books by Julie Miller

HARLEQUIN INTRIGUE
588—ONE GOOD MAN*
619—SUDDEN ENGAGEMENT*
642—SECRET AGENT HEIRESS
651—IN THE BLINK OF AN EYE*

*The Taylor Clan

THE TAYLOR CLAN

Sid and Martha Taylor: butcher and homemaker
ages 63 and 62
respectively

Brett Taylor: contractor
age 38
the protector

Mac Taylor: forensic specialist
age 37
the professor

Gideon Taylor: firefighter/arson investigator
age 35
the crusader

Cole Taylor: the mysterious brother
(the family's not quite sure
what kind of work he does—
undercover)
age 30
the lost soul

Jessie Taylor: the lone daughter
antiques dealer/buyer/restorer
age 29
the survivor

Josh Taylor: police officer
age 27
at 6'3", he's still the baby of
the family
the charmer

Mitch Taylor: Sid's nephew—raised like a
son
police captain
age 39
the chief

CAST OF CHARACTERS

MacKinley Taylor—His brilliant mind and legendary control can't help him see. But they might help him see the truth.

Julia Dalton—How far will she go to help a childhood hero? She's willing to risk her life—but does she dare risk her heart?

Jeff Ringlein—Mac's protégé. Just who was he afraid of?

Melanie Ringlein—How much does a public servant's pension pay, anyway?

Inspector Joe Niederhaus—An Internal Affairs investigator due to receive his gold watch. He plans to get his man one last time. Even if it's the wrong one.

Inspector Eli Masterson—Joe's partner. This Internal Affairs man has learned from the best. But who is receiving the benefit of his inside information?

Wade Osterman—A uniformed police officer with a bad habit of betting on the games.

Arnie Sanchez—Missing evidence would get his case dismissed.

Martha Taylor—Meddling mother #1. Is this matchmaker in over her head, trying to rescue her second son?

Barbara Dalton—Meddling mother #2. She is only trying to help her daughter.

Mitch Taylor—There's a cover-up going on in his precinct. Is the traitor's identity closer to home than he realizes?

For Scott and Ryne

Prologue

Mac Taylor adjusted his gold-rimmed glasses on the bridge of his nose and studied the slim band of light beneath the door to the Fourth Precinct Crime Lab. He glanced at his watch to check the time again. 1:13 a.m. A shuffle of movement drew his focus back to the door at the end of the hallway opposite his office.

"I thought I was the one married to my job." Who would be in the lab at this hour? As sure and even as his footsteps down the deserted corridor, his mind clicked with possibilities.

Custodian? No. They weren't allowed in the lab itself. Thief? In a police building with officers on duty twenty-four hours a day just one floor down? Not likely. Technician? The Fourth was a satellite unit that kept regular office hours. Only the main lab south of town stayed open around the clock.

With the possibilities systematically rejected, only one option remained. Trouble.

Tucking the manila envelope with the technical data he carried under his arm, he turned the knob and opened the door, identifying the intruder before he allowed himself to be heard.

"Jeff?"

His quiet voice startled the ponytailed chemist in the

white lab coat. Jeff Ringlein hunched his compact shoulders over the stainless-steel counter, righting the instrument tray he'd hit with his elbow.

"Mac." His hands stilled their work, but he didn't turn around. "You're here late."

"So are you." Mac strolled over to the center table, his long legs giving him an easy stride that belied the eagle-sharp observation of eyes that missed nothing.

A Bunsen burner on steady heat. An assortment of liquids in beakers. An open evidence bag, its label written in his own illegible scrawl. One of the perks of working as a forensic pathologist for the Kansas City Police Department was that he could delegate routine tests to a staff lab tech, and concentrate on assessing the crime scene and piecing together the entire case.

He didn't recall this particular assignment.

"You on to something interesting?" he asked. Jeff had been right out of college when he started at the lab. Though technically proficient, he lacked the instincts to make his investigative work anything more than routine. His eagerness to please, though, had ingratiated him to his co-workers and earned a bit of indulgent patience from Mac.

So his rushed, toneless answer sounded perfectly normal. "I'm running a dye test."

Mac eyed the twist of threads lying inside the bag, then surveyed the counter once more.

No microscope. How did he expect to ID the sample without one?

Mac leaned his hip against the table, banking his inquisitive nature in an effort to put Jeff at ease. "I don't think the criminals will overrun the city if we knock off and get a few hours of sleep now and then."

Jeff finally turned, but his dark-eyed gaze never quite met Mac's. "What are you doing here?"

Fair question. "I'm testifying at Ned Prosky's hearing later this morning. I wanted to double-check my facts."

"He's the alleged hit man?"

"Yeah. If I can put him at the scene of the crime, we can at least nail him for accessory. Dwight Powers is going after him as the trigger man, though."

Jeff's chin sank to his chest at the mention of the assistant district attorney's name. He returned to his work. "Powers is pretty ruthless. Think you'll win the case?"

Mac shrugged. He loved the immutable laws of science, the simplicity of seeing facts in black and white. But he accepted that most of the world evaluated things in shades of gray. "I just interpret the data. The rest is up to Dwight and the jury."

"Yeah, well, good luck."

"Thanks." Mac shifted his weight onto both feet and fished in the pocket of his jeans for his keys. "Look. Whatever I gave you to do can wait until morning. Knock off and go home."

"I will. As soon as I get this cleaned up. Good night."

The anxious farewell pricked Mac's curiosity even more than the incomplete experiment setup. "Everything okay?"

"Fine." Jeff opened the cabinet above his workstation and lifted the box where samples were stored. Maybe he'd screwed up a test earlier, and was here to rerun it without the teasing of his fellow technicians. Mac's prying wouldn't help get the guy home to his wife any faster.

Mac squeezed the envelope in his hand. His company tonight would be printouts of DNA strands and microfibers. Jeff had a flesh-and-blood woman waiting for him. He couldn't blame the guy for being impatient.

"Be careful, then." He headed out the door, his curiosity unappeased, but his confidence in his staff intact.

That's when the smell hit him. The sharp sting of mismatched chemicals stung his nose and made his eyes water. "Jeff, what are you...?"

Startled by Mac's reappearance, Jeff lurched. A beaker flew from his hand and shattered on the countertop. "Leave me alone!"

When he spun around to confront Mac, his elbow hit the Bunsen burner and toppled it.

"Kill the flame!" Mac ordered. His report flew into the air as he snatched the fire extinguisher by the door and dashed across the room.

"Just let me do my job." Jeff's hand curled into a fist. He cocked his arm back to take a swing at Mac. Mac ducked, but avoiding the flying fist wasn't necessary. Jeff froze, halfway through the roundhouse punch, and stared at the wisps of flame consuming the sleeve of his white lab coat. "Oh my God—"

"Move!" Mac pulled the trigger and doused Jeff's arm with the suffocating foam. "Get out of here!" He nodded over his shoulder and turned the extinguisher on the counter. "What the hell...?"

Mac shoved his fingers beneath his glasses to wipe the burning film clouding his eyes, and looked at the counter a second time to be sure his vision wasn't playing tricks on him. An assortment of plastic evidence bags floated in a pool of clear amber liquid inside the metal tray. "It's all contaminated."

Destroying evidence.

Incompetence? Or sabotage?

Acting on instincts ingrained more deeply than self-preservation, Mac reached for the bags. Hair, filaments, cloth, fingernails and more—he rescued them from the toxic pool and tossed them aside.

He saved two, five, six bags before the sharp thwack at the base of his skull knocked him, belly first, onto the counter. An explosion of fireworks shot through his brain.

He staggered to his feet and turned to see the missing microscope—raised high in Jeff's fist, ready to strike again.

Mac reached behind him for the first available weapon to defend himself against the unexpected attack. His fingers touched the metal tray. He gripped it in his fist and slung it straight at Jeff's face.

The flying steel knocked him back a step. But the corrosive liquid that splattered across his face proved even more effective. The microscope crashed to the floor as Jeff doubled over, clutching at his face and screaming in pain.

"What the hell were you thinking?" Slightly breathless from the combination of poisonous fumes and the blow to the head, Mac staggered over to Jeff and turned him toward the door and fresh air. "Let's get out of here."

"You can't know." Jeff wheezed through the stinging pain. "He'll hurt Melanie."

"Who?" Mac recognized the name of Jeff's wife, but the plea made no sense.

"I have to do my job." Jeff shoved Mac into the wall and swayed back to the counter.

Mac followed a step behind.

A step too late.

Jeff hit a switch, pulled a lighter from his pocket, and click...

The gas from the Bunsen exploded into a fireball.

The toxic air ignited, consumed Jeff in its fiery claws. The names on the plastic bags shrivelled and died as they melted into a puddle. Like relentless, grasping hands, the flames reached out for their next victim.

Mac backpedaled his feet and tried to retreat.

But the shockwave tossed him across the room and slammed him into the wall. The impact of shattered glass and scorching metal pierced his skin like gunfire.

Those immutable laws of science followed their true nature, and plunged Mac into oblivion.

Chapter One

Six Weeks Later

"What have you gotten me into this time?"

Julia Dalton paused at the threshold of the sturdy rock house and held her breath. Literally.

Nestled among two-story relics from the 1920s, the high ceilings and oak floors spoke of the leftover charm of this once-wealthy neighborhood near the Kansas City Museum. But this sweet little cottage just northeast of the Market area where she grew up had lost something over the years. What time and urban fatigue hadn't done to the house, an interior tornado bent on destruction had.

Her mother, Barbara, followed a step behind. "Oh, my. What's that smell?" Her scrunched-up nose brought an unexpected grin to Julia's freckled face.

The faint pungency of formaldehyde hung in the air. "The sewer's not backed up, is it?" asked Julia.

She lifted her foot over the crumpled doormat and led the way into the living room. Her mother's best friend, Martha Taylor, closed the door and joined them. "No. Everything in the house works fine." She shrugged her shoulders, clearly embarrassed by the mess, but ready with an explanation. "My oldest son, Brett, bought this place to fix up and resell. He's just getting started on the remodeling, but the plumbing is fine. It's the current tenant—''

''Martha.'' The clear snap of her mother's voice captured Julia's attention as well. She caught the unsubtle message flashed from hazel eyes to blue.

Martha, taller, and a tad thinner, shook her head. ''She's bound to notice.''

Julia knew the dynamic duo was up to something, but she could never be sure where her mother's good intentions might lead, much less when she was in cahoots with her lifelong pal since kindergarten.

She'd been home only a few days, but the urgency the two older women had used to get her out of the house that morning made her wonder if she had already overstayed her welcome.

''Anyone want to offer an explanation yet?'' she asked. ''You said you needed a nurse, not a housekeeper.''

Martha perked up at Julia's comment. ''As a professional health-care worker, do you think living like this presents a health risk?''

''Not if you're a cockroach or a rat looking to make a new home.''

Julia stacked the magazines strewn across the couch and set them on the end table. She checked the dark stain on the seat cushion beneath for dryness before plopping her backpack that served as both purse and overnight bag on the empty spot.

Then she folded her arms across the front of her denim jacket and switched roles from daughter to authority figure. ''So who's going to fess up? You told me to pack a bag and my credentials because you had an emergency at home. But we didn't walk across the street to your condo, Martha. We drove here. What's going on?''

Though humor had always been her first best line of defense, she hadn't managed the night shift of one of Chicago's toughest emergency rooms without learning how to throw around a little intimidation. She knew how to draw up all five feet, six inches of her blocky figure into a not-to-be-messed-with show of force.

Unfortunately, she'd learned the trick from her mother. Barbara mimicked her daughter's stance. "Don't get mad at Martha. I agreed with her totally on this. I thought it was a good idea."

"I'm not mad. I just want to know—" A solid thump from the back of the house rattled the chandelier above her head. Julia jumped in her boots. But other than a quick catch of her breath, she didn't let her mother see how the unexpected sound unnerved her. A sense of impending dread pulsed through her at the uneven tread of heavy footsteps advancing toward them.

"Who's the patient, Martha?" These women were not given to lying. But they might fudge a little bit if they believed it would help someone they loved. "Mom?" she prompted.

"Ma?!"

She knew that voice. Years ago she'd memorized the quiet authority, the distinct pitch of it. The deep tone had a raspy, strident ring to it now. But she'd know that voice anywhere.

Once, it had saved her life.

Today, it could destroy her.

"I'm not ready for this."

Shreds of panic plummeted to her toes, robbing her of conscious thought and reliable self-assurance. She snatched her bag and flung it over her shoulder. Her mother hadn't known then. She didn't know now. Julia had never told a soul. Her humiliation ran too deep. The futility of her feelings was a raw, vulnerable wound, barely shielded now after all that had happened in Chicago.

She had to go. She had to...

"Ma, you there?"

She froze in her tracks when she came face-to-face with the man braced in the archway where the living and dining rooms joined.

Mac Taylor.

As tall and lean as she remembered. The broad shoulders and endless stretch of legs beneath the gray sweatshirt and faded jeans were the same. The long, dextrous fingers still fascinated her. But the lack of meat on his angular frame gave him a hard edge. And the tight slice of his mouth across the golden scrub of a beard indicated he was angry.

She'd never seen him angry before.

"Ma?"

"I'm here, son." The fatigue in Martha's voice distracted Julia's attention for a moment. Like her own mother, Martha would be in her early sixties. But the heartbreak that suddenly creased her face made her seem years older.

"Who's with you?" Julia turned back at Mac's demand.

Time and injury hadn't been kind to her childhood hero. His sandy blond hair had lost its burnished lustre. All trace of curl had been cut away, leaving it a short, spiky length. Jagged streaks of newly healed, baby-pink skin branched out over his left cheek and across his forehead in an intricate web of fresh scars.

But it was his eyes that held her captive.

Beneath the cut that bisected his eyebrow, a tiny white blemish blotted the symmetry of pupil and iris in his left eye. And the right looked through her, past her, without seeing her.

He was blind.

Those cool chips of granite, once silver behind the gold of his glasses, that she'd fantasized about through her teenage years, were blind.

Her fears scattered as shock rendered her silent. Her lips worked to mouth the question, *Why?*

"Ma? Who's with you?" he repeated.

Tears of sorrow, and maybe even pity for all he had lost, stung her eyes.

Martha shrugged off her son's harsh tone. "Barbara Dalton."

He tipped his face up, sniffing the air with an almost feral focus. "Who else?"

Julia blinked back the moisture in her own eyes, sensing sympathy would not be appreciated. "It's Jules, Mac. Julia Dalton."

"Son of a bitch." His face flushed with emotion, and he whipped around. His shoulder banged into the archway, knocking a picture crooked on the wall. A string of succinct, damning curses accompanied him as he stormed back through the house.

"MacKinley Taylor!" Martha dashed through the archway, scolding after him. "She's a nurse, son, she can help—" A door slammed, cutting her off, leaving Julia and her mother standing in shocked silence.

Several moments later, Martha returned. The strain on her face aged her even more. "I'm afraid I brought you here under false pretenses." She rolled her gaze heavenward and clenched her mouth in an effort to stem her tears. "Of all my children, that one was never a bit of trouble. Never once gave me cause for concern. And now, when he does need me, he won't let me help."

"He needs bandages on those eyes." The practical professional inside her kicked in. But decades-old friendship softened her scold to a gentle reprimand. "The damage to that tissue is recent enough that it could still breed infection. At the very least he should wear dark glasses. The light must be killing him."

Martha went to the picture on the wall and straightened it. "I almost think he enjoys it. The pain, I mean."

With an instinctive empathy, Julia knelt down to retrieve the wadded newspaper pages from beneath the coffee table. "Why would he punish himself that way?"

"I think he feels responsible for the accident."

Julia straightened, hating her natural curiosity and abundant concern. Why couldn't she just let things go? "What happened?"

Martha's back seemed to creak with the effort of bending down and picking up a pillow that was half a room away from the chair to which it belonged. "There was an explosion at the lab where he worked. He suffered chemical burns, shrapnel wounds." The hopelessness in Martha's voice tore at Julia's heart. Then her voice brightened a bit with a shallow smile. "There's a chance the blindness isn't permanent. He nearly lost one eye. It's damaged beyond repair. But his right eye can be retested once he's healed. He may be eligible for a lens transplant. If the eye's strong enough. But he's so stubborn. He's so... defeated."

Julia shoved the newspapers into the trash can beside the desk, turning away from her mother who was hurrying to Martha and sweeping her into a comforting hug. She tried to remain clinical. "Transplant operations are fairly common, and generally quite successful. Partial or complete sight is restored, and the postoperative healing process isn't too traumatic."

"Don't quote me facts." Unfocused anger replaced the quaver of tears in Martha's voice. "The success of the operation makes no difference if he won't take care of himself! Look how he lives. Half the time he hides out in his room behind a locked door. He crashes around this house without regard for his safety, and has a temper tantrum whenever someone tries to help. He's chased off three nurses already.'' The anger receded behind a plea from the heart of a desperate mother. ''You're my final hope. Please. As a favor for old times' sake?''

Julia clutched the straps of her black leather pack and squeezed until her knuckles turned white. She eyed her mother, whose arm draped in support and protection around Martha's shoulders. Why hadn't her mother done the same for her?

She choked back the traitorous thought. She hadn't told her mother about Chicago. About that humiliating morning in Anthony's office. She'd simply shown up on her parents' doorstep last Saturday morning, a welcome, though unexplained, surprise. She'd resigned from her job at the hospital, closed up her apartment and headed for home. She needed time to think. Time to heal. Time to be safe.

She shook her head and, palm raised as though warding off the threat of danger, backed toward the door. ''I can't handle a serious case right now. I'm sorry Mac's in trouble. I'm sorry for your whole family. But I can't do this.''

Julia spun around and shot out the front door into the crisp autumn air, anxious to escape the pressure, the disappointment, the guilt. Halfway down the front walk to her car, she heard the door shut behind her.

''I didn't raise a quitter.''

Julia halted at the sound of her mother's voice. On a deep breath, she turned and pleaded with those eyes, part gold, part green, just like her own. ''Someone else can help Mac. There must be hundreds, thousands, of qualified nurses in the Kansas City area. Reliable, tough—''

''I'm not talking about Mac.''

A bit of the concern she'd seen etched in Martha's face now lined her mother's. ''What do you mean?''

Barbara closed the distance between mother and daughter. Physically, and emotionally. ''I've never seen my little girl tuck her tail between her legs and run home to hide before.''

Julia held her tongue, not knowing what to say. She'd tried to be cheerful, talk of good times, help around the house. But she could see now that she hadn't fooled her mother for one instant. "I'm sorry if I worried you. I didn't mean to.''

Barbara smiled. "I'm a mom. Even after thirty years, it goes with the territory.'' She reached out and brushed one of the short curls that crowned Julia's head off her face. "I don't know what happened to you in Chicago, but I'm sorry it hurt you. You are always welcome at home, and I am always ready to listen, if you decide you need to talk. But, in the meantime, I think you should do something. Keep busy, don't just brood.''

Julia clasped her mother's hand and squeezed it tight. "I love you for your concern, but I don't think this is the right thing for me to do.'' She looked up to the house, seeing it as a distant symbol of lost hope and shattered dreams. "He needs so much. And I don't just mean nursing care. I don't think I have it in me to give him enough of anything right now.''

The answering silence brought Julia's attention back to her mother's face. Those hazel eyes looked sad in the grim expression Barbara wore. "Martha Taylor has been my friend longer than you've been alive. You and her son Cole were classmates and good friends for many years. That family's in desperate trouble now.'' Julia sighed right along with her mother. "I won't insist on anything that would put you or your feelings in danger. I just want you to remember that, sometimes, *giving* is what enables us to move beyond the fear or sorrow, and allows us to find a way to heal ourselves.''

Julia rolled her eyes heavenward, seeking the strength that seemed to have abandoned her. Growing up hadn't been easy for her mother. But that life experience had given her a wisdom and insight that had surprised her daughter more than once. Maybe she did know something about healing the spirit, about mending a shattered self-image, about piecing together the will to move forward with her life. She looked at her mother, wanting to believe in that wisdom.

"I don't remember you being this philosophical, Mom."

"I don't remember seeing you in this much pain."

Julia considered the importance of family and friendship, of loyalty and love. She weighed the value of her actions in Chicago and what they had revealed about her true character. Her instincts had failed her, and she'd been too stubborn to listen to common sense. She had fallen short of her parents' expectations of her, far short of her own expectations for herself.

Maybe she owed them a bit of penance until she could figure out how to make things right again.

If only she wasn't so afraid of making things worse.

But Barbara Dalton *hadn't* raised a quitter.

"All right." She stepped forward and wrapped up her mom in a hug. The tight embrace around her own shoulders might be the only strength she'd have to sustain her through this. "I'll give you twenty-four hours. We'll see how it goes. But you and Martha need to be looking for a backup plan."

She felt the tension in her mother relax. "Thank you, Jule."

Embarrassed by the simple gratitude, Julia separated and trudged up to the door. "Twenty-four hours," she reminded her.

To do a favor for an old family friend?

Or to survive a sentence from hell?

MAC WAITED A GOOD ten minutes after his mother's good-bye before leaving the sanctuary-slash-prison of his bedroom. At least he thought it was ten minutes. His internal clock seemed to have gone haywire in the same instant the toxic flames and lacerations scarred his throat and tore the sight from his eyes.

Ten minutes. Five. Twenty.

What did time matter to a man who served no useful purpose?

The dull ache behind his left eye was a constant reminder of all he had lost. And no amount of scientific or medical training could bring back the competency of a man who had lived by his senses, his powers of observation, his ability to see something once and identify its attributes. He was a man of science, a man of thought and reason. He'd never worried about how to get from point A to point B. How to find the toilet across the hall. How to pick out socks that wouldn't clash with his jeans.

He'd never thought about living without his sight.

Mac swung his bare feet off the edge of the bed and slipped into the beaten loafers that had become his uniform of late. He inhaled a deep, fortifying breath and stood, steadying himself by grabbing on to the headboard. He waited for the waves of dizziness to pass, knowing damn well these vertigo attacks were a result of panic and disorientation, and had no bona fide physical cause.

Only when his shadowed world stopped spinning did he move. Three steps from the bed to the dresser. He trailed his fingertips along the scarred oak top, sticking a moment where the old varnish had pooled, sliding past the spot where there was no varnish at all. His hand hit a smooth, hard object and glass clinked against glass.

Tempting defeat, he turned his hand, lifted the glass to his nose and sniffed. Nothing. Plain water. Maybe the other…

His stomach rumbled in protest at the lone leftover doughnut he had scrounged for breakfast. Despite his abysmal welcome, he hoped against hope that his mother had left a sandwich for him to eat. Restoring the clutter on his dresser, he reached for the door.

Two steps more across the hall to the bathroom. He followed the wall until he hit the dining room. Then he was in no-man's-land as he buffeted from chair to wall to sideboard. When he stubbed his toe on the break in the carpet beneath the archway, he knew he'd reached the living room.

He clutched at the molding that framed the arch and paused to get his bearings. He needed to learn the number of steps into the kitchen, or move the bookshelves and recliner so he could simply follow the perimeter of the wall without breaking his foot, his face, or any of those knick-knacks his mother had entrusted to him over the years.

As if thoughts of his mother triggered the response, guilt reared its ugly head. He'd never realized how much temper simmered inside him. He'd always prided himself on maintaining an even emotional keel. But since the explosion, he'd learned he could be a beast. Reactive. Out-of-control. And his mother, meddling saint who had raised six boys and one girl under her roof, didn't deserve to bear the brunt of his sour moods. Once he had some food in his stomach, he'd call home and apologize.

And make Ma promise not to spring any more surprises on him.

Feeling even that small bit of mastery over his life once more, Mac extended his arms as feelers and braved the booby-trapped path to the kitchen.

One step. Two steps. He butted his shin against the recliner and stopped, rotating his arm like a compass needle in his search for the clear path. His outstretched fingers hit the floor lamp and knocked it at a tilt. He caught it and straightened the shade, experiencing a silly little rush of triumph that he hadn't destroyed it. With a trace of positive energy whispering through him for a change, he moved with more confidence, stepping to the left to avoid the obstacle.

He plowed into something warm and soft and solid, with two hands that latched on to his wrist and elbow to catch him from recoiling backward.

"Mac?"

He wrenched his arm away from the firm grip and smacked the lamp with his fist, sending it crashing to the floor.

Jules.

"I thought I told you to leave." The condemnation in his scarred voice sounded harsh, even to his own ears.

"You never got around to that. You were rude to your mother, and then you stormed out."

The teasing retort came from below, and he realized she had squatted down to pick up the lamp. "Bent, but not broken." Her voice sounded nearer. Had she stood? "No wonder it looks like a demolition derby in here. Didn't you get a cane to walk with?"

"I don't need a cane."

"Right." Her clear, low-pitched voice danced with a smug humor. "It would be easier to just rent a bulldozer and trash the whole place in one fell swoop, instead of wrecking one little corner at a time."

A flood of indignation surged through him. How dare she joke at his expense! Did she have any idea how embarrassing it was to flounder around his own home like a fish out of water? He couldn't even hold a decent argument with her, not knowing whether he was talking to her face or her belly button.

"What are you doing here?" he demanded.

"Helping out a friend."

Right in front of him. Mac turned his scarred visage on her. "I didn't ask you to come."

"I was talking about your mother. She needed my help."

Ouch. An appropriate comeback escaped him. Jules had been one of the neighborhood kids. Hanging out at his dad's shop or in the rooms upstairs they called home. Of all those adolescent interlopers who interrupted his work and study time, she had been…which one? He thought his way through the maze of comings and goings that had been a part of their everyday lives back on Market Street.

It had been useless to try to concentrate on his books when Cole and his buddies descended upon them. They'd gather around the kitchen table and raid the fridge and play cards, or perch in the living room to watch sitcoms on TV. Accepted as one of the guys, Jules had always been at the center of their laughter.

Her sassy wit hadn't dulled over the years.

Mac wondered if anything else about her remained the same.

But he filed away his curiosity to return to later. A more pressing question needed to be answered as a fist of concern gripped his heart. "Is Ma holding up okay?"

A faint rustling sound answered him. "If dark circles under her eyes and new wrinkles beside her mouth are normal, then, yes, I'd say she's doing fine." That tart voice was a shade more distant. She'd moved.

"I owe her an apology."

"Probably." The gentle agreement nicked at his conscience. He owed Jules an apology, too. But she never gave him a chance to organize those thoughts. "If you take half a step to the left, your path is clear to the kitchen." Like a beacon, her concise directions called to him from a distance. She must have gone into the kitchen herself.

Not yet trusting that the edge of a rug or leg of a chair wouldn't leap into his path, Mac stood rooted to the spot.

In an effort to form an image of what she looked like now, he tried again to picture the Jules he'd once known. Having graduated in Cole's class, she'd be seven years his junior. "Braces. Freckles." He tapped the memories out loud. He'd watched a couple of coed league games one summer to support his brother. "You played second base. Killer arm. Shag hitter, always made contact with the ball."

He could remember details of a fifteen-year-old softball season, but couldn't remember the layout of his own house. Frustration made his damaged voice tight. "So what have you been doing all this time, playing for the majors?"

Her voice returned to the living room. "Nah, I got cut last week. Right after the braces came off." The husky music of her laughter defused the tension that had paralyzed him. "You coming?"

He heard the rustling sound again. Then the clank of pots from the broiler pan beneath the oven. She'd abandoned him once more.

A trace of scent lingered in the air. Something crisp and fresh, like autumn air and sunshine. With arms outstretched, he followed that scent into the kitchen. Just as she had promised, there'd been nothing in his path to stumble over.

But his victory was short-lived. When his feet hit the smooth linoleum, shards of pain shot through his eyes. He reeled back a step, squinting against the bright overhead light. He shielded his eyes with his hand and cursed. The remnants of torn and burned tissue contracted at the glare, an autonomic response of organs that still did everything they were supposed to do—except see.

"Sorry. I'm a nurse. I should know better." Julia's hasty apology registered the same time that crisp sunshine smell floated past him. He heard the tiny click of the light switch, then the gentle rasp of cotton on cotton coming toward him and circling around him. Mac dipped his head to follow the faint rustling sound. It had to be Jules herself.

He tried to anchor himself to her scent, pinpoint her heat. Though finely tuned to compensate for his blindness, he had yet to master control of his other senses. Julia's proximity was a bombardment of sensation—warmth and scent and sound.

And touch.

Strong, supple fingers pulled his hand from his eyes and Mac froze. "I read the write-up from your doctor."

She gently probed the tender new skin at his cheek, temple and brow. "He prescribed bandages on your eyes until the end of the week." In his mind, the inspection of her fingertips was a timid caress against sensitized skin, a stark contrast to the confident strength with which she still held his hand. "If you wore them the way you're supposed to, the light wouldn't aggravate your condition."

His condition? He was a crippled-up cop. A cop who should have seen the accident coming. Who should have seen a lot of things before he ever lost his sight.

Mac snatched her hand from his face, putting an end to the unwelcome examination. "My *condition* is called blindness. I can't see your hand in front of my face. I can't see you. I can't see a damn thing!"

Their fingers twined together as he shook his fist to make his point. "You can push and poke and prod all you want, but I'm still a blind man."

Unknowingly, he clung to her while he spoke. Long enough to detect the uniquely feminine combination of soft calluses inside her palm, and even softer skin on the back of her hand. Long enough to note the blunt, functional fingernails at the tips of lithe, lineal fingers.

Long enough to feel the fine tremors trembling within his grasp.

Was that Jules's shocked reaction to his spare, unadorned words? Or the remnants of his own anger running its course?

But almost as if she sensed the instant he began to analyze the subtle movement, she freed herself. "You're a man, Mac. Pure and simple. A man who happens to be blind. Millions of people live with that handicap every day and lead full, productive lives—"

"Spare me the inspirational speech."

He'd heard the same lecture from his doctors, the police psychologist, his parents—even his big brother. He should be grateful he was alive. Hopeful he had a 50-50 chance of regaining sight in one eye.

But a friend was dead.

His career was finished.

His life had flashed before his sightless eyes.

He didn't need some freckle-faced Florence Nightingale doing the neighborly thing for old times' sake. He needed to be alone to figure out where he'd made his mistake, and devise a plan to make everything right again.

"Go home, Julia."

There. He'd made himself perfectly clear.

He turned toward the open doorway. He hoped.

"I found a pair of sunglasses with the price tag still on them." She started talking again without comment or argument, as if his succinct command had been an invitation to make herself at home.

Mac halted his grand exit. With his fingertips, he reached out and verified that he had found the door. The worn contours of sculpted oak reassured him. *He* wasn't the one disoriented this time.

The clang of metal on metal and the suction pop of the refrigerator door opening behind him indicated she was preparing a meal. He ignored the sudden anticipation that wet his mouth and rumbled in his stomach, and concentrated on her words. "Somebody's trying to take care of you. At least the glasses would protect your eyes from the light, if not from infection."

The glasses had been a gift from his youngest brother, Josh. Along with some lame advice about making him look cool, and turning him into a babe magnet.

Such questionable laws of nature no longer applied to him.

"You don't have to be here, you know."

The racket behind him stilled, followed by a long, controlled whisper of air. "Yes, I do. For twenty-four hours."

Twenty-four hours? What was that about?

He heard the rustling noise again. Julia was moving.

Wrapping his fingers around the doorjamb for balance, he tipped his ear toward the intriguing sound. In his mind he pictured a pair of legs, dressed in soft, snug denim, the thighs gently touching with each step.

He closed his eyes unnecessarily and envisioned her as a fifteen-year-old. She'd had a stocky, muscular build, perfect for snagging grounders and blocking base paths. He wondered what she looked like now. If she'd filled out in the right places over the years. If those muscles had turned into curves. If those long legs he heard brushing together were rounded or straight. Or...good God, what the hell was he thinking?

This was a fine time for his intellectual curiosity to rear its head. He wanted to get rid of her, not study her like some unidentified lab specimen.

Then the import behind her odd pronouncement registered through his instinct to analyze and identify. "If you don't want to be here, then why are you?" he asked.

The pungent odor of gas catching flame told him she had gone back to the stove. "Your mother was worried about you. My mother was worried about me. Their solution was to put the two of us together."

"They're not matchmaking, are they?" His older brother Brett had recently married, and Martha Taylor seemed to have developed a fever now to find mates for all her brood. For Mac, her timing couldn't be worse.

Julia laughed. "Are you kidding? Have you seen me lately?"

Her self-deprecating joke turned full circle in the dead air that followed. He knew the instant that her gaze searched his back in apology. Mac straightened. Six feet, three inches of stiff back ought to finally get rid of her.

"Can't say as I have."

"I'm sorry. I didn't mean—" An immediate flurry of activity covered the silence. "I'm fixing an omelette for a late breakfast. It'll take just a few minutes. Have a seat, the chair is two steps to your left. I'll get some coffee going, too."

Hell. Her attempts to distract him from her apology pricked his defenses. He'd rather do battle with her than endure her pity. He already carried enough of his own to choke on.

He ignored the pangs in his stomach and the curiosity of his mind, and tramped back into the living room. He hit the trash can and kicked it aside, not giving a damn about the mess he'd inevitably made.

That enticing whisper of denim followed quickly behind him. "You don't have to like this," said Jules. "But we should make the best of it."

"Fine. You make the best of it. I'm going to my room."

"Dammit, Mac, be reasonable." She snatched his

sleeve and tugged him around. Half a turn, maybe. Or was it all the way around? He squeezed his eyes shut against the dizzying confusion. As if the complete darkness was somehow more comforting than the shadowy nothingness of his vision.

"You look like hell. You need a shave and clean clothes. This scruffy look never was you." A second hand grasped his chin and tilted his face to one side. "At least let me bandage your eyes. We can't risk infection."

He jerked his chin free of her soft, firm touch. "I can risk anything I damn well please."

"What about breakfast? I didn't see any dirty dishes. Have you eaten at all today? What about fresh air? Sunshine? Do you ever get outside?"

The woman was relentless. "Too many damn questions!" He twisted his arm from her grip and swatted the air, clearing the space around him, and hopefully scaring some sense into her. "Just leave me alone."

Mac headed for the dining room, intending to leave Nurse Jules and her annoying determination behind him. On his second step he banged his shin against the coffee table and let out a stream of curses that would have made his mother grab the soap and wash out his mouth.

He spun around, planning to skirt the table. His knees butted into the sofa. He took a half turn to the right, ignoring a flare of panic, and ran into the overturned trash can.

Just like that internal clock, the compass inside him had gone haywire.

Mac choked back a frisson of fear that erupted within.

Lost in a spinning world. Trapped among the unknown terrors of his own home.

Imprisoned by his handicap.

For a man who had relied on cool, concise thinking his entire life, this continual buffeting of emotion played havoc with his sense of reason. Guilt. Fear. Anger. They were all his enemies now.

And for the first time in his life, he could think of no way to fight back.

Chapter Two

"With a cane you could tap your surroundings and find the way out." Julia's calm suggestion made a mockery of Mac's own common sense.

"Shut up."

He could control this. He could figure a way out of the maze of his own living room.

The rustle of sound barely registered as he concentrated on getting his bearings. He detected her unique scent, coming from behind him now, an instant before her hand latched onto his.

For an unthinking moment, he folded his fingers around hers, clinging to her sure grip, anchoring himself in the spinning disorientation of darkness. For all his crude words and rude behavior, he was grateful for the undeserved patience in the gesture.

"This way."

Her gentle voice beckoned and he followed. He allowed himself to be led a few steps, until he was free of the embarrassing hazards of his own home. He stopped when she stopped, but she tugged on his hand and pulled him forward another step.

His remaining senses buzzed into full alert as she guided his hand to the crook of her elbow. A practical gesture, he supposed. But the skin on the back of his hand and wrist bristled with acute awareness after brushing against the bountiful softness of what had to be a breast. In contrast, her strong shoulder nudged against his chest as she positioned herself to guide him. About chin height, he estimated, judging how she measured up against him. Maybe a shade taller.

The scent he had detected earlier and identified as her own pooled at nose level. It was her hair, he deduced. Her shampoo, to be more precise. Nothing perfumy. Clean, but not antiseptic. Fresh. Sassy. Just like…

Mac snatched his hand away and stepped back, shocked to realize he'd been analyzing Jules in a way that had nothing to do with science, and everything to do with the primal way a man checked out a woman.

As if he had any business checking her out.

As if she'd have any interest in being checked out by a scarred-up waste of a man like him.

"I don't need you to be my guide dog." His raspy voice, already ruined by the toxic fire that had destroyed his lab and killed a friend, sounded harsh in the monstrous quiet of the house.

He expected her to pack her things and run. The other nurses had refused to put up with his churlish behavior. He wanted to be alone right now. He needed his solitude.

But he'd met his match when it came to bullheaded determination.

Jules had somehow moved behind him. She touched his shoulders and turned him slightly. But she released him before he could justify any protest. "The archway's about five steps directly in front of you." Could he trust her guidance? He took two tentative steps, then three more. Her crisp, no-nonsense voice remained behind him. "The wall's just to your right now. Put your hand out and use it to guide you."

Mac reached out. The wall was there, just as she'd said.

Hiding his tentative sigh of relief, he made his way through the dining room without bumping so much as a shinbone. His pulse quickened in anticipation as he entered the hallway. Close to escaping her, or close to reaching his sanctuary, he couldn't tell. He simply knew she wouldn't have to see him, and he wouldn't have to deal with *not* seeing her. He wouldn't have to deal with anyone or anything if he could just reach the relative security of his room.

His fingers curled around the doorjamb. An overwhelming sense of relief rushed through him, making him lightheaded. He ducked inside and turned to shut the door.

"What's with the mad scientist routine?"

Startled by her voice, he spun toward the curious question.

He heard the clunk of glass on wood, and knew she was inspecting the beakers on his dresser. "Pew! Formaldehyde isn't exactly standard air freshener."

"Get out of here." He defended his makeshift lab with a hollow whisper.

She'd snuck past him somehow. Hell. How easy was it to sneak past a blind man?

Anger swelled inside him, quickly replacing the embarrassment of being caught and questioned like a little kid. He felt the same need to defend his ideas and actions as he had the day his mother caught him trashing her kitchen to perform a series of experiments as an eleven-year-old. That same indulgent curiosity, blended with a gentle reprimand, colored Julia's voice.

"I'm guessing hydrochloric acid on this one. Alcohol." She went down the line, correctly naming the contents of each beaker. "What are you trying do here?"

He reached for that voice. He hit her neck first, idly noting the cropped wisps of curls that indicated how short she wore her hair. His fingers glided down a swanlike arch of neck and he cursed himself for noticing anything about her at all.

Damning the fact that he could be distracted by something so unattainable as the discovery of a pretty woman, he slid his hand down to her shoulder and turned her. He clamped his fingers around her so she couldn't escape.

"Ow!"

Despite her squirming struggles, he found the other shoulder and pushed her into the hallway. Her hands flattened against his chest and resisted, but he had superior strength and momentum on his side. He backed her up until she hit the wall.

"Get the hell out and stay out," he ordered.

But now momentum worked against him. He cursed the law of science that carried him forward into Julia's body. For the briefest of instants, his thighs and torso crushed into hers, giving him a fleeting impression of muscles and curves and soft spots that gave way beneath his harder body.

"Damn, damn, damn!" He jerked away from the contact and staggered back to his room, escaping the subversive distraction of discovering the tomboy-next-door from his youth had matured into a full-figured woman.

So much for intimidation. Even the ability to hold a decent argument with her frustrated him.

Breathing hard, from emotion as much as exertion, he closed the door behind him. He leaned his shoulder into the aging wood, absorbing the brunt of her furious knocks until his fingers could find the lock and turn it.

"I don't do room service! If you want to eat, you come to the kitchen." Mac stood where he was, savoring his victory. Let her fuss and fume. He wouldn't have another thing to do with her.

The doorbell rang, a distant call from the outside world that made him realize he hadn't really escaped at all.

"You want me to get that? Or should I throw them out on their backside, too?"

"Give it up, Jules." He pushed away from the door, feeling trapped in the place where he'd sought freedom only moments ago.

"I don't give up on people, Mac."

Mac laughed at her vehement promise. It was a sick sound, raspy and unnatural. She'd learn soon enough about lost causes.

Six weeks ago he'd learned the hard way.

I DON'T GIVE UP *on people, Mac.*

Julia listened to her words echo off the closed door and backed away. She clutched her arms across her middle, nearly doubling over at the hypocrisy of what she'd shouted.

I don't know who the hell you think you are. There's nothing between us. We had our fun. Now be an adult and move on.

The harsh, horrible words rang fresh and true inside her head, spreading salt on an age-old wound that refused to heal.

Well, maybe she'd given up on just one person.

The doorbell rang a second time, forcing her to leave the downward spiral of self-recriminations and put on a pleasant facade to greet the outside world. Still charged from the fury of doing battle with Mac, and drained by the unexpected memory of the mistake she'd made in Chicago, she wiped her damp palms on her jeans. She took a deep, steadying breath and headed for the front door, practicing different versions of a smile along the way.

She opted for a polite but distant grin. Securing the chain on the door first, she opened it a few inches and looked out at the two men in suits and ties on the front step. "Yes?"

The older one, with snowy white hair and a bulbous nose that indicated a fondness for alcohol, pulled a thick, chewy cigar from his mouth and answered. "KCPD, ma'am. I'm Sergeant Joe Niederhaus, Internal Affairs. This is my partner, Eli Masterson."

Two decades younger and packing muscle where his partner packed fat, the dark-haired detective tipped his head in greeting. "Ma'am."

Julia clamped down on a genuine urge to smile. These two were a real life send-up of the *Dragnet*-duo her father loved to watch in reruns on TV. "What can I do for you?"

Sergeant Niederhaus took charge of the visit. "We're here to see Mac Taylor. He's an officer in the Crime Scene Investigation unit. Is he in?"

Did they expect a blind man to be off on an afternoon drive? Her amusement at their plain, polite talk faded with a nagging sense of unease. What sort of questions did cops ask other cops? What sort of answers did they expect to get from Mac?

"Could I see your badges, please?"

Detective Masterson reached inside his jacket, revealing the curve of the black leather holster strapped across his shoulders. Seeing the firepower he carried shouldn't have fueled her suspicions. She'd seen cops with guns before, both uniformed officers and detectives. Plenty of them showed up to question victims and suspects in the ER. Two had even shown up as patients during her tenure there.

Maybe it was just the lingering tension of spending time with Mac that made her so jumpy. She quickly read the pertinent facts about Eli Masterson and nodded her thanks. Sergeant Niederhaus tapped his cigar ashes out on the stoop, ignoring her request.

But with Julia's staunch refusal to open the door any

farther, and Eli's questioning glance, he reached inside the rotund silhouette of his jacket and pulled out his badge.

Satisfied that the two had official business to conduct, Julia stepped back to unchain the door. She nodded toward the sergeant's thick stogie. "I'll ask you to put that out before you come in."

"Dammit, lady—" His face reddened as he caught himself. He could cuss loud enough to alert the entire neighborhood, if he wanted. Julia had certain rules around her patients. And certain personal tastes. She simply expected him to cooperate. Once the cigar hit the step and was ground out beneath his shoe, she closed the door and released the chain. Then she stepped back to usher the two men inside.

"I don't mean to be unfriendly," she explained, "but I've lived the past several years on my own in Chicago. You can never be too careful about who you invite in."

Detective Masterson smiled in approval. "It pays to be smart, ma'am."

"Is Taylor here? We have to ask him some questions." Clearly, Niederhaus was from the old school. Maybe he didn't approve of single career women or small talk. Maybe he simply didn't like to be kept waiting.

Julia had dealt with all kinds of curmudgeons in her line of work. This old fart might be lacking in the charm department, but he deserved her patience and respect until he proved otherwise.

"Sorry about the mess. I was hired just this morning and haven't had a chance to clean up yet. Feel free to push something aside and have a seat."

"Thanks." It was Eli who answered.

But as she crossed through the dining room en route to Mac's locked door, she noticed that neither officer chose to sit.

That unnerved feeling crept along her spine again. Not

for the first time that morning, she wished she was home, locked in her own room with her books and the mementoes from her childhood. Locked up in the past where she didn't have to deal with men and their egos and all the games they liked to play.

Fearing the volume of Mac's scarred voice would reach their guests in the living room, Julia gritted her teeth and knocked quietly on the old oak door.

"Mac, there are two police officers here to see you."

"Nice try." His tortured rasp reached no farther than her own ears. "Leave me alone."

She glanced down the hallway and offered an embarrassed smile to the two officers whose watchful gaze she could feel, even at this distance.

She knocked again. "It's Joe Niederhaus and Eli Masterson from Internal Affairs. They need to speak to you."

She rested her ear against the wood and listened for sounds of activity on the other side. She heard the creak of a mattress. But was he getting into bed or out?

When another minute of silence answered her, she assumed he'd gone to bed and dismissed her. Her disappointment hissed out on a breath of air. Great. Now she'd have to come up with some excuse to get the detectives out of the house. Something like, Mac's on his pity pot right now and won't come out. Or, the professor's in the middle of an experiment, and doesn't want any company until hell freezes over.

She jumped at the unexpected click of the lock. Her breath came in shallow, sporadic gasps as the door opened a slit and Mac's blank gaze glowered into the hallway.

"If you're lying to me…"

The accusation hurt. If only. If she was a better liar, she could have saved herself a lot of pain over the years. "I'm not. It's one of my shortcomings."

His eyes swiveled from side to side, as if searching. But for what? "Is that supposed to mean something?"

She looked up into his face and shrugged, behaving as if he could see her reaction. Acting as if the expression on her face could tell him all about how much believing in lies had cost her.

But he couldn't really see her. Nobody could see inside to the insecurities of a lifetime. She covered the awkward moment as she always did. By turning it into a joke.

"It means your company's waiting in the living room. It's a hazard area, so we don't want to leave them there for long."

His shoulders rose and fell with a deep breath, as if the effort to figure her out made him weary.

"Internal Affairs?" he asked.

Julia nodded, then realized the foolishness of the gesture. She gave the verbal answer he needed. "Yes."

The door opened wider. She watched in curious fascination as his long, eloquent fingers reached out through the doorway. She stepped aside when she realized he was coming on out, but didn't move quickly enough to avoid the graze of his fingers across her cheek in an unintended caress.

Mac snatched his hand away as if he'd been burned. "Sorry."

"No problem." She failed to keep the catch from her voice. But at least she could spare herself the embarrassment of him seeing how the pink blotches of self-consciousness heating her face clashed with the honey-tan freckles that covered her skin.

For years, she'd fantasized about Mac Taylor touching her in a personal way. They'd collided more than once today, but she knew his hand skimming her breast or cheek meant nothing.

Whenever a man touched her, it meant nothing.

"We'd better get out there." He nodded at the reminder. Julia swallowed what was left of her battered pride and made doubly sure to get out of his way as he marched Frankenstein-like across the hall.

When his hand hit the wall, he turned. Trailing the fingers of his right hand along the panelling, he reached out with his left, moving it back and forth in the uneven sway of a broken pendulum. Julia followed a step behind, chomping down on the urge to take his arm and guide him safely out to his guests.

"You really should have the rugs removed," she admonished, when he stumbled on the dining room carpet. "Streamline the arrangement of furniture so you don't have as many turns in your pathway."

Mac stopped midstride and turned his face over his shoulder as if he could peer at her. "Drop the fix-it-up routine, okay?"

"I'm surprised the other nurses didn't make those recommendations." He turned so that his body faced her, and opened his mouth for another terse remark. But Julia cut him off. "I'll bet they did. You're just too pigheaded to let anybody try to help."

"If you're trying to goad me—"

"Officer Taylor?"

Mac stilled at the question from behind him. Julia's combative energy whooshed out at the transformation on Mac's face. Even sightless, even scarred and stiff, his features changed from defensive to startled to suddenly wary.

"Mac?" One golden brow dipped at the corner. She wondered what thoughts crossed that clever mind of his. "Mac?" she repeated.

Remembering their last encounter, when Mac reached out, she backed up. "No."

Responding to body heat or instinct or pure luck, he clamped his hands around her shoulders and kept her in place. A fourth expression altered the contours of his face. The man was tucking away his pride.

Curious, yet disheartened at the same time, Julia held still as he trailed his fingers down the sleeve of her cotton sweater to the crook of her elbow. He held on and circled around her. She realized his intent when he aligned himself behind her left shoulder.

"Take me to the living room."

Considering his aversion to any kind of help from her thus far, this display of trust surprised her. "You sure?"

"Internal Affairs never pays a social visit. I'd better find out what they want and send them on their way."

"That sounds comforting." With a shade of sarcasm coloring her voice, she covered her hand with his. She held off reminding him how his less than pleasant demeanor had been more than enough to chase away several people. These two cops shouldn't be a problem. She led him on a straight path down through the dining room, without once allowing him to bump into anything.

The two detectives exchanged curious glances as they entered the living room.

"Recliner or sofa?" she asked, ready to forge a path to either seat.

Mac straightened behind her, standing almost a head taller than she, as if he could sense the surprised scrutiny of Niederhaus and Masterson. "I'll stand. You boys never see a blind man before?"

Niederhaus seemed genuinely surprised to see the extent of Mac's handicap. "We heard you were in the explosion that killed Jeff Ringlein."

Mac's grip tightened around her arm, betraying a tension that put her on guard. Was he about to bolt? Should she get rid of these two men?

But Mac patted her hand, and sounded perfectly at ease

when he answered. "I was there, all right. What can I do for you?"

Amazed at the transition from hotheaded patient to cool-under-pressure cop, Julia disengaged herself from Mac. "Would you gentlemen like some coffee?"

Eli Masterson smiled and dismissed her at the same time. "Thank you. Black, please."

"Yeah. Me, too," said his partner.

Fine. Man talk. With her skin still tingling where Mac had held her, she could use some time to herself in the kitchen to regroup. She only hoped Mac was up to an interrogation. She couldn't tell what the sudden change in his behavior meant. Was this a cover? Or was the Mac she'd known from the old days in the neighborhood finally showing himself?

Julia searched the cabinets, locating a tray and three matching mugs while the coffee brewed. With Sergeant Niederhaus's booming voice, she couldn't help but hear snatches of conversation from the living room.

"We believe Ringlein may have been involved in something illegal. Did you suspect anything? Is that why you were there that night?"

"Jeff may not have been the most skilled technician, but he was loyal." Mac's voice reflected a calm detachment that had been absent from her encounters with him. "I can't see him being a part of what you're suggesting."

Julia tuned out the conversation and looked about for a snack to serve with the coffee. It might be a way to sneak some food into Mac's stomach and rebuild his strength.

"Did he say anything to you that would indicate he was suicidal?" That sensitive-as-nails question came from Niederhaus.

"He wasn't suicidal. He was in trouble. He mentioned that someone had threatened his wife."

"Who?"

Julia put grocery shopping high on her list, right behind cleaning. The only suitable food she found to serve with the coffee was a box of stale doughnuts. The stereotype of serving doughnuts to cops didn't bother her as much as the crusty shells that had hardened around the sugary confections.

Caught between the choices of serving old doughnuts or making sandwiches, Julia stuck her head into the living room, intending to ask Mac which he preferred. But she pressed her lips together and said nothing. Like the coffee, her temper brewed at what she saw.

Mac had perched on the edge of the recliner while Sergeant Niederhaus pressed him for information from his spot on the couch. Eli Masterson, it seemed, had little interest in the interview. He circled the room on silent feet, his head tilted at an intent angle to lift and study photographs, and thumb his way through the books and CDs behind Mac.

How dare he take advantage of Mac's handicap by sneaking around like that! Julia cleared her throat and garnered the attention of all three men. But her focus was on Eli. "Don't you need to have a search warrant?"

"Excuse me?"

Julia's take-charge voice kicked in. "Can I help you find something?"

He shrugged his shoulders like he'd done nothing wrong. "I was looking for the restroom."

Behind the bookshelf? Though she didn't believe his quick response, she pointed him in the right direction. "Down the hall. On your left."

She watched him to be sure he reached his destination, then glanced back at Mac. Had he even realized Detective Masterson was snooping around the living room?

Just who was under investigation here, anyway?

Joe Niederhaus rolled to his feet, leaving Mac staring

at the place where he'd been sitting. "Your deposition claimed Ringlein set fire to the lab himself. Do you think he was trying to eliminate you?"

Mac tipped his head to the sound of Niederhaus's voice, then stood when he realized his inquisitor had done the same. "What are you getting at?"

The toilet flushed in the back of the house, and Niederhaus shrugged, seeming to lose interest in his questions all of a sudden. He smiled for the first time. "Don't get in a sweat. Whenever an officer dies, it's I.A.'s job to check it out. Rule out any criminal activity."

"You should check into his wife's safety."

Eli returned to the living room, his quiet voice approaching Mac from behind. "You believe that claim?"

Startled by the second officer's approach, Mac turned himself sideways, shifting on the balls of his feet as if he felt penned in by the two men. "It was one of the last things he said."

"What was the *last* thing he said?" Niederhaus's question sounded like a taunt. Judging by the defensive angle of Mac's shoulders, he heard it the same way, too.

Julia knew little about police investigations, even less about male posturing. But she was an ace when it came to protecting her patients.

She joined Mac in the center of the room, changing the unsettling topic of conversation and giving Mac an ally to face off against the two investigators. She put on her best innocent expression and smiled like a diplomat. "I know it's early in the day, but I thought I'd see if you wanted sandwiches with your coffee?"

Niederhaus looked at Julia as if really seeing her for the first time. He made a noise that was half laugh, half grunt, and shook his head. "We need to be going."

A few defensive instincts of her own made Julia turn to

keep Detective Masterson in her sights. "It wouldn't take me a minute," she offered.

"Thanks, anyway." Eli crossed the room to join Niederhaus at the door. Side by side in the small living room, the two men formed an opposing front.

But they wore badges. That made them the good guys, right? So why did she feel the need to take a step back toward Mac?

Her shoulder blade bumped against his chest, and she shivered at the unexpected contact. But she didn't get a chance to move away. Mac's searching hand tapped first on her arm, then slid up to rest atop her shoulder. His long fingers splayed across her collarbone and down to the V-neckline of her sweater.

Masterson's gaze zeroed in on the spot. Then he looked at Mac's face and spoke as if Mac could see him. "Sorry you got hurt. I'm sure this will turn out to be a routine investigation. We appreciate your cooperation."

"Yeah." What part of Eli's words was Niederhaus agreeing with? "Sorry you got hurt, too."

With a nod of their heads, the two detectives left, closing the door softly behind them. Julia curled her arms around her middle, wondering if her imagination had gotten the better of her. Had she read something into their visit that wasn't there because she was already such an emotional wreck? She'd discovered she was a pro at misreading men and their intentions.

That's when her skin started to burn beneath Mac's hand.

Though the pressure of his hand never increased, what had seemed like an intimate stamp of possession, of protection, at the very least, now weighed down upon her like a confining manacle.

Maybe Mac sensed the change in her from wary to self-conscious. Maybe the involuntary shiver that shook her was enough to repel his touch.

He lifted his hand. The throaty whisper at her ear startled her, yet rooted her in place. "Easy, Jules. Your heart's racing like a comet. Something wrong?"

She couldn't help but think of that night, half a lifetime ago, when he whispered to her so gently. The voice was deeper now, more hoarse than it had been back then. But the effect was still the same. The unadorned words comforted her battered soul, and her mind raced with hopeless possibilities.

But she was no foolish teenager anymore. She was smart enough to recognize compassion for what it was. She was smart enough to walk away.

She walked all the way to the front door, where she locked the dead bolt and reattached the chain. "I'm okay," she reassured him, trying to reassure herself. "I spooked myself somehow. Probably fatigue. It's been a long couple of weeks for me."

She turned around to see Mac's questioning look. A crease formed in the scar tissue beside his eyes as he squinted to focus on something he could not see.

"You *are* a rotten liar."

She longed to put a complimentary twist on his words, but could only come up with sarcasm. "Gee, thanks."

"They spooked me, too." He stepped out, stumbled through the obstacle course, with a clear destination in mind. Julia went to help him, but he clamped down on her arms when he felt her touch, and gave her a little shake. "Tell me exactly what Masterson was doing."

The sharp clip in his raspy voice was a welcome relief to the tender touch of a moment ago. She could handle Officer Taylor, crime-scene investigator, a lot more easily than Mac, the hero, who triggered those silly, sentimental feelings from her youth.

"Nosing around. He seemed interested in the stuff on your bookshelves."

"I have crap on my bookshelves." He cast her aside with a sense of urgency, an intellectual ferocity that wasn't directed at her. He headed toward the corner of the room, rammed his hip into the desk and cursed. Julia hurried to his side as he fumbled around the desktop, rearranging the existing mess by creating another.

"Mac, what is it?" This frantic burst of energy worried her more than her suspicions surrounding Niederhaus and Masterson. She captured both of his hands in hers to stop his search. "What's wrong? What do you need?"

"Where's the damn phone?"

Chapter Three

Mac waited with exhausted patience while he was transferred from the Fourth Precinct desk to his cousin, police captain Mitch Taylor.

"Mac." Did he imagine the caution in the phone greeting? Or had he developed a paranoid mistrust of all his senses?

"Am I under investigation?"

"So much for small talk."

Mac shook his head, bemoaning his crass impulse. He hadn't asked about Mitch's pregnant wife, or checked how the precinct was getting along without their forensic chief. He breathed in deeply, trying to slow down the rest of the questions careening through his brain.

Autumn air and sunshine teased his nose. Jules. Sticking by his side to keep him from totalling his body and ruining his recovery.

The suspicions he'd sensed in her had put him on guard in the first place. He remembered her rapid pulse, beating beneath his fingertips. The way she'd backed into him, seeking safety.

He'd reacted on instinct, holding on to her, offering her a bit of reassurance, as if he was like any other man.

As if he could protect her from any real threat.

"Mitch? I know I'm officially on leave. But if you've got any answers for me—"

"I know, I know. You've got plenty of questions." Mitch was more than a cop. He was an adopted big brother. They'd grown up together. Mac drew on that connection to get a glimpse of the truth.

"I just had a visit from Internal Affairs. They wanted to know if I thought Jeff Ringlein's death was suicide, and if he intended to kill me. What's going on?"

The heavy sigh at the other end of the line wasn't a good sign. "Jeff was under investigation at the time of his death."

This was news to him. "Then why are they just getting around to asking me questions now?"

"You were in the hospital for five weeks, bud."

"Before that. Why the hell didn't anybody tell me there was trouble in my department?"

"You know I don't have any influence with Internal Affairs. They're a separate investigative unit. I can't tell you anything."

Intellectually, he knew his cousin's hands were tied. But the frustration eating through Mac's reserve of patience threatened his ability to think rationally. And, dammit, he needed that ability right now. He needed to think, to ask the right questions, to put the clues together in a way that made sense.

And then he felt the gentle grip at his elbow. The strong hand to anchor himself to in a flood of fear and panic. Jules.

Just as she had reached for him when he'd been so disoriented earlier, she reached for him now. Even that most impersonal, professional of touches grounded him in the chaos of his own personal darkness. Julia's strength allowed him to tap into his own strength.

In a much calmer voice, he pressed Mitch for information. "I'm guessing this has something to do with missing or tainted evidence."

"Mac—"

"There's no other reason to destroy a crime lab. We're not street cops. We're not first on the scene. We're the detail guys. The nitpickers. We don't arrest people and send them to prison."

"Your testimony can."

"We're the scientific backup to a good case." He shook his head, running on pure speculation at this point. "I think Jeff was in trouble. I.A. seems to think so, too. He was destroying evidence the night I found him in the lab."

He heard the whistle of breath from Mitch. "You sure? That would definitely interest Internal Affairs."

"What interests me is why Jeff would do it. Was he taking a payoff? Protecting someone? Afraid of someone?"

"You're getting ahead of yourself, Mac. This isn't your case. They were probably just checking you out as a character witness."

Mac remembered Julia's bossy accusation when she'd caught Eli Masterson snooping through his things. He couldn't equate that protective tone of voice with any innocent activity. "They wanted something more. I'm just trying to figure out what."

"You think Jeff altered evidence before that night? I could run a check of cases he worked on. See if any of them have been dismissed because of the lab work."

"No, I've got that information..." Mac's self-assurance faded on a sobering thought. He couldn't read through his files or access his computer. "Can you copy them in braille?" His sarcasm was too sharp to be funny.

Mitch's patient sigh deflated the remnants of Mac's ego. "You can't—"

"I know. I can't read braille."

The grip at his elbow tightened, summoning his attention to the woman standing quietly by his side. "I could read a report for you," she whispered.

His fractured pride warred with his mind's need to find answers. "It's pretty technical stuff." He tried to warn her away, get her to retract her offer.

"So? I'd just be reading the words. You're the brain."

Meaning she wasn't? Nobody got through college and earned a registered nursing degree without their fair share of intellect. Julia's teasing at her own expense nagged at his subconscious mind, but he filed away the casual observation to analyze later.

He turned his mouth back to the receiver. "Send me the files. Maybe I can find a pattern of some kind."

He doubted there was much he could do toward proving Jeff's motivation for destroying the lab, but it would give him a break from trying to identify the chemicals which Jeff had been using the night he died. "Jeff had a tray of lab samples swimming in a pool of corrosive acid. I suspect it wasn't an isolated incident. Either he was taking a bribe, or he was in big trouble. From his words and behavior I'd say he was coerced."

"You think somebody was blackmailing one of my cops?" A territorial authority that made Mitch Taylor one of the most respected captains of any Kansas City precinct almost elicited a smile from Mac.

"If I.A.'s on it, they may suspect corruption somewhere else, too."

Mitch's curse was choice and succinct. "You watch your back, Mac. I know you're not involved in anything illegal. But you were the last person to see Jeff alive. Whoever was blackmailing him may think you figured out what he was up to."

He could hear the snap of paper, the click of a pen at the other end. He could envision Mitch taking charge and taking action—in a way Mac could not. "I'll put out some feelers from my end, see if we can dig up anything else about Ringlein and his connections. I'll send someone over to keep an eye on Melanie Ringlein's place.

"And I'll post a guard at your house, too, just in case anyone comes snooping around. If nothing else, they can give you advance warning if I.A. returns to ask more questions." Once, Mac would have protested such take-charge, big-brotherly behavior. Now he accepted it as a practical matter of course for a blind man.

"Fine."

"You there by yourself?"

The question drew Mac's attention back to the steady hand on his arm. "No. Jules is here."

As if mentioning her name had the same impact of one of his defiant arguments, she released him. The scent of sunshine faded as the whisper of denim took her away from him.

A new emotion worked its way into Mac's brain. Regret. He didn't want her close to him, didn't want to need her the way he apparently did. But he'd felt strengthened when she was at his side. He felt like something was missing when she walked away.

Before he could fully analyze those new and discomforting thoughts, Mitch laughed. "Jules? You mean Julia Dalton? That tomboy across the street who ran around with Cole? I guess they all grow up, don't they?"

"Yeah." Though most of what Mac remembered about Jules were her skills as a second baseman, he'd learned a lot about the grown-up version of the girl next door in the past few hours. Julia Dalton had matured into a sweet-smelling woman. And the way his nerve endings sat up and took notice of her sharp wit and shrewd tongue breathed energy and sunshine into his dark, gloomy world.

Not that he was ready to deal with energy and sunshine yet.

His body heated with the memory of her figure imprinting into his. His imagination hadn't pictured anything close to a tomboy then.

His face and body had been diced and burned and sewn back together, while she'd matured into a soft-skinned woman, with strong shoulders and rounded hips, and eyes...

What color eyes did she have, anyway?

And why did it matter?

He had no better chance of solving that mystery than he had of making sense of Jeff Ringlein's death.

"They grow up, all right." He ended the trip down memory lane. "Thanks, Mitch."

"I'll keep in touch."

Mac pressed several buttons before he disconnected the phone and could lay it on the desk. Some nagging bit of information, buried in the dark recesses of his mind tried to make itself known, but failed to make sense. He'd seen Julia's eyes before. He'd seen them, but he couldn't remember them.

He added that to the list of mysteries a blind man could never solve.

OFFICER WADE OSTERMAN ate more than enough to fill his six-foot, six-inch frame. He weighed in at a bulky two hundred eighty, only fifteen pounds under his playing weight, as Julia had learned while sharing dinner with the uniformed policeman. He'd played semi-pro football. Defensive lineman.

On his third helping of mashed potatoes, she found out he could have played in the pros if his knees had held up. "And my wife had stayed with me," he added. It was more a philosophical remark than an expression of remorse. "She was always my best cheerleader, even when she wasn't wearing that cute little skirt."

Julia wondered if his confession needed some kind of response. Did she express sorrow over his dissolved marriage? Ask if he'd had his knees scoped? Since she didn't know what to make of the big, blustery charmer, she ended up simply asking, "Do you have room in there for dessert?"

She'd finished her pork chop, green beans and potatoes a while back, but had remained at the kitchen table to keep Wade company.

And to wait for Mac to make an appearance.

She'd given her mother a very specific list of groceries to bring to the house, hoping to lure Mac out of his room with the comforting scents of home cooking. But the enticement had failed. He'd gone without anything to eat all day, unless he had something stashed in his bedroom.

Hell. Something could be rotting in that room, and no one would smell it because of the assortment of chemicals he kept on his dresser.

What was *that* all about, anyway?

"I smelled that pie when I came in this afternoon. I can hardly wait. Usually, on a job like this, I get stuck with takeout." Wade had been on duty for only four hours, but already he'd made himself at home. "You got ice cream to go with that?"

"Sure."

Julia cleared the dishes and took the ice cream out of the freezer to soften up. She couldn't help but look through the archway that led into the rest of the house. She'd stuck to her professional guns today, refusing to take any food to Mac. But his suffering pulled at her personal heartstrings.

He needed medical attention, food and liquids. But first she'd hoped he could work through the chips of guilt and self-pity and anger that burdened his shoulders. A patient had little chance of healing if he didn't make the effort to heal himself.

"Who do you think is gonna win the World Series this year?" Wade interrupted her thoughts. Normally, she loved discussing sports. But tonight she had to force an interest in the topic.

"Braves, probably." She repeated a line she'd heard her father say more than once. "Good pitching beats good hitting."

"You think they can take the Yankees? I got half a paycheck riding on New York. I got a tip that says they're making a trade for another left-hander in their pitching lineup. That'd make them a sure thing."

Wade was off on another conversation that required no input from herself. How could the guy be so amiable while discussing divorce and throwing away his money on a bet?

She served his pie and ice cream, biting back the urge to ask if risking half his paycheck had anything to do with his wife leaving him. But Wade was just a casual acquaintance. She had no right to comment on his personal life.

Besides, she had a more important task to accomplish. She dished up another serving in a large bowl, grabbed a spoon, and stiffened her backbone for the upcoming battle. "Excuse me, Wade. I need to check on Mac."

"S'okay," he said with a wad of food in his mouth. "It's seven o'clock. Better check the perimeter again." He stood, towering over Julia and swallowing up the space in the kitchen. He held up his dish like a starving waif. "S'okay if I take this with me?"

She still wasn't quite sure what Mitch Taylor wanted to protect Mac from, but she didn't question the security of having this friendly giant on guard outside the house. "Go ahead."

She followed Wade to the front door and locked it behind him, then walked to the back of the house. She'd spent the afternoon cleaning, so the path was clear, but she'd need some muscle to move the furniture into an easier layout for Mac to negotiate. Maybe she'd just sent a prime recruit outside with pie and ice cream. That small bit of good fortune carried her all the way to Mac's locked bedroom door.

The battered oak could be turned into a beautiful piece of wood if it was stripped and refinished. She wondered what it would take to break it down. Maybe Mac's hard head. But she'd try other means first.

She didn't bother knocking. No sense giving him the opportunity to be rude. "Mac?" No answer. "Your dinner is cold. I brought dessert. Apple pie and ice cream. Can you smell it?"

"Go away."

Julia breathed deeply. She knew this wouldn't be easy. "Your sense of smell should be more acute now." She passed the bowl along the seam of the door, shamelessly tantalizing him. "It's still warm. Take a whiff."

"Acute?!"

A couple of quick footsteps preceded the sound of a skeleton key twisting in the lock. She jumped back when Mac wrenched open the door. His hand shot out. Julia dodged a poke in the jaw, and barely managed to switch the pie from one hand to the other before his searching fingers clamped down on her wrist and dragged her inside.

"Smell these."

He spun her toward the dresser. Toward the parade of glass beakers. He moved his hand to the back of her neck, pushing her forward, forcing her to inhale the mishmash of toxic vapors. Her sinuses burned. She shook her head, but his grip held fast. "Can you tell which one is flammable? Which one is safe?"

"You're hurting me." Her plea fell on deaf ears. His

hand tapped across the dresser and picked up a beaker with a surety that made her think he'd done it several times before.

He thrust the glass beneath her nose. "Do you think this is the one that Jeff used to destroy those samples? Is this what blew up in his face? I can't tell the difference anymore. Can you?"

"Dammit, Mac!" Forgetting any rule about treating the patient with care, Julia defended herself. She shoved the beaker away from her face and twisted within his grasp. The beaker flew into the air and he released her.

Reflex actions made her lunge for the glass to try and save it, but she stumbled over Mac's foot. Her legs knotted with his when he tried to move away. And then they were falling. The beaker shattered on the floor the same instant Mac hit the bed and she landed on top of him.

Fortunately, he'd taunted her with water. Nothing dangerous. But manhandling her was a crime she would not forgive. Patience be damned. The man was going to eat.

Julia plopped herself on Mac's stomach, keeping him off balance when he tried to rise to his feet. She scraped the spoon through the bowl, splashing melted ice cream onto his shirt. She aimed for his mouth and hit her target, startling him into swallowing the food. Her victory fired her up for a second try.

But blind or not, Mac proved amazingly quick. He rolled. The bowl and spoon hit him in the face, but he knocked them aside and pinned Julia beneath him. "You want to take advantage of a blind man, Jules? Is that what you want?"

In a heartbeat, the breath rushed out of her and she froze. Long and lean, Mac's body stretched beyond the length of hers. Their legs tangled together, his hips fitting snugly over hers. His hands had found her shoulders, and the tip of one long thumb branded her across the top curve of her breast. His face hovered mere inches above hers, close enough to feel each fevered breath brush across her cheek.

The heavy sensation that rushed to where his thigh sank between hers made her forget all about defending herself. How many times had she kissed her pillow and dreamed it was Mac Taylor?

If she wrapped her arms around his waist or lifted her lips, she could turn their position into an embrace.

If.

An instinctive rush of self-consciousness stole into her mind, killing the thought before it could take wing. Lying on top of her, could he gauge the dimensions of her figure? Could he remember the freckles that made her plain? The shape that made her easy to overlook?

I'm not just your last chance. I'm your only chance. A nightmare from long ago whispered into her subconscious mind.

Sturdy. I like that in a woman. Not exactly Dr. Casanova's slickest line. But she'd fallen for it, anyway.

Julia squeezed her eyes shut against the ugly voices inside her head and tried to pull herself back to the present.

"Jules?" His terse, ruined voice demanded a response.

To be this close and know he thought of nothing but besting her, nothing but rebelling, nothing but proving a point, kept her from giving in to her hopeless fantasies.

She sought out reason, the way the Mac she'd had a crush on all these years would.

"In what way exactly do I have the advantage?"

His sightless eyes zeroed in on her crisp articulation. She felt an answering stiffness work its way into his arms and legs.

And then she was free.

Of course she was free. He'd come to his senses, after all.

Eventually, every man did.

He sat on the edge of the bed and Julia crawled to a seat beside him. She hid her disappointment, sternly reminding herself that she was his nurse, not an old flame. Hell. She barely qualified as an old *friend*.

She straightened her sweater and smoothed a wisp of hair above her ear. "If you want to identify the chemicals, I'll help do the research. But my first priority is your health. You have to take care of yourself before you can take care of anything else."

He buried his face in his hands and rocked from side to side as if suddenly caught up in a wave of dizziness. "I'm useless. Out of control and useless. There's a crime to solve, and I can't do it."

Julia tried to follow his mood swings. She rose to her feet beside him and planted her fists on her hips. He was way too stubborn. Way too down on himself. She shook her head, battling through her own frustrations so she could deal with his.

"How well did you know Jeff Ringlein?"

"You, too, huh?" Julia folded her arms and glared back at his accusatory smirk. She didn't know what crime consumed him so. She was just trying to help him work his way through whatever was putting his recovering eyesight, and maybe even his life, in jeopardy. His broad shoulders lifted in a weary shrug before he finally answered her. "I took him under my wing when he joined the department. He was a nice enough kid. I tried to be a mentor to him."

"Sounds like he'd have a lot of respect for you. If something was wrong, maybe he thought killing himself was better than disappointing you."

"If something was wrong, I should have seen it. I should have helped him." He pounded his fist in the palm of his hand. "I should be working right now to find out why he had to die."

"Why don't you?"

He tipped his face up to her, his handsome, scarred visage flushed with self-righteous anger.

"One guess."

"You're not the only person who's had to cope with pain in his life. You find a way to deal with it. You don't wallow in it."

"Pain?" Mac rose to his feet. He was slow and unsteady getting there, but tall and straight and utterly inscrutable once he found his balance. Despite the cloudy lack of focus in his eyes, his cold expression still managed to pierce her good intentions. "What do you know about pain and suffering?"

She hugged herself against the verbal blows he unknowingly inflicted. Pain came in many forms. It could tear an ego to shreds. It could destroy a heart's hope. It could make a mockery of even the most basic of trusts.

She couldn't do this. She absolutely couldn't heal this man when she had too many wounds to heal herself. "Damn you, Mac Taylor. I was only trying to help."

Julia turned away before the tears in her heart overflowed and provided her final humiliation. She left him in her dust and marched straight to the phone. She punched in a number she'd known since childhood. "Martha?"

The long breath at the far end of the line told Martha Taylor she knew exactly who was calling and why. "I'm sorry, Julia. You know he's not really this way. It's the injury talking. He just doesn't—"

"Don't apologize for him. He's thirty-seven years old. A grown man. He has no excuse for treating people the way he does. Not you, not me, not anybody. I've had it. I want out of here. Now. Let him bang around this place on his own."

As she raised her voice, a metallic echo screeched across the phone line. Julia pulled the receiver away from her ear until the harsh feedback receded. Struggling for self-control, she quieted her voice and tried a heart-to-heart plea. "You know I love your family. I'd do anything for them. But I'm not at my best myself right now."

"You promised me twenty-four hours."

The absolute fatigue in Martha's sad voice finally registered. Mac wasn't the only injured person in this family. As a nurse, she should have been aware of how her tirade could hurt. "I'm sorry."

How could she tell this kind, loving mother that she wanted to abandon her son?

She couldn't. And even if she could say no to Martha Taylor, she could never really say no to Mac.

She owed him too much. Maybe even her life. He might not remember that awful night so long ago, but Julia could never forget it. Her hero might have fallen from his pedestal in the meantime, but she had yet to repay him.

Tonight that debt would come due.

"I'm sorry to have bothered you, Martha. I just had a weak moment. We'll get through this tantrum."

"You'll stay, then?" She detected a hint of renewed energy, maybe even hope in Martha's voice.

"I'll stay."

MAC LAY IN BED, looking up toward the ceiling, and wondered if there were any other sins he could commit before the earth swallowed him up and put him out of his misery. No, he wouldn't be that lucky.

He deserved every bit of guilt and suffering the devil threw his way. He hadn't been observant enough to catch on to Jeff's trouble. He should have detected the scent of corrosive acid sooner that night. He could have saved Jeff's life if he'd been thinking.

Thinking.

Seems he hadn't been able to do much of that lately.

Not with his mother pestering him to take care of himself. Not with Internal Affairs paying surprise visits.

Not with Julia Dalton running around his house, talking fresh and smelling like sunshine in the middle of his dark world.

He didn't know whether to be pleased or concerned that she hadn't packed her bags and left like the others.

Of course, none of the other nurses had fallen into bed with him. Or backed their curvy little butt into his thighs, expecting him to be some sort of ally against Niederhaus and Masterson, some sort of protection. None of the others had forced food on him.

The unused muscles in his face creaked into a smile. His hungry stomach had finally won out over pride. The dessert Julia had brought him had slopped out across the bedspread, and the spoon was somewhere on the floor. But he'd followed the tart scent of Granny Smith apples and used his fingers to eat every bit of the concoction left inside the bowl.

In his youth, knowing something that delicious existed inside the house would have been motivation enough for Mac and his brothers to sneak into the kitchen for a midnight raid to polish off the rest of it. He'd love another slice of Julia's pie.

But his sneaking days were over.

He rubbed his palm across his beard and felt the sticky crumbs of piecrust and caramel sauce caught there. He didn't just feel like hell. As Julia had said, he must look it, too.

In the rational part of his brain he could still tap into, Mac knew she was right. He was feeling sorry for himself. But not for the reason she thought. It wasn't the blindness. Sure, that aggravated the hell out of him. Retraining himself to do the simplest tasks he'd once taken for granted taxed his patience.

It was the guilt.

One of his men had died, and Internal Affairs suspected foul play. They'd come to ask him questions and, according to Jules, had given his house a superficial inspection. Did I.A. think he was part of Jeff's business, too? Was anyone else on his staff destroying evidence? Why couldn't he figure this out?

He'd always been able to figure things out.

Maybe Julia was right. Maybe he needed to take care of his own needs first, before he tried to deal with anything else.

Not trusting his internal clock, Mac had waited until the sounds of the house had stilled for a long time. Officer Osterman was in his car out front. Julia was asleep in the guest room down the hall.

He stood and clutched at the headboard, waiting for the dizziness to pass. He did have one slight advantage with his blindness. He wouldn't have to turn on any lights to go for a midnight walk.

Barefoot, Mac risked the safety of his toes by slipping across the hall into the bathroom. He needed a shave, a shower, a chance to brush his teeth and some clean clothes.

He found his toothbrush and toothpaste in the holder above the sink. He squirted the paste onto his thumb before finding the bristles. But after running the water slowly to make less noise, he managed to pull off that task with very little mess.

Allowing that small victory to soothe his ego, he moved on to shaving. He let the water run until it was hot, and opened the cabinet door, looking for his razor and the shaving cream.

He managed to get the foam on his neck before the first mistake happened. "Ow. Damn."

The razor caught not once, but twice. The foam dribbled

into the cuts, making them sting. He scooped up two handfuls of water to wash away the irritating lather. The water ran straight down his neck and soaked the front of his shirt.

Was the blade old and rough? Or had he just misjudged the angle in this dangerous shave by touch routine? He pressed his thumb against the blade and winced. "Damn."

Definitely sharp enough to cut.

With his thumb in his mouth, he dropped the razor into the sink and reached for the can of shaving cream. Now the devils were working against him. His hand hit the can. His fumbling attempt to catch it knocked it across the room. Metal made an embarrassingly loud noise when it crashed onto tile.

Resigning himself to the inevitable, Mac sank to his knees and crawled around, searching the floor for the shave cream.

He was reaching between the tub and the toilet when he smelled her.

Outdoor fresh in the musty confines of the bathroom.

"Need some help?"

Was the deep-pitched huskiness in Julia's voice due to interrupted sleep or amusement at his expense?

"Do you mind if I turn on the light over the sink?" she asked. "It won't be as bright as the overhead."

He laughed at that one. "Doesn't bother me."

He used the moment when he thought she'd turned away to climb to his feet. At least he'd found the shaving cream.

Two gentle fingers pressed at his neck before he could get his bearings. "Yikes. Looks like you cut yourself." The can was pried from his hand before he could speak. "I've done this a hundred times at the hospital. I'll have you shaved in no time."

Mac turned to either side, feeling confined, lost. He could hear her at the sink, moving items around. Running fresh water. How had he lost control of the situation? Oh, right. He couldn't sneak anymore.

"Sorry I woke you."

"An apology, huh?" Had he been that awful to her? He bowed his head. Of course, he had. And she still wanted to help him? "I wasn't sleeping very well, anyway."

"You don't have to do this."

Her hands caught him above his elbows, angling him slightly. "You want me to let you cut up that handsome face even more? Sit."

Her teasing undercut his apology. The soft sounds of her moving around with such confident care made him a little less self-conscious. If he was smart, he'd let her help. And he desperately wanted to feel smart. "Where do you want me?"

"Right behind you. Knee level." Could he actually hear a smile? "Don't worry, the lid's down."

He heard the swoosh of foam as he sat, finding the toilet seat exactly where she'd indicated. He started to relax when he felt her knee touch his, nudging it aside.

Like a magnet reaching for its polar opposite, Mac's skin tingled through his jeans and shirt. She moved in close, with one leg on either side of his right thigh. An impersonal bit of practicality, he supposed.

But there was nothing impersonal about her heat meshing with his own. His body woke up and took notice of her tantalizing warmth, responding to an intangible beauty his eyes could not see.

Her hands cupped his cheeks and slid down across his jaw. She had too much foam, but he didn't mind the waste. She smoothed her palms into the indentations beneath his cheekbones, and her skin caught in the scruff of his beard, creating friction that sensitized his pores all the way down to his toes.

She tipped up his chin and stroked her fingers down his throat. Mac's mind reeled with questions. Was he looking up into her face? Was she looking down at his? Her breasts should be at eye-level, if he'd judged her height correctly. With a secret sight known only to those devils who plagued him, he dropped his gaze, trying to imagine what stern nurse Julia Dalton wore to bed.

Her arms were bare, so she hadn't put on a robe. Just how intimate was his no-nonsense nurse being with him? Just because he couldn't see didn't mean he couldn't imagine.

When she reached for the razor, her thigh pressed into his, and something very male, very unexpected tightened within his body. He hadn't felt competent or capable since the accident. But tonight, with Jules standing in front of him with her robeless body and bewitching hands, he felt incredibly normal. Instinctively male. He felt stirrings inside him he hadn't felt since long before the accident.

When her finger touched his chin and tilted it for her to reach his neck, he closed his eyes and reached out. He settled his hands at her waist. Soft cotton, he discovered. She wore a big cotton T-shirt to bed. He squeezed his fingers imperceptibly and analyzed further. Something with thick elastic rested beneath the T-shirt. Pajama pants.

Sensible Julia wore sensible clothes to bed. Only there was nothing sensible about his body's reaction to each sweep of the razor, cleaning his neck and jaw and cheek like a sensual caress. There was nothing sensible about the healthy heat firing deep in his belly as her thighs nudged his again, and her waist flexed within his hands. There was nothing sensible about the overwhelming desire to pull Julia into his lap and kiss her.

"I've made a mess of your shirt." She had to speak before he realized she'd finished the job. And before he could do anything sensible—like release her, or protest, or push away—she had the shirt up and over his head, skimming her fingers and palms along his flanks and shoulders along the way. He swallowed hard. Now she was undressing him. "Did you want to get in the shower, too?"

Mac stood, fighting off the drugging sensation of the fantasies he'd spun around Julia. She was doing her job. That was all.

He tried to sound unaffected by the intimacy they'd just shared. "Yeah. I can get it, though."

She bustled around some more, opening and closing a door. His hearing picked up on every sound, making his body long for her to return. "Here's a fresh towel and washcloth. I laid them on the toilet lid."

Next he heard the water running. Felt the steam rising in the air around him.

Felt her hands at the snap of his jeans.

Mac's body lurched in response. He snagged her hands and pulled them away from the betraying evidence in his pants. "I said I could handle it."

He felt the recoil in Julia's muscles and knew he had spoken harshly. Then he felt the tiny jerk in her arms, from shoulders shrugged as if they didn't care.

"I've been a nurse for eight years, Mac. It's not like I haven't seen everything."

This she didn't need to see.

He owed her something. Anything. At least an explanation.

"I'm not thinking of you as my nurse right now." He said the words slowly, giving her a hint of his reaction to her. "And I'm sure not thinking of you as the little girl who used to live across the street."

"Then what's wrong? I strip you down, you get in the shower, I bring you fresh clothes, we're done." Though her crisp voice held no trace of innuendo, the scene she conjured fired him up all over again.

"Jules—" He trailed his hands up her arms until he braced them at either side of her face. His fingers caught in a crop of short, silky curls that hugged the elegant shape of her head.

She wrapped her hands around his forearms and he felt the question in her touch. She still didn't understand. He angled his head to hers, hoping he had her face in his focus. "I'm thinking of you as a woman."

When the light dawned, her fingers tightened in a painful grip that pinched the hair on his arms. "No, you're not." Then she was pushing him away, backing away. "You can't."

"Can't what?" He tried to follow her, but ran into the sink.

"You must be thinking of someone else. You'd be disappointed if you could really see me."

By the time he'd negotiated the hallway, she'd shut her door in his face. He didn't try to open it or call to her, though he wanted an explanation. He'd hurt her too many times already.

Mac pressed his forehead against the panelled wall and wondered how else he could screw up today. He'd fought her at every turn, and then, in the middle of the night, he'd gone far beyond noticing her as a woman, and started lusting after her.

He was the blind man here. Couldn't she see how she affected him?

While he stood and considered all his mistakes, Mac's ears attuned to the tiniest of sounds.

The brush of a footstep? He heard it only once. He tilted his head to listen. There it was again.

It wasn't from Julia. She was stomping around in her room, cursing his confession, somebody named Anthony and men in general.

He heard the sound again. Soft, stealthy. Wade Osterman was on patrol outside and the doors were locked. Right?

With the sixth sense that only a blind man could possess, Mac turned.

Someone was in the house.

Chapter Four

Mac tapped softly at the closed door and whispered. "Jules."

"Leave me alone."

He wished he could.

"I need you." He swallowed his pride and made the plea. Through the wood he heard silence that seemed to last for days, punctuated by a heavy sigh.

He shifted his weight onto the balls of his feet, not knowing what to expect when the door opened with a rush. "What? I'm not on duty twenty-four hours a day, you know. I mean, I'm sorry if I embarrassed you in there—"

"Shh." Mac sought out the source of the reprimand turned apology. His fingers fumbled across her chin, then settled over her open mouth, cutting off a startled breath. "I need a set of eyes."

Julia pulled his hand away but latched on to it with that gentle authority he was learning to admire. The sudden hush in her voice told him she had picked up on his suspicion. "What's wrong?"

"Someone's in the kitchen."

"You're sure? Maybe it's mice in the woodwork. You haven't exactly been living up to code—" The shuffling he'd heard became the definite click of a cabinet door. Julia's fingers jerked around his, as if she'd heard the sound, too. "I guess that rules out mice." She braced her free hand against his chest for balance and stretched up on tiptoe to whisper right into his ear. "Should I call someone? My cell phone's in my bag in my room."

Mac shook his head and stepped away from her searing fingertips. It was hard enough to keep his speculations logical without the unexpected distraction of even her most innocent touch. "I don't want to look like an idiot if there's no one there." Mitch's vague warning about watching his back made him cautious. But he couldn't imagine what anyone hoped to find in his kitchen. "Let's check it out first."

"Okay." Dropping back to her feet, she pushed against his hand and moved him back a step. "I'll go look."

"No." He grabbed her shoulder as she scooted past him. "*You* don't go. *We* go." He couldn't provide much protection for her if there was an intruder, but he'd be damned if he'd let a woman go face a danger alone he wasn't willing to face himself. "I just need you to get a glimpse of who or what it is. Then we'll come back and phone it in if we need to."

"Okay."

Her shoulder rolled beneath his hand, and he realized she was steeling herself for whatever confrontation lay ahead. *Don't worry. I'm right behind you,* he wanted to say. But, somehow, that seemed like little comfort coming from him.

Mac slipped his hand down the soft cotton of her sleeve and wrapped his fingers through the crook of her elbow. "Let's go."

Angling himself behind her so that her shoulder butted against his, they stepped off together—both barefoot, and both blessedly silent as she led him through the dining room and around the corner into the living room. He found her easy to follow, not just because she kept her steps slow and evenly paced, but because they fit together so well. It was as if his arm—from the notch of his elbow to the pillow of his shoulder—was a perfect cradle to hold her arm from elbow to shoulder.

The sounds in the kitchen switched to a quiet shuffle, interrupted by the stealthy slide of a drawer and the rasp of metal dragging against…damn. The sound stopped before he could identify it. Someone was searching. But for what? Mac shut his eyes and tried to think.

Like a magician, he concentrated on conjuring an image of his kitchen and its contents inside his head. Dark wood cabinets. White appliances. Shadowy, faceless strangers.

He shook his head, silently damning his handicap. Once, he would have looked at a situation, assessed his options immediately and taken action.

Now he had to rely on Julia for the basic facts. He was useless. Damn, damn useless. It was easier to give her the lead and simply follow.

When she stopped, he stopped. He anticipated it in the movement of her arm and sent up a thankful prayer that he hadn't plowed into her or anything else and alerted the intruder to their presence. When she turned slightly, he stepped back with her. In one fluid movement she had them both backed against the wall just outside the kitchen.

He tore his mind away from the half-formed image of the kitchen and the intruder's intent, and focused on the woman standing at his side. He sensed her hesitation. The rallying of courage, the weighing of options.

God, she was a trooper. She'd put up with his foul mood all day, cleaned his mess, aroused his body like a lusty adolescent's—and now he was asking her to put herself in potential danger on his behalf.

And what had he done to repay her? Nothing. Nada. Not a damn thing. Not even a simple thank you.

Maybe he wasn't completely useless.

Thirty-seven years of being raised a Taylor wound its way into his conscience. Somewhere between the guilt and concern and simmering frustration that plagued him, a bit of the old Mac Taylor showed himself. He slid his fingers along the smooth warmth of Julia's forearm and found her hand folded into a quaking fist. He wrapped his fingers around hers and squeezed.

"You don't have to do this. I shouldn't have asked."

"I'd feel better if I had a baseball bat." He smiled at her brave sarcasm. At least, that's what it felt like the rusty muscles around his mouth were doing. And then he heard a thump that erased the brief smile. A crunching noise reverberated in some dark recess on the other side of the wall. Mac craned his neck to identify the new sounds. The tug at his arm pulled his focus back to Julia. "What is it?"

"I think he's eating."

"Eating?" Julia's entire body stiffened. "What kind…? Her muscles bunched wherever he touched her, ready to spring into action. "Oh, no."

Before Mac could piece together the meaning of her response, she'd marched off into the kitchen. He reached out for her, but caught nothing but air. "Jules!"

"Wade Osterman! What the hell do you think you're doing?" Even Mac snapped to attention at the crisp command in Julia's voice. He heard a flurry of activity and a bass-deep curse. Then a heartbeat of silence pounded in Mac's darkness before Julia continued. "You scared me to death. I thought someone had broken in."

"I was hungry and you're a good cook." The police officer's voice was muffled, as if he had food still stuffed in his mouth.

"Skip the flattery, Wade. You're supposed to be guarding us, not sneaking around the house." Mac flattened his palm against the wall and followed it to the kitchen archway.

"I found the back door open when I was making my rounds. I checked it out. Nothing's been disturbed. I'm watching things."

Mac joined the conversation. "Not very well."

The hushed rasp of his stern pronouncement echoed through the room. He stayed near the door, out of the light that so tortured his eyes. From the responding creak of leather, which he supposed was a holster or utility belt, the officer with the full mouth was standing straighter and taking notice of Mac.

He heard the gulping sound of too big a bite going down a man's gullet. "It's after midnight. I didn't realize anybody was still up. I was trying to be quiet."

Mac matched what he assumed was the guard's defensive stance. He hadn't drawn his gun, or Julia would have reacted. Instead, he could tell she'd taken a step back toward him, judging by the proximity of that familiar sunshine scent.

From the angle of his voice, he guessed Wade to be a good three to four inches taller than he was. But the big man was unsure of himself, facing off against Mac and Julia. He didn't know what to make of being caught with his hand literally in the cupboard like this.

Mac's chest expanded with a calming breath.

Not so useless, after all.

It was ridiculous to think he had any kind of advantage here. But he felt it, anyway. Maybe it was the rank he'd once carried, that would put him above a street officer like Osterman. Or maybe it was the edgy shifting from foot to foot that Mac could hear in the other man's soft-soled shoes.

"You came in the back door, you say?"

"Yeah. I've been walking the perimeter every half hour.

I thought you'd be asleep. You really ought to do a better job about locking up.''

So Osterman had come up the back porch and through the hallway—when? While Mac was sulking in his room? While he was in the bathroom with Julia?

How had he heard him in the kitchen, but not walking through the house?

Suddenly the tension in the room shifted, and Wade's voice brightened. ''Was I interrupting something?''

Mac recognized the abrupt, wink-wink apology of one man to another. With his concentration focused on finding the source of the sounds in the kitchen, he had forgotten he was dressed in nothing but jeans and briefs. While Julia wore…

Mac muttered a damning curse and his pulse quickened with a protective beat. Julia's luscious figure was covered with nothing more than that old soft T-shirt and pajama pants. And Wade was probably taking in an unfair eyeful.

''What we were—''

''No, of course not.'' Julia's vehement denial bounced off his ego and plunged the room into an awkward silence.

''Hey!'' An instant after Wade's protest, Mac heard the light switch. He guessed she had turned it off out of consideration for his sensitive eyes, but wondered if she, too, had suddenly become aware of how much Wade could see.

Of all the things she'd endured today, Mac was determined that embarrassment not be one of them. He walked toward Julia's scent and found himself behind her. He put his hands up and cupped her strong shoulders. Without a clear sense of direction, he didn't know if he was hiding her from Wade's view or simply offering his support.

But one thing was clear. He could feel the chill of her skin through her shirt. Answering a vague alarm inside his head, he automatically began to rub her shoulders, offering his heat, his strength—whatever she'd been robbed of at that moment.

But apparently his touch was not what she needed. Or wanted. She slipped away, and the next moment he could hear her at the sink, running water, busying herself cleaning up a few dishes.

Wade had followed her movements, too. "That was good pie, ma'am. I hope it's okay that I polished it off."

"Sure."

Mac pinpointed the source of Wade's voice, and turned to face the sound. "I don't mind if you eat the food, Osterman. But next time you come in, announce yourself. There's no sense giving Ms. Dalton a fright."

"Sorry, ma'am. I'll just, uh, take this last bit with me." The water continued to run and Julia continued to work, oblivious to Wade's apology or Mac's defense.

Her sudden silence was a stark contrast to the woman who had barked orders at Wade only moments ago. What was it about conversations taking a personal turn that made her withdraw like that? With too many thoughts to analyze, Mac opted for the one he had the best chance of understanding. He turned to Osterman. "I'll walk you out."

"You can do that?"

Mac bristled at the officer's surprise, but didn't respond. "Let me hold your arm."

Reluctantly, Wade let him grab on and led him into the living room. Mac used the opportunity to learn the dimensions of their ravenous bodyguard. He discovered Osterman was right-handed since there was no gun on his left side. He wasn't sure why he wanted that information, but the time it took to find it out gave Julia a moment to recover from whatever had made her blood run cold like that.

Seven steps from the kitchen Wade stopped. The chain

lock rattled and the dead bolt slid into the open position with an authoritative thunk. "Can you lock up behind me?"

Mac nodded as the door opened and a brisk breeze from the damp autumn night cooled his naked torso. "You're on duty until eight in the morning?"

"I get a replacement at noon."

Mac had been a scientist and a cop. The natural instinct to press for answers until his curiosity was satisfied kept him asking questions. "What did Captain Taylor tell you about this assignment?"

The breeze diverted, hitting Mac in the arm now. Wade must be blocking the doorway. "The captain?" Hesitation gurgled in Wade's throat. Was he searching his memory for Mitch's orders?

"Captain Taylor *did* tell you why you were here, right?"

"Right." Wade sucked in an audible breath. "He said I should watch the house. Said maybe the explosion at the lab wasn't an accident. That somebody might be gunning for you, too."

"So you're here to protect me, not keep an eye on me."

Mac got the impression that subterfuge wasn't easy for this big tank of a man. He had less trust of Osterman's next answer. "That's right. Look. I'm sorry if I overstepped my bounds and all. It's just, I haven't had home-cookin' in a long while. Not since my divorce. It was hard to resist. You're not going to report me for leaving my post, are you?"

"Not this time." Mac braced his hands on his hips and trained his unfocused gaze on the words from Wade's throat. "Just keep in mind what I said about announcing yourself. And report anything you see to me, all right?"

"Yes, sir." The breeze swirled around him as Wade

hesitated in the open doorway. "You'll, uh, smooth things out with Ms. Dalton, right?"

The boyish plea in that incongruously deep voice almost made Mac laugh. But giving in to humor might shatter the illusion of authority he'd established with the uniformed officer. "I'll do what I can."

"Thanks. Good night."

"Good night, Osterman."

The last of the cool air was cut off when the door closed. Mac searched until he found the dead bolt, then pulled the door open again. He wrapped his fingers around the outside edge and ran his fingertips along the keyhole itself. A set of eyes couldn't give him a clearer impression. The brass felt smooth and cold. And solid and unblemished as the day his brother Brett had installed it.

No sign of forced entry.

He set aside his curiosity for the moment and locked the door. Once he had the chain fastened, he extended his arm and turned. He hit the back of the sofa and used it to orient him in the direction of the kitchen.

When he bumped the old oak molding framing the archway into the kitchen, he shifted into the opening. Julia was still busy at the sink. Washing dishes, from the lemony smell of things.

"What's wrong?" he demanded.

"Nothing."

"Don't lie to me. I'm at enough of a disadvantage as it is." He lifted his arms and shuffled, Frankenstein-like, across the kitchen. "Osterman said something that bothered you. Your body temperature dropped a good five degrees."

The surprise in her voice was clear as she faced him. "You could tell that?"

At least she didn't deny her reaction. Her wet, soapy

fingers latched on to his elbow and guided him to the counter beside her before quickly releasing him.

"I'm discovering I can tell a lot about what's going on around me if I put my mind to it. What was wrong?"

A moment passed before she answered. "He said the door was open. But I swear I locked them both. I double-checked them before I turned in. It's a habit from living alone in Chicago."

A smart one, in his opinion. And one that made him all the more suspicious of their so-called bodyguard. He reached for her elbow, soap suds and all. "Take me to the back door. Now."

He was quickly getting used to the subtle sway of her body moving in synchronous step with his. Twenty-four hours ago he'd been stumbling around his house, cursing anything that jumped into his path. Now, with Julia at his side, those hazards fell by the wayside. He could move. He could think. He could act.

As he suspected, the door to the back porch was bolted tight.

Julia tried to rationalize Wade's entry into the house. "That proves nothing. It would be simple enough to lock it behind him once he was in. Should I check for broken windows?"

"No, we would have heard that. Examine the lock again. Are there scratch marks around the keyhole itself?"

"You mean like it'd been picked?"

"Yes."

He waited. "I don't see anything."

Forget solving Jeff Ringlein's death. Mac couldn't even solve this simple problem. Yet.

Out of instinct, he started to pace. Two steps and a solid wall cut short that avenue. In a flash of frustrated anger, he turned on Jules. "Did you give Osterman a key?"

"No. I don't have one. Your mother let me in."

What was going on here?

"Then how the hell did he get inside my house?"

JULIA ROLLED UP the sleeves of her olive green canvas shirt before pulling the toaster down from the cabinet beside the fridge. A ham and cheese omelette bubbled in the frying pan on the stove and the coffee was ready to be poured.

Though she hadn't gotten to bed until nearly 2 a.m., sleep had been an elusive thing. But Wade's mysterious midnight visit had been the least of her concerns.

I'm thinking of you as a woman.

She'd only been doing her job, helping out a patient who needed her assistance. But, in all honesty, she hadn't been entirely professional about helping Mac with his toilette. She'd never gotten to touch him like that before.

She'd never touched any man like that.

She never thought she could.

Fingertips tracing the angles and dipping into the contours of his rugged face. Her palms receiving a jillion little jolts of electricity as she rubbed them along his beard.

Not even Dr. Anthony Cardello's six-month seduction had made her so aware of a man. Anthony had been her last hope. Her last hurrah.

Her biggest mistake.

Last night, she'd almost set herself on a similar collision course with doomsday.

In those brief, charged moments with Mac, something inside her had awakened. All her schoolgirl dreams of what it might be like to be truly intimate with a man had escaped the little Pandora's box she kept tightly locked deep inside her heart. That little locked box had saved her from humiliation more times than she cared to remember.

I'm thinking of you as a woman

She'd been thinking of Mac as a man.

She'd known it had been wrong to stare at the lean angles and planes of Mac's bare chest. She'd marveled at the healing power of pink scarred skin. The damage from the burns he'd suffered reached down like an angry claw from his right shoulder. But the talons of marred skin faded into healthy flesh tones and a golden mat of hair that nestled between his pectoral muscles and thinned into a long line running down to the snap of his jeans.

Definitely a man.

He'd suffered so much pain, yet he remained so strong. She'd been wrong to mourn the fractured beauty in his dark granite eyes. Wrong to wonder if his thin, firm lips would soften when he kissed a woman. Or whether they'd be as hard as the rest of his features, which were chiselled a bit too sharply into gaunt lines after his hospital stay.

Her pulse had raced. She couldn't even remember breathing.

She'd admired and wondered—with the safe barrier of his blindness between them. His sightless eyes hid her shortcomings and made it easy to drop her guard. She could imagine herself any way she wanted. Pretty. Thin. Sexy.

He was the one who had knocked some sense into her. Reminded her of her professional duty.

I'm thinking of you as a woman.

Julia nearly laughed out loud at his pitiful misconception of reality.

It was absolutely time to leave. She'd packed up her bag and her schoolgirl fantasies and counted the minutes until Martha Taylor would relieve her of duty.

Because of all the men in this world she was destined to disappoint, she didn't want Mac Taylor to be one of them.

With the bread in the toaster and a mug of hot coffee

and cream in her hand, Julia leaned her hip against the counter and waited for Mac to make an appearance.

Just like last night's dinner, she refused to wait on him. She was willing to cook, but he needed to make an effort toward his recovery. Deciding to clean himself up was a first step. Now she needed to get him to wake up at a decent hour and eat regular meals to rebuild his strength.

At least he'd finally taken an interest in something besides the chemicals sitting on his dresser. The coolly rational Mac of old had finally returned for a brief time last night. Like a dog with a new bone, he'd replayed and studied and silently considered just how Wade Osterman had broken into the house to finish off the leftovers from dinner.

The man had gotten a key from somewhere, Mac determined. The *where* was the mystery. Mac's key ring was still in the top drawer of his dresser, and he'd given a spare set to his parents after his accident.

This morning, Julia had found things out of place in almost every drawer and cabinet. Maybe it was just the sloppy work of a man who didn't know his way around a kitchen. Or maybe Mac had reason to be suspicious.

First, Detective Masterson had been snooping around. Now, Wade had gotten into a locked house.

A chill rippled down her spine. As she carried a plate of toast and jelly to the table, she couldn't help but look over her shoulder at the row of cabinets she'd set to rights that morning.

She was alone in a house with a blind man. Yet she couldn't shake the feeling that somehow she was being watched.

"Smells good."

Julia jumped at the rasp of Mac's voice, and the plate of toast clattered onto the table top. Her startled heart beat like a rabbit's. She automatically clutched her hand above it before turning to see him standing in the archway.

"How? How did…?"

Mac's spiky short hair glistened with the moisture from a recent shower. He'd dressed himself in a clean pair of jeans, white socks with his beat-up loafers, and a gray Mizzou Tigers sweatshirt that hugged his broad shoulders and draped loosely over his lean torso.

"I'm not the brain of the family for nothing. I can be taught." He walked in, his arms out in front to act as feelers. A pair of sleek, black, wrap-around sunglasses masked his damaged eyes. "I'm learning to count steps. Plus, having a clear path through the rooms helps."

Julia's heart rate slowed with an infusion of pride and amusement. "Should I tell you the price sticker is still on the left lens?"

"Ruins the studly look, huh?"

No. Nothing could ruin the effect of intellectual sun god Mac Taylor smiling with that wry self-assurance of his again.

A moment later Julia remembered it wasn't her place to wear a silly, indulgent expression, so she pushed back her sleeves and went to work. "I can fix them easily enough for you." She pulled the blinds over the sink window to dim the light in the room, and took his glasses. She could tease right back as long as she knew it was all about a nurse-patient relationship. "Now. Are you also going to let me medicate and bandage those eyes like I'm supposed to?"

"One step at a time, Jules." He knocked his thigh against one of the chairs at the table and stopped. "Where do you want me?"

She pulled a soft dish towel from a drawer and dried his glasses. "Right where you are. Pull out the chair. There's a place setting there."

"I usually sit at the head of the table." He slid around the corner of the table. "I'm more out of the way here, aren't I?"

"You don't have to be out of the way. It's your hou—"

"What's this?"

Her black leather backpack hung from his fist. Too late, she realized she'd left it lying in the chair.

The frown that creased the raw skin around his eyes was more curiosity than confusion.

Julia felt like a traitor. "That's my bag."

"Judging by the weight of it, it's all packed. Are you that eager to leave me?" His voice had dropped a notch in pitch, and any humor that had lightened his tone got lost in the wounded timbre of his damaged vocal cords.

Julia crossed the room and made a quick exchange of his glasses for her backpack. She hugged the bag to her chest, using it as a bulky shield to protect her from the ice that spread across his features.

"I only promised your mother twenty-four hours. I was just filling in until she could find a permanent replacement."

"Permanent." Mac flicked his sunglasses onto the table. If he could see, his eyes would be drilling holes through her. "You mean I have to break in somebody else? I felt comfortable with you."

Comfortable?

She had to look away from the frozen granite. Comfy was the story of her life. Comfortable. Fun. One of the guys. She'd had way too much *comfortable* and not enough *special* along the way.

But that was hardly Mac's problem. He had bigger issues to deal with than her iffy ability to deal with a man on a personal level. Desperately needing the awkward moment to end, she set her bag down and carried their plates to the stove.

Busier was always better. "I came home to see my parents, not to work." It was a white lie that softened the feeling of letting him down. George and Barbara Dalton had been the destination, if not necessarily the reason, for her return to Kansas City. "Besides, you need someone trained in home health care. I'm a trauma nurse. Now if you chop off your finger or fall off the roof, I'm your woman. But this day-to-day stuff—you know—there's just not enough excitement for me."

She cut the omelette in two and dished it up, not realizing her joke had fallen on deaf ears until she heard the scrape of a chair leg behind her. She was too late to save the ladder-back chair from crashing to the floor. Too late to stop Mac from stalking out of the kitchen.

She followed, hot on his heels, dashing in front of him before he reached the dining room. "Where are you going?"

"Back to my room." He halted in his tracks, knowing she blocked his path. But she stood her ground beneath the assault of his sightless glare.

"Mac, it's not you." She hastened to apologize. Tried to explain without really explaining anything. "I didn't mean—"

The doorbell rang, giving her a chance to think, giving him a chance to push past her.

He banged his shoulder against the archway as he escaped too quickly. "I don't want to see anybody."

Julia's temper flared at the abuse he endured in the name of self-pity. "Dammit, Mac, if you want to duke this out, then stay and fight. You can't afford to make three steps of progress and then run away."

"Run away?" He whirled around. He swayed at the fast movement. But Julia didn't help him. She retreated a step as he lurched forward and braced his hands at either side of the archway to steady himself. "Look who's talking."

"I am not running away." The skewed lie choked in her throat. "I told you. I made a deal with our mothers. Twenty-four hours."

The doorbell rang a second time, followed by a sharp knock and Wade's voice. "Detective Taylor? Miss Dalton?"

Julia swallowed and took a deep breath. She didn't want her stay with Mac to end with a shouting match. "That's Wade with your mother now, I'll bet."

"Free of the ogre at last, huh? I want to talk to her and set her straight on her crazy ideas about taking care of me." He knocked his shin against the coffee table as he set a course to avoid Julia.

She headed for the door herself when Wade knocked again. "She asked me to help because she loves you, Mac. She wants you to heal. I do, too. It's just that I can't stay."

"I thought we were friends, Jules."

He halted at the end of the couch, using his hand to steady himself there. His gravelly soft whisper cut short all her arguments.

Friends?

Acquaintances, perhaps. Neighbors, for sure. A naive damsel in distress and her stalwart rescuer—who'd gone their separate ways after that one terrible, frightening night.

"I owed you a favor, Mac." Now that she was about to leave, she could at least tell him that. She turned to look him in the eye, as if facing him would somehow allow him to see how fifteen years of gratitude and shame had left her with feelings impossible to explain or fulfill. "I needed to repay a debt. But your brother Cole's my buddy. You and I barely know each other."

"What favor?" he demanded.

Had she really expected him to remember the incident that had forever shaped her life?

But that much she would not give. She left his question unanswered and turned back to slip off the chain lock and open the door to Wade.

"Good morning, ma'am. Everything all right?"

She glanced beyond him to welcome Martha, but stopped short. The only person on the front step was Wade himself. She didn't recognize the sporty black Mercedes-Benz in the driveway. Burying a flare of panic, she delivered her good morning to Wade. "We were just having a difference of opinion."

"I see." The glazed expression in his red-rimmed eyes told her that if he did truly understand, he was too tired to care.

Julia took a moment of compassion for the big man. "There's some breakfast on the stove if you're hungry. Why don't you go on in and help yourself."

Wade's weary expression perked up immediately. "Sounds great."

Mac made his presence known by coming up beside Julia. "What's going on, Osterman?"

The uniformed officer straightened to something resembling attention. "You have a visitor, sir. A Mrs. Melanie Ringlein."

"Jeff's wife?"

"Mac? Is that you?"

A petite woman skirted around Wade. Dressed in black leather pants and a matching jacket, she walked straight to Mac. Her dark brown hair hung in perfect glory past her shoulders, and framed her tear-stained face. Both Julia and Wade took a step back as she threw her arms around Mac's neck and hugged him tight. "Oh, Mac. I need your help."

She stretched up on tiptoe, pressing every inch of her trim figure into Mac's long body. "You may be the only one who can."

Chapter Five

"Oh, Mac. I just don't know who to turn to."

A despair that bordered on panic seemed to color Melanie Ringlein's tears.

Mac's hands hovered in the air about her shoulders. And if the stunned look on his face was any indication, he didn't know whether to hug her or push her away. Julia watched as he reached a logical compromise. He wrapped one arm around Melanie's back and turned her toward the sofa. "Have a seat, and tell me what's wrong."

She answered with a cry that covered three syllables and several pitches. She turned her face into Mac's chest and sobbed again. "Jeff never meant to hurt you. He always thought of you as a friend. I do, too. This is all such a terrible mistake. He didn't mean to do anything wrong."

"I believe the explosion at the lab was an accident." Mac stretched out his left hand and located the sofa. "I don't blame Jeff for my injuries."

"Then you'll help me?" She threw her arms around his shoulders and hung on to his neck. "Oh, Mac, I knew I could count on you."

He guided her down to a cushion and sat beside her. "Don't be so sure. I'm not up to full strength yet. And you still haven't told me what the problem is." Patting her back, he rocked her back and forth. But Melanie only leaned into him and wept, babbling on about being left alone and being unable to cope.

The dark-haired beauty was petite and delicate and utterly feminine. A striking foil to Mac's golden coloring and masculine dimensions.

Julia crossed her arms in front of her and turned away, squashing a rise of futile jealousy. The woman was in mourning, after all. She wouldn't be the first to turn to rock-steady Mac Taylor for solace or advice.

Hadn't she done the same fifteen years ago?

"Melanie." Mac's clipped voice betrayed his scientist's need for understanding. "You have to tell me what's going on. Has something happened?"

"Yes."

While Melanie sniffled, Mac patted his pockets, searching for a handkerchief. But he'd done well to get himself dressed that morning. Packing such an accessory hadn't occurred to him.

His lips pressed into a thin line, and the scars beside his eyes furrowed, revealing his mounting frustration at finding a solution. With a muttered curse he stuck out his hand, poking the air, reaching out for…her.

Startled by the demanding request for her assistance, when she'd thought he'd forgotten her presence, it took a moment for Julia to react. If he'd been sighted, he could have seen the questioning look on her face. That silent question that asked how he could hold a beautiful woman in his arms and still know she existed.

But more deeply ingrained instincts overrode that perennial self-doubt. He needed her help. And as long as he was her responsibility, she couldn't deny him. She picked up the box of tissues from the desk and brought it over. She set the box in his lap and pressed a couple of tissues into his hand.

In the instant their hands touched, he turned his fingers

and squeezed hers. His grip on her tightened as his shoulders lifted with a deep breath. Julia held her own, feeling the tension radiating from his body into hers, like a bolt of lightning dissolving into a handful of charged atoms as it hit a lightning rod and grounded itself. His grip slackened as the tension eased from his shoulders.

But he didn't release her. He tilted his face toward hers, as if he could study her reaction to his simple touch. As if he, too, had somehow felt the same electric current that rooted her to the spot.

Melanie seemed to sense that his focus had shifted from her, however briefly. Her chin quivered as she pulled back, struggling to contain the emotions that overwhelmed her. "Mac?"

He turned his head back to that quavering voice. "I forgot to make introductions. Melanie Ringlein, this is Julia Dalton. She's a…"

What? An old friend? A roommate? His verbal sparring partner?

Mac released her hand. A resigned mask settled across his features. "She's my nurse."

Julia curled her fingers into her palm and clutched it to her stomach, withering beneath his final choice for defining their relationship.

What had she expected, anyway? She hardly qualified for anything beyond her temporary job description. That brief, charged need they had shared was nothing more than a patient's panicked quest for assistance. And like the good nurse she was, she had delivered. Anything more personal had simply been the wishful thinking of that traitorous Pandora's box hidden deep within her heart.

Moving past the disappointment, she extended her hand to Melanie. "It's a pleasure to meet you. I'm sorry it couldn't be under better circumstances."

Melanie took her hand in a light grip, lifting her puffy red eyes to Julia. "Did you know Jeff?"

Julia shrugged an apology. "No."

"Oh." Melanie frowned. She snatched the tissues from Mac's hand and dabbed at her eyes, reclaiming his full attention and dismissing Julia from the conversation. "They've tied up all of Jeff's money."

"Who has?"

Resigning herself to her subservient position, Julia busied herself straightening items on the desktop that she'd straightened the day before. She watched her patient from a distance and eavesdropped on his conversation, while the lingering aftershocks of his needy touch ran their course out through the tips of her fingers and toes.

"Internal Affairs." Julia began to imagine a pattern in the other woman's tears. A soft sob or catch of breath punctuated each tidbit of information. "They say I can't use Jeff's bank accounts as long as he's under investigation. But I have bills to pay."

Instead of reacting to the helplessness that was so evident in Melanie's pouty mouth and the sad tracks of mascara that had run down onto her cheeks, Mac responded like the investigator he was. "If they're examining his accounts, they must suspect he was taking a payoff of some kind. He *was* destroying evidence when I found him."

"He wouldn't do anything wrong," Melanie insisted. "Not on purpose. Jeff wasn't like that. He was working extra hours to buy me nice things, that's all. He always took care of me." Melanie's breath stuttered and caught on a silent sob. "Who's going to take care of me now?"

When the tears flowed in earnest again, Julia wondered if Mrs. Ringlein had ever considered working a job herself to pay the bills.

As soon as the uncharitable thought registered, Julia regretted it. She'd been supporting herself since college graduation, but then she'd never had any other choice. Melanie had found a good man to love, a man who supported her. And now she had suffered a devastating loss. She'd read of cases, involving older women mostly, in which a widow who'd been supported throughout her marriage faced a double loss when her spouse died. She lost not only the man she loved, but her way of life.

Who was she to begrudge Melanie that kind of grief?

Still, it hurt to see how Mac held Melanie's hands in both of his. He wasn't a man who used soft words and sweet reassurances, but the effort he made to gentle the harsh natural rasp in his voice triggered an embarrassing memory.

Even fifteen years ago, he had been kind to women in trouble.

We'll get a steak from Dad's shop to put on that lip. The words weren't suggestive. Not even remotely romantic.

But the words weren't what had made the difference that night.

Julia had hung her head in shame while the tall, gallant son of a butcher had draped his jacket around her shoulders. Mac's tone had been clearer then, without the hoarseness of damaged vocal cords. But he'd been no less gentle.

His long supple fingers had touched her chin and lifted her ugly, wounded face up to be studied through his golden glasses. His beautiful gray eyes had looked right into hers. She'd squirmed like a specimen under a microscope beneath that look.

But then Mac had smiled. It was a half-moon-shaped grin that said everything would be all right. That promised *she* was all right.

And she believed him.

For a few precious minutes that night, she believed she was all right.

A man like Mac Taylor wouldn't lie.

Melanie's sniffles jerked Julia back to the present. "They can't do that, can they? Couldn't you talk to someone?" Melanie probably recognized Mac's integrity, too.

Right now he was looking at a spot over Melanie's right shoulder. Maybe he'd misplaced her position. Or maybe he just didn't know what to say. "I don't think I can help you. I'm on leave from the force right now."

"I don't need a cop." Melanie frowned at his faraway gaze. She reached up and turned his face to hers. "I need a man."

Excuse me?

Julia froze at the brunette's bold suggestion. She must have made some slight sound because Mac looked her way, dragging his attention away from Melanie.

But Mrs. Ringlein needed consoling. She demanded his full attention right now. "Mac?" She clutched at the front of his shirt and dropped her voice to a seductive pitch. "Please say you'll help me."

Julia watched, feeling helpless herself, as Mac succumbed to the other woman's needs. Soon he was promising phone calls and recommending a lawyer's name. All the while holding Melanie's hands tight within his own.

Julia forced herself to look away. Her heart sank in her chest, weighed down by a familiar set of emotions that she had never quite been able to shake. They pressed into her lungs, making it difficult to breathe.

Loving a man she had no chance with was one thing. Watching him with another woman was a punishment she didn't have to endure.

"I'll be in the kitchen if you need me." Julia bid what she hoped was a polite excuse, and hurried out of the room.

Her company there wasn't much better.

"What do you mean it's off?" Wade snapped the question into his cell phone. But with his mouth full of eggs he was eating straight from the frying pan, his accusation lost some of its punch. "You promised me twenty to one."

Julia didn't know whether to laugh or frown. He made an amusing picture, but something about his phone call upset him. She decided she'd better make her presence known. "I can put that on a plate for you," she offered.

Wade spared her a glance over his shoulder. The wild look in his eyes didn't seem to recognize her. Instead of answering, he turned the width of his formidable back to her and huddled over the phone.

His intense emotion made his whisper loud enough to overhear. "No. Don't call her. My money's good. You make the damn bet."

With one hand he flipped the phone shut and slid it back onto his utility belt. With the other, he stabbed a forkful of eggs and shoved them into his mouth.

His eyes, bleary from a night on watch, nonetheless reflected his charming smile when he finally turned to face her. "Sorry about that. I had to take care of some personal business."

"Everything okay?"

"Fine." Though his face smiled, his big shoulders still radiated the tension he'd displayed during the phone call. *Nice cover,* thought Julia. If she wasn't so used to picking up the nuances of her patients when trying to diagnose them, she might have believed his answer. "I'd better get back to my post. Do you mind?"

He inclined his head toward the table. Julia followed his gaze to the stack of buttered toast that had probably cooled to room temperature by now. "Uh, no." She picked up the plate. "I could make you fresh."

"This is fine." He crossed to the table in one long

stride, swooped down and left the room, leaving Julia standing with an empty plate in her hand.

"You're welcome." She called the phrase to an empty room and the double click of the front door opening and closing behind him.

Julia set down the plate, surveyed the damage left by the feeding frenzy of Wade Osterman, and decided she had no other calling in this world than to clean up after a pair of messy men.

She made quick work of the dishes and countertops, and was drying the last pan when she noticed the utensil drawer to the right of the stove was open an inch or so. She went to close it with a butt of her hip, but something inside caught her eye. In the tiny gap between drawer and counter she saw serving spoons, a tape measure, a can opener, two wooden spatulas, and...

A key.

A house key. A spare made from a generic slug instead of one bearing the brand name of the matching lock.

Julia hung up the towel and the pan before returning to the drawer. Perplexed by the discovery, she opened the drawer farther and simply stared. She had cleaned this place from top to bottom this morning. She'd gone through all the drawers herself to make sure there were no steak knives or other sharp objects for Mac to accidentally grab. She'd run across a lot of junk in these drawers—it was a man's kitchen, after all, a scientist's kitchen at that—but she didn't remember finding a key.

Wade had gotten into the house last night with no signs of forced entry. It was his word against her memory that she had left the back door unlocked.

Julia opened the kitchen blinds and gazed out. She saw the back half of Wade's black and white police cruiser parked on the street beyond the hedge surrounding Mac's yard.

Was it normal for a cop to be so hungry while on guard duty? To make himself so at home in a stranger's kitchen?

Was it normal for a jovial giant to get so angry and distressed after one phone call?

A shiver of unease raced down Julia's spine. She grabbed the key and closed the drawer. Too many things didn't add up. She might be leaving Mac's house with her ego in shreds and her heart aching with unrequited feelings. But dammit, she was going to leave with her sanity intact.

With no desire to rejoin Melanie and Mac, she palmed the key, pulled on her jacket and decided to test the locks herself.

In the living room, Melanie stood in front of Mac's seated form and smiled down at him. "If you'll excuse me a minute, I'm just going to borrow your bathroom and—powder my nose." The hitch in her voice promised that she was done crying. Julia paused just long enough to see the petite beauty bend down and plant a lingering kiss on Mac's cheek. "Thank you. For everything."

Julia's pulse stopped, then pounded inside her veins. She had no right to be jealous. No right.

"It's just down the hall." Mac waved his hand in the general direction of the bathroom and Melanie danced off to freshen up. Obviously, their guest was feeling better. Much better.

Julia tried to make a quick exit, too, but Mac's voice stopped her from behind. "Jules?"

She hadn't made a sound. How did he know? It didn't matter. Julia shook off her curiosity as he stood. She wanted to spend as little time with Mac as possible until her replacement arrived. Less time meant fewer false hopes. Fewer stirred-up memories. Less chance of certain disappointment. "I'm going out for some fresh air," she answered, already on her way out the door. "Holler if you need me."

If Mac had any response, she didn't give him a chance to say it. Julia closed the door and pressed her back against it, using the recuperative moment to look down the front walk. Wade sat inside his cruiser, on the phone again, caught up in yet another heated discussion.

Good, she thought. It was just as well he didn't see her snooping around. After all, if her instincts proved correct, she'd caught him in a lie. Though he'd been more polite than not with her, she didn't imagine Wade would handle an accusation of lying particularly well.

Julia quickly slipped around the house to the back door. Holding her breath in anticipation, she inserted the key into the keyhole—and unlocked the door.

A cool whirlwind whipped the curls of her hair about her face while she stood there with her hand frozen on the key in the lock. "Why?" she whispered, her question carried away on the breeze.

She knew the key hadn't been in that drawer until after Wade's breakfast visit. Was he so embarrassed by his appetite that he felt he had to steal a key and lie? Did sneaking into the house have anything to do with his angry phone calls?

Julia relocked the door and pocketed the key. She needed a detective to figure this out.

Though the man with the obvious deductive skills waited on the other side of this door in the living room, Julia wasn't eager to ask for his help. Why stir up a mystery when Mac had other things to deal with right now? No one had gotten hurt by Wade's intrusion. The only thing missing was her caramel apple pie.

Maybe she would go ask Wade for an explanation, after all. She blew out her breath on a sarcastic sigh. Didn't that sound like fun?

Julia took her time returning to the front of the house.

Though the morning air was crisp with an October chill, the sun beat down upon her face and warmed her. Just like the house, Mac's yard had a lot of potential. The surrounding hedge was healthy, turning from green to golden yellow. It had been trimmed to a waist-high level, but needed to have the blown trash picked out of it. And though the grass was turning brown with the change of the season, there were still a few mums holding their color in a row along the front of the house. Gold and salmon and crimson red.

She wondered if Mac had planted those flowers. Had he been able to enjoy their rich autumnal color? Or did visible aesthetics like that even interest him? It was at that moment Julia realized she knew a great deal about Mac's character, but almost nothing about his personal tastes. His personality. His day-to-day habits in life.

She still judged him by who he had been that night so long ago. He'd been twenty-two then, a med student at the University of Missouri-Kansas City. This Mac was harder and leaner, and a lot less patient than her hero had been. Yet for all his scars, all his resentment, all his rough talk, she still thought of him as that young man who had saved her.

She still owed him.

And if she had no other way to repay him, she could at least offer him the truth.

With the key clutched inside her fist deep inside the pocket of her denim jacket, she headed for the front door.

She stopped just shy of the porch, though, as the door opened. Melanie Ringlein, with her arm linked through Mac's, waltzed out onto the top step. "You've been great about this, Mac."

"Consider it a favor to Jeff." He stopped short when

they left the shade of the porch and stepped into the full sunlight. Mac squeezed his eyes shut and ducked his head.

Automatically, Julia took a step forward, but Melanie beat her to the problem. "What's wrong with you?"

"The light hurts my eyes." He thumbed over his shoulder. "I need my glasses."

"Oh. Well—" Melanie stretched upon tiptoe and pressed a kiss to Mac's jaw. "Thanks. I'll call you later, okay?"

Julia bit her tongue at the other woman's self-centered inconsideration. Instead of complaining, Julia pushed past them both and picked up Mac's sunglasses from the kitchen table.

By the time she returned, Melanie had climbed into her Mercedes and was backing out of the driveway. The woman was as sleek and stylish as her car, but Julia was glad to see her go. "Are you coming in?" she asked.

"No. The sun feels good." Though his eyes were still closed, he had angled his head to bask in the clear autumn rays.

"Here." She pushed his glasses into his fingers.

When he had them on, he lifted his face to the sunlight. "Much better. Thanks."

Julia blinked as the sun reflected off the lenses. The bright morning light glistened along the remnants of gold in his hair and bathed his skin in a healthy glow. She wondered if he had any idea how handsome he was despite the disfigurement on his face. Probably not.

"So—" she began, feeling an awkward need to cover her tendency to stare. "You must have said the right thing to Melanie. She sure seemed perky all of a sudden."

"The woman's going through a hard time. If she feels a bit of happiness, let her." He lowered his focus and turned toward her. "Her husband's not only dead, but he's accused of betraying the police department. That could wipe out Jeff's pension, not to mention his reputation.''

''Do you think he's guilty of taking a payoff to destroy evidence?''

''What I think doesn't matter. Melanie needs our patience and understanding right now.''

''Not *ours*. She's only interested in yours.''

He folded his arms across his chest. A dare crept into his voice. ''What's that supposed to mean?''

Julia bit down on her lip, wishing she'd had the sense to choose a less volatile line of conversation. But the stubborn tomboy in her refused to back down. ''She showed up here weepy, needy, unable to cope, she said. The minute you agreed to help her—boom—she got better.''

His hands slid to his hips and he leaned toward her. ''And you find that unbelievable? Maybe I'm not as washed up as you think, Ms. Dalton. I still have connections. I can make a few phone calls on her behalf.''

Julia matched his stance. She tilted her face up and refused to accept his flare of temper. ''I don't think you're washed up for one minute, detective. You could do a lot more than make phone calls, if you wanted. *She's* the one I question. Don't you think a lot of strange things have been going on around here the last twenty-four hours?''

''You mean stranger than a visit from Internal Affairs or a break-in to steal a piece of pie?''

Julia reached into her pocket. ''How about a spare key in your kitchen drawer that wasn't there last night?'' She set the key in his palm and wrapped his fingers around it. ''It fits the back door.''

''Wade?'' Mac's temper dissipated and a new kind of frustration set in. It was evident in the grim set of his mouth and the almost manic inspection of his fingertips on the key. ''I wish I could see it all. Then I could pinpoint what feels out of place.''

"You feel it, too?"

His hands stopped. "Feel what?"

Julia hoped she didn't sound completely foolish. "Like we're being watched."

EVEN AS SHE SAID the words, Mac felt an uncomfortable sixth sense kick in.

He was a man of facts. Of reason. The only instincts he believed in were the ones that led him from one clue to the next when evaluating the details of a crime scene.

So he didn't completely trust the unnerving sensation sweeping open the pores of his skin. Someone could be watching the house from a distance. Or Wade Osterman might be looking their way as he stood guard over them. Or maybe Mac's subconscious mind had reacted to Julia's suggestion, and the only person studying him was Julia herself as she waited for him to answer.

"Everything feels weird to me right now," he confessed.

The only thing that had felt remotely normal since coming home from the hospital was Julia. Her steady reassurance. Her sharp tongue. Her curvy figure.

But her bag was already packed. She had no intention of staying with him and helping him sort out the chaos of his dark world.

So yeah, he was pretty much reduced to flinging around the house on his own without any clue as to what was going on.

"I feel it, too. And I'm not blind." He heard a short gasp of air from her lips. Was that an apology? Impatience? A plea? "How well did you really know Jeff Ringlein? Maybe he was in bigger trouble than you think. His wife was driving a Mercedes just now. Either she inherited money or he made a lot more than most cops I know. Isn't there some way to check that out?"

Jules was asking the questions he should be asking, searching for answers the way he used to.

"You'd subpoena the bank records, just like I.A. has. Ask questions of family and friends." He tugged each answer out of the murky quicksand of his brain. "You check his case logs. I don't know."

Though the dark glasses prevented his eyes from contracting against the sunlight, he still lifted his fingers and rubbed at the tender new skin surrounding them. There was no external itch at the moment, no current pain. But the feeling of useless incompetence ate away at him like a scar that refused to heal.

"Don't." Two strong, gently calloused hands wrapped around his own and pulled them from his eyes. "You might accidentally break open the new skin. You can't risk any infection if you want a chance at a successful lens replacement operation."

Mac latched on to her fingers when she would have pulled away. At first it was for comfort. Touching Julia seemed to have this inexplicable effect on him. She calmed him. Centered him. Took away the panic that seemed to paralyze his thought processes.

Though he had his fears and doubts, he desperately wanted the healing process to be a success. He pulled her hands up and spread them flat against his chest, capturing them there, soothing himself with her gentle warmth. "We can't risk that, can we."

Then he held on for curiosity. With her pinned to the front of his shirt, he used the sensitive tips of his fingers to explore the shape and size of her capable, caring hands. He recorded the symmetry of short, rounded fingernails. The skin was soft and smooth across the back of her hands, supple and sinewed across each joint and knuckle. Her feminine proportions intertwined perfectly with his larger, longer fingers.

"Let me go."

Her voice was a honeyed plea that sank into his brain and turned this simple holding of hands into something more. His breathing seemed to stop, and he was aware only of her. The delicate scent of a lotion she used. The subtle rise in temperature along the surface of her skin where he touched her. He skimmed along the curve between her thumb and index finger and felt a vibration in his chest as she trembled against him. Or maybe that was the sudden intake of his own breath coming to life.

There was something magic in this woman's hands. Something warm and caring that would soon be denied him.

"Mac."

He shook his head. He didn't want to talk, he didn't want to think. He only wanted to explore. His mouth went dry with the need to do more than touch. He wanted to taste her.

He pulled her left hand up to his lips and brushed them against her palm. Her fingers tugged, then curled around his. She warred with the same sensations he did. And, like him, she succumbed to the unexpected temptation.

Mac touched his tongue to the tiny dimple near the base of her palm. He came away with a subtle tang of salt, a subtle morsel of heat. He tasted the spot once more, then traced the crease that ran vertically up toward her fingers and felt her shiver.

"Mac." Not a protest this time. A plea.

Her right hand came up around his neck, her fingers cupped his jaw and grazed the tender skin behind his ear. His jeans tightened as he felt her shift a step closer. He was making love to a woman's hand. Tasting and taking and getting aroused by the fine textures of her skin and the sensual response of her wonderful body.

Jules made him feel strong. She made him feel like a whole man again.

He didn't want to think about handicaps or goodbyes or investigations he couldn't pursue.

He wanted to kiss her.

On the lips.

He wanted to explore that part of her just as thoroughly, using every sense available to him.

She was close enough, he thought. And judging by the direction of heat, she was right in front of his downturned face. He only had to calculate the distance, be gentle in his approach, draw himself toward that delightful scent of creamy coffee on her breath.

With a sudden jerk, she pulled away. No kiss. No hands. No nothing.

"We have company."

Mac felt her withdrawal like a winter chill over his heated body.

"Who?"

He heard the sound of a car engine in the driveway just as Jules made the announcement.

"Our mothers."

They groaned in unison. He was still raw from the sensations of that almost kiss. He'd never been caught in the act of seducing anyone before. Certainly not the daughter of his mom's best friend. "Makes you feel about fifteen years old, doesn't it?"

He heard her shaky sigh, mistook it for a nervous laugh. But it wasn't enough warning to brace himself for her words.

"It's time for me to leave."

Chapter Six

For a wounded man trying to seclude himself from the pitying glare of society, Mac was suddenly extremely popular.

As he stood in the open doorway beside his mother, Joe Niederhaus slapped a folded document into his hands. "Search warrant. We're going to take a look around."

The smug superiority in Niederhaus's tone was intended to make Mac feel like a criminal. Since he wasn't one, the strong-arm tactic only ticked him off. When the Internal Affairs detective tried to push his way into the house, Mac flattened his hand against the man's chest and shoved him back beyond the threshold.

"Just a second." He handed the paper to Martha. "Ma, read it. Make sure it's legit."

"You're interfering with a police investigation," warned Niederhaus.

"I *am* a police investigator. I know the procedure."

"Joe, back off." Eli Masterson's calm, rational tone buffeted his partner from the opposite side. "He has the right to read the warrant before we go in."

"I've been doing my job for over forty years." Niederhaus's winded breathing from an unhealthy lifestyle and the stench of cigar smoke on his clothes made his angry movements easy for Mac to track. "I don't have to take orders from any lab tech. Especially some college-boy hot-shot like you.''

''My son is the director of CSI services for the Fourth Precinct.'' Mac resisted the urge to smile at Martha Taylor's stern defense of her second-born child. Spoken like a true mom.

''*Was,* ma'am.'' Detective Masterson made the correction. Though his tone held more respect than his partner's, he still made it clear that he had a job to do, and that he intended to do it. ''Detective Taylor here is on indefinite leave. We need to know why the explosion occurred in his lab, why evidence has been damaged, destroyed or misplaced, and if Officer Ringlein was working alone or had accomplices within the department.''

''Are you accusing my son of being an accomplice?''

''We're just gathering facts at this point, ma'am.''

Mac heard a snap of paper and felt Martha's shoulder brush against his arm as she straightened. He had a feeling the Taylors weren't going to win this argument. Her long-winded sigh confirmed it. ''It's a legitimate warrant. It's been signed by Judge Engelman.''

Niederhaus's laugh stirred up stale air. ''Move aside.''

Mac linked his arm through Martha's and pulled her out of the detectives' path. Though her words had been brave, the clench of her fingers on his forearm revealed her fear. He didn't know how yet, but Niederhaus would pay for upsetting his mother.

Barbara Dalton was worried, too. ''Mac, is there something we should do?''

Her presence behind him reminded Mac instantly how Julia had abandoned him so quickly. Leaving him to greet their moms outside, she'd run into the house for her bag, returned, keys in hand, wished him a quick *Take care of yourself,* and then was gone. She'd pulled her small-engined car away from the curb and vanished beyond his hearing.

Gone. Just like that.

As if she couldn't wait to escape the monster he'd become. As if he'd been left with the face and needs and personality that only a mother could love.

Some friend she'd turned out to be.

Before he'd had time to decide if he was angry or hurt or just plain stupid for caring whether or not she stayed in the first place, Niederhaus and Masterson had arrived.

Mac had nothing to hide. Still, a second visit from Internal Affairs was enough to put any smart man on guard. He gave his mother's hand a reassuring squeeze. "Get Mitch on the phone."

Even if the only news came from the rumor mill, he wanted some kind of answers.

"I'll come with you while you make the call," Barbara offered, as Martha picked up the cordless phone and the two women walked into the kitchen together.

Good. At least his mom had Barbara here to support her. Mac would monitor the two detectives on his own.

"What are you looking for?" he asked.

"We'll know it when we find it, won't we?"

Mac stood behind the sofa and gripped the back in his tight fists. He buried the debilitating feeling of helplessness that spun his world on its axis and concentrated on his sense of hearing. Eli Masterson's even tread carried him to the rooms down the hallway while Joe Niederhaus pawed through the living room.

Mac wasn't sentimental about too many of his things, but the fact that Niederhaus was going through them with the unrestrained finesse of a drunken bull warred with his own need for order and understanding.

Internal Affairs had the thankless job of policing the police, of making sure the men and women who protected the citizens of Kansas City weren't corrupt themselves. He owed the man respect on that count. But he didn't have to like him.

"How old are you, Niederhaus?" Mac asked.

The I.A. detective laughed at the question. But since it seemed unrelated to the situation at hand, it was safe to answer. Just as Mac had hoped. Get the old grouch talking. "Sixty-four."

"Gettin' set to retire, huh?"

"End of the year, I'm out."

Mac heard the abrading rasp of wood sliding against wood, and knew Niederhaus was going through the drawers of his desk. "You got a good record?"

The papers in his desk would be completely trashed by the time Niederhaus finished rifling through them. "Like I said, I've been doin' this forty years. I make clean arrests, and I make a lot of them." The challenge to contradict him was as clear as the pride in his voice.

"Ever had the lab work let you down on a case?"

A drawer slammed shut, and Mac suspected he had Joe's full attention now. "You think I got a grudge against CSI?"

Since the crime scene investigation unit seemed to be the target of his inquiries—yes.

Mac wished he could tell whether or not he was holding the detective's gaze. "You're making a mistake. Jeff Ringlein was in trouble. I think he was being blackmailed. I don't know why or how, but I can't think of any other reason why he'd destroy evidence."

"Blackmailed, huh?" That labored breathing came closer and Mac could tell Niederhaus was checking under the sofa and around the cushions. "You ever been blackmailed, Taylor? Anybody ever pressure you to misplace some evidence?"

"No."

"Any of your people report to you that they'd been pressured into compromising evidence in the lab?"

"My people get approached from time to time. They're overworked and underpaid, but I believe they're honest."

Niederhaus's crepe-soled shoes squeaked on the exposed wood floor as he approached Mac. "Did Ringlein tell you he was being blackmailed?"

"Not in so many words."

"What words *did* he use?"

Mac closed his eyes and replayed those last few hellish minutes of Jeff's life. Jeff had been desperate enough to attack him. Desperate enough to choose death over discovery.

"He was worried about his wife." Mac dragged the words past the image of shooting flames. His breath caught in a shallow gasp and he wrinkled his nose against the memory of toxic air. He forced his eyes open, as if that would allow him to see out beyond the boundaries of his nightmare. Beyond those last images of Jeff setting the air on fire. But he remained trapped with the darkness. "He said 'I couldn't know.'"

Crepe-soled shoes and stale smoke circled around Mac. "So you walked in on him as he was destroying case samples. And then he tried to cover it up."

Mac turned toward the sound and smell, feeling an increasing need to defend himself. "I'm sure you have my statement."

"I've read it." Old stogie breath came closer and Mac backed off a step. "How did that make you feel? Knowing your protegé had betrayed you?"

"I was busy at the time."

All his senses screamed that Niederhaus had leaned forward, standing too close, invading Mac's personal space. "You didn't get angry? You didn't react to that betrayal?"

"Jeff mixed those chemicals, not me. I tried to save his life."

"Did you now? He makes a mighty easy scapegoat since he's not here to defend—"

"Joe." Eli Masterson's curt, low voice silenced his partner with a single word.

While Mac had been holding his own against Niederhaus's manipulative version of grilling a witness, he'd missed Eli's return. The distance of the living room separated them, yet Mac felt the need to turn and face off against the younger detective.

Something was wrong.

There was an endless moment of awkward quiet, until Niederhaus answered with a breathy, grunting sound. His version of a dismissive sigh, Mac speculated. "I got nothing in here."

"Don't go anywhere, Mr. Taylor."

Seriously wrong.

Mac went rigid at Eli's command. There was something more troublesome in his quiet, controlled warning than in Niederhaus's blustery barrage of questions. "Joe, you better come take a look at this."

If a grunt could sound triumphant, Niederhaus had just scored a victory. He shuffled out of the living room behind his partner, leaving Mac to wonder what Eli had found.

"Ma?" No sense waiting for the bad news to come to him.

Using the sofa to guide him, Mac stumbled toward the kitchen and the closest pair of friendly seeing eyes. He ran into her halfway there. Catching her by the shoulders, he tipped his face down to hers. But the height felt different. "Ma?"

"No, it's Barbara." Mac released Julia's mother, feeling as awkward as the apology in her voice. "Martha's talking to Mitch. Do you want me to get her?"

"No. I—" That damned vertigo set in, cancelling out all rational thought. He shoved his thumb and middle finger up under his glasses, knocking them to the floor. "I need to think."

He rubbed at the skin beside his eyes and tuned in to the rustle of Barbara Dalton's dress as she bent down to retrieve his dark glasses. The meager attempt to focus calmed him enough to pose a few questions. But he remained lost in a world where he couldn't find answers.

Niederhaus's search warrant made no sense. Like Jeff, he'd been a victim of that explosion in the lab. He was the witness to Jeff's crime of interfering with police procedure. Assigning Wade Osterman to guard him meant the police considered him a valuable resource on the case. Why come here? What could they hope to find?

Unless something else had happened.

But he was so damned far out of the loop, he had no idea on the status of the case.

"Planning on destroying some evidence yourself?" Eli's quiet voice thrummed through the living room. A waft of stale cigar smoke indicated Niederhaus had returned as well.

Mac adjusted the glasses on his face before answering. "I can explain the beakers. I was trying to identify the chemical Jeff was using that night. It was toxic. Corrosive. And in the right combination, it was explosive."

"Then how do you explain this?"

What, he was supposed to read minds now? What was Eli taunting him with? "Barbara?"

He shifted toward the two I.A. detectives while Barbara Dalton described what Eli held in his hand. "It looks like a clear plastic sandwich bag with some thread inside. There's writing on a label—"

"An evidence bag."

Eli echoed his deduction. "An evidence bag."

The sound of moist, shallow breathing preceded Niederhaus's question. "You sign this out from the lab, Taylor?"

Mac swore, a simple, succinct curse under his breath. Yes, he often brought his work home. Papers. Reports. Documentation.

But the actual evidence stayed in the lab.

"It's labeled Case Number 2514, Exhibit B." Joe practically smacked his lips. "It's from that case Dwight Powers is trying next week. You wouldn't be helping that baby-killer go free, would you?"

"You son of a—"

"Joe." Eli took control of the room one more time. "Mr. Taylor, you're within your jurisdiction to transport evidence. You have the clearance to check it out of the lab." He paused for maximum effect. "Or rather, you did."

The use of the past tense wasn't lost on Mac. How the hell did he explain possessing key circumstantial evidence on a murder case? Especially when he didn't know the answer himself.

All eyes were on him. He could feel it. A confused glance. A questioning glance. A taunting glance.

And something more.

He *felt* her. In the heartbeats it took for the cooling breeze to register, he smelled something more. Crisp air and autumn sunshine.

Jules was here.

She'd come back.

He tipped his nose toward her sweet, wholesome scent and absorbed her presence like a steadying hand.

When he turned back to the two detectives, he'd centered himself in his world again. Instead of denial or self-defense, he seized his curiosity. "Where did you find it?"

"Back of the bathroom closet." At least Masterson gave him answers. "*Did* you check this out of the lab?"

Mac avoided implicating himself. "I thought Jeff was the one you were investigating."

Niederhaus's breathing quickened into excited gasps. "You were the last person to see him alive. He may have passed you incriminating information that you're trying to hide so your department looks clean. Or maybe you killed him to hide *your* crime. Ringlein's death might not have been an accident, after all."

"MacKinley." Martha interrupted with a name sure to get his attention. She hurried into the living room and pressed the phone into his hand. "Mitch says not another word until you talk to a lawyer."

AT LEAST THEY hadn't handcuffed him and hauled him in for further questioning. But Mac wasn't ready to breathe a sigh of relief yet. If anything, the tension within him was strung even more tightly.

What the hell was going on here?

Detective Masterson took the misplaced evidence bag with him, and bade a polite goodbye to the ladies. Joe Niederhaus had thrown a terse, *Don't leave town,* his way before stalking out the door.

Mac sensed that Eli Masterson was a tough, but fair, man. But maybe he and Niederhaus were simply playing a good cop/bad cop routine, trying to get Mac to drop his guard and reveal something. Clearly they suspected him of compromising evidence, if not the actual murder of Jeff Ringlein. The fact they hadn't arrested him meant they didn't have the grounds to prove it. Yet.

Or maybe the only reason they hadn't taken him downtown was because his cousin Mitch Taylor, Captain of the Fourth Precinct, was on the other end of the line.

"What can you tell me about Case Number 2514?"

Mac demanded, putting the phone back up to his ear while Julia locked the door behind the two detectives. "Dwight Powers is taking it to trial next week."

Mitch's bracing sigh put Mac on alert. "That's the Arnie Sanchez kidnapping case."

Mac closed his eyes and mentally sorted through the files of information he stored in the recesses of his mind. "He's that advertising wiz who claims his stepson was kidnapped? He paid a ransom, but the people who did it were never caught?"

"Right. Allegedly, the child was a victim of abuse, by either the mother or Sanchez himself."

Mac ignored his emotional reaction to the memory of the toddler's body, half-buried in the woods southeast of the city. He'd worked that crime scene himself. Gruesome didn't begin to describe what he'd found. But he'd conquered the urge to punch his fist through a tree or toss the contents of his stomach by remembering that if he did his job right, he could nail the son of a bitch who had hurt such an innocent child.

Just like then, he concentrated on maintaining an objective, routine discussion of the work. He chose his words carefully, not wanting to alarm the three women gathering in a semicircle around him, eavesdropping on the conversation. "The D.A.'s case is based on the idea that Sanchez covered up the crime by staging the kidnapping himself."

"Oh my God." He reached his hand out toward the pleasing, home-cooked smells that identified his mother. When she latched on to his hand, he held on, offering whatever strength and comfort her handicapped son could provide.

"That missing child's name was in the news for a week last winter." Barbara seemed to be explaining the tragic story to Julia.

"How awful." Julia's response came from beside his

left shoulder. He hadn't had time to ask why she'd decided to come back. Even if her reasons weren't personal— maybe she'd forgotten her toothbrush or some other inane thing—he was glad she was here. Despite the distraction of her clean, sweet smell, her presence enabled him to think more clearly. He'd ask the whys later.

He refocused his attention on Mitch. "Do you know the status of the trial?"

"Powers is out for blood on this one. Ever since he lost his own kid, this is the one type of case he refuses to lose." Mitch paused, probably working past the same anger that Mac and every other law enforcement official dealt with when facing such an injustice. "What's your interest?"

"I found fibers that place Sanchez at the scene with the body."

"I remember. That's why the D.A.'s office went ahead with the indictment. Combined with the ex-wife's testimony, they'll put him away for a long time."

"But if that circumstantial evidence is missing—"

"What do you mean, 'missing'?"

"—Sanchez could walk."

"Is that what that man just took from here?" Martha echoed the same shock and anger as her nephew.

"What's Martha saying?" asked Mitch.

Mac sucked in a deep breath and counted to five before releasing it. "Internal Affairs just found those fiber samples in the back of my bathroom closet."

Mac held the receiver against his chest, muffling the fluent string of curses that answered him.

The vertigo that spun through his imagination seemed to be taking a very real turn. He carried the phone back up to his ear. "I didn't take that evidence bag, you know that."

"I know." Mitch's gruff expression of faith spurred him on.

"I need you to do me a favor, Mitch."

His cousin's response got lost in the static that suddenly erupted into Mac's ear.

"Mitch, you there?"

"...name it." The static cleared for an instant.

"Mitch?"

Mac jerked the phone from his ear at the decibel-breaking screech that reverberated across the line. His sensitive ears waited for the noise to fade before attempting to speak again.

"Was that from your end?" Mac whispered.

Don't you feel like you're being watched?

Julia's question jumped into his mind as if she'd just repeated it out loud.

He knew the answer with sudden, chilling clarity.

"Jules. I need your cell phone." There was a beat of hesitant silence before she moved. "Mitch, I'm calling you on another line."

He pressed the off button and ran his fingers along the rectangular perimeter of the phone, searching for the seam where the outside casing joined together.

"Here's my cell." Julia touched the phone to the back of his hand. He grabbed it and held it out to his mother. "Ma, call Mitch again."

"What's going on?" Martha asked as she took the phone from him.

"I'm not sure. But I don't want to take any chances. Call."

With a pair of working eyes, he would have had the advantage over an inanimate object that refused to cooperate with him. "I need a screwdriver."

"I'll get one." He heard the quick swish of Julia's jeans as she dashed into the kitchen. Thank God she was here.

Maybe he was just going stir-crazy, imagining conspiracies where none existed. But with Julia, sensible and competent in so many ways, here, he'd soon have his answers. Then he could either apologize for being an idiot and send her on her way, or he could thank her for standing by him just as she had last night when Wade Osterman had let himself into the house uninvited.

"Let me." She took the phone from his hand. "What am I looking for?"

"Open it up."

He heard the strain of plastic bending and resisting, and then he heard a pop. Mac found her shoulder and leaned over it, anxious to know what she'd found. The soft curls of her hair caught on his nose when she turned to speak. She took an abrupt step away, but made no comment. "There's something inside. Is it a listening device?"

The idea that she found his proximity so discomforting was as frustrating as not being able to see what she was talking about. Maybe he should tell her that her scent and sound kept her from being as anonymous as she'd like to be.

But this wasn't the time to challenge her on it.

"Let me hold it." Julia laid a tiny box, no bigger than a pencil eraser, in his palm. He curled his hand around it and explored it with his fingertips. The size was right. But how could he be sure? "Describe it to me."

Julia possessed the same penchant for observing details that he did. "It's a small square of grayish plastic with some short wires sticking out of it. It has several silvery crisscrossing lines on it, like a computer chip."

Mac squeezed the traitorous device in his fist. "It's a bug, all right." Government issue. Like cops or district attorneys or anyone buying government surplus might have access to.

"Here's Mitch." Martha thrust the phone into his right hand.

"What's going on, Mac?"

He didn't know the big picture yet, but he could answer the immediate question.

"My house is wired."

"I don't like the smell of this." Mitch's suspicions matched his own. "Any idea who or why?"

Mac ran down the list of visitors he'd had in the past twenty-four hours. Any one of them could have planted the bug *and* the evidence bag from the Sanchez case. Hell. A stranger could have come in at anytime. Julia had already proved how easy it was to get around a blind man's defenses. "I can give you suspects, but I don't have any motive."

"I'll send someone to do a sweep for other bugs."

"Someone you trust," Mac insisted.

"He'll be handpicked and he'll be there in twenty minutes."

"I owe you."

"Pay me back by finding the truth."

By the time he'd hung up, Mac had already begun a mental list of what needed to be done to ensure his safety and eradicate the susceptibility of being set up in his own home.

"What can we do?" asked the two moms.

He didn't want them or their good intentions in any potential line of fire. "Don't touch anything."

"Jules," he went on, "I need you to get rid of those beakers. Flush the contents, one at a time, down the toilet. Then I want to find out where Osterman got his key—"

"Mac." Martha's cautious fingers touched his arm. "Julia was leaving. Remember?" Barb and I are here to take care of you until we can hire a replacement."

The bottom dropped out of his world for a heartbeat. "I...forgot."

"It's okay, Martha." He heard a rustling sound, denim on denim, that was distinctly Julia. She was already moving to carry out his demands. He only wished her answer sounded a little less fatalistic when she added, "I'll stay."

WITH THE KNOWLEDGE that his own mother had removed her spare key to his back door and left it in the kitchen drawer for Wade to find, and the promise that he would, indeed, eat the casserole she'd brought and call whether he needed anything or not, Mac listened to Julia close and lock the front door behind Martha and Barbara.

She'd had a brief conversation with her own mother and he'd tried not to eavesdrop. But with his acute hearing, he'd picked up a few words like *sacrifice* and *debt* and *will you ever be able to tell me what happened in Chicago?*

Was staying on as his nurse the sacrifice? And what debt, what favor, was she so determined to repay that she was willing to make that sacrifice?

And what the hell had happened to her in Chicago? Clearly something serious enough to worry Barbara. Unexpectedly, that same unknown factor worried him.

Jules had been such a cool kid growing up. He hadn't known her all that well, but she'd always held her own with the boys that Cole had run around with. How many high-school girls had he known who could throw a man out at the plate, then turn around and discuss geometric proofs with a college student?

Mac blinked his eyes and tried to snatch the afterimage of a memory that hovered at the fringe of his conscious mind. *He'd* been that college student. Strolling down the sidewalk on Market Street with Julia at his side. A lot of years ago. She'd have been too young for them to have been on a date, but he'd walked her home.

They'd discussed geometry, Royals baseball and the color of her eyes.

Why couldn't he remember the color of her eyes?

The scars of his body seemed to have worked their way into his brain, destroying random remnants of his past. He remembered enough of that one night to make him curious enough to want to remember it all. Mac forced his eyes open. He remembered enough to make him suspicious. Was that her debt? Was something about that night the favor she felt she owed him?

As Julia's crisp scent drifted through the living room toward his position in the kitchen archway, Mac snapped back to the present. He decided the direct approach would be the best way to assuage his curiosity.

"Why did you come back?"

She pushed past him into the kitchen. "Your mother's not going to get any other help under these circumstances."

"What circumstances are those?"

"A police investigation. Those two Internal Affairs detectives are after you, not Jeff Ringlein." Judging by the sounds she made, she was putting the casserole in the oven. Working. The woman always seemed to be working. While he admired her ethic, it wasn't a crime to take a few moments to relax. Unless...

"Do they make you nervous?"

He understood the "duh" in her sigh and almost smiled. "They think you're part of whatever Jeff was involved with. And somebody's doing their best to make it look like you are."

"They might just be doing their job, and whoever was blackmailing Jeff is using the opportunity of his death to pin the missing evidence on me."

Her movements stopped, and Mac got the feeling she had turned to face him. "That evidence bag wasn't there when I cleaned yesterday morning."

"I know. I'm being set up." Part of him wanted to go to her and soothe the helpless concern he heard in her voice. But a more rational part of him saw her vulnerability as a chance to get some answers. "Why did you change your mind about leaving? What favor is so important that you feel you have to get mixed up in this?"

An awkward rush of activity followed the silence after his question. "Niederhaus and Masterson showed up. I wasn't comfortable with them when they were here yesterday. I wouldn't be a very good nurse if I left my patient—and our mothers—to deal with them on their own. So I parked in the alley around back and came in to check on you."

Mac called her on her noble excuse. "Just to check on me?"

"I couldn't leave you in danger." The atmosphere in the room suddenly changed. The racket stilled on the heels of her surrendering sigh. "You never left me."

"Remind me what happened that night." He took a step toward her, but sensed her drawing away. "Yes, I remember some of it." Mac patiently retreated, and tried to negotiate a deal, instead. "C'mon. I'll even let you doctor my eyes if you'll talk to me."

He interpreted her shaky laugh as a hopeful sign and sat at the table. Taking off his glasses, he turned his chair and tilted his face toward the ceiling, exposing that rawest, most damaged part of himself as a gesture of sincerity and trust.

An interminable moment passed when he thought she might refuse. But the professional in Julia—if not her good heart itself—couldn't pass up the opportunity to tend to her patient.

After washing, she went to work, hesitantly at first, but then with the sure movements of those beautiful hands. At first there was only the work as she gently rinsed his wounded eyes and tipped his head back to administer antibiotic eyedrops.

Maybe there was something in the vulnerability of his own position that finally prompted her to speak. "My first date in high school was my only date. I mean, I always had friends who were guys, but no one special. You know."

Whether he did or didn't, Mac chose not to answer. He didn't want to say or do anything to stop her from telling the story. With her fingertips gently massaging the scarred skin around his eyes, she used a cotton swab to apply an ointment. It was a pungent medication she assured him would stave off infection as well as keep the healing tissue soft and pliable.

"I was chosen to be part of a senior prank, called a 'dogfight.'" Mac grit his teeth together when she leaned over him, brushing a full, rounded breast against his temple as she doctored the other side of his face. There was nothing honorable in the way she pronounced 'chosen'. "That's where a group of boys challenge each other to bring the most homely date to a party."

Oh God. Mac cupped one hand around the generous flare of her hip and pushed her back a step. He knew where this was going. But no way in hell could he reconcile this sensual beauty with the remembered emotions exploding inside him like a lit box of fireworks.

"Ray Wozniak." He remembered the young man's name. Not a man. A jerk. A piece of scum. An adolescent nitwit who wouldn't have recognized a lady, much less known how to treat one.

"Good ol' Ray." Her self-deprecating laugh hurt. Mac settled a hand at the other side of her waist. Supporting her. Apologizing. Wishing like hell he hadn't brought this up. "I was so flattered that he had asked me out. So naive. I had braces and freckles and I was built like a linebacker. I should have known he wasn't really interested in me."

Julia's curves flexed within his grip as she reached across him to pick up the gauze strips that would eventually cover his eyes. "I was walking home from the bus stop after class," Mac recalled. A frisson of the fear, the anger, he'd felt then coursed through him now, making his breath come in erratic gasps. "He had you backed up against a brick wall. Your mouth was bleeding."

Now she stood stock still between his hands. "You remember that?"

He felt the tremor in her voice all the way down to his fingertips. "He wasn't too pleased that you wised up and walked out on him. You cost him a bet."

"A hundred dollars. That's what I was worth to him." The tremors danced beneath his fingers again, deeper and more rapid. "He said I owed it to him one way or another. I was so stupid."

"No." She couldn't really think that, could she? "You were young and trusting, and he took advantage of that." Mac trailed his right hand up along her arm and neck and found her face, flushed with heat. He patted his fingertips across her cheek and discovered the feverish moisture in the corner of her eye.

Ashamed that his intellectual curiosity had caused her this emotional distress, Mac tugged with his hands and pulled her into his lap. He wound his arm around her waist and pressed her cheek into his shoulder. Offering such comfort was foreign to him, but he did all he could think to do. He brushed his fingers against her hot skin and rocked her back and forth.

"I shouldn't have asked," he apologized again, turning his lips to the wispy curls that framed her face. "I remember it now. He was kissing you. No—he was assaulting you when I walked up.''

''You asked me if I wanted to be there, and I said no.'' He hugged her tighter at her stuttered breath. ''You made him leave me alone.''

Melanie Ringlein had wept buckets of tears that morning, and he'd hurt for her. But he hadn't felt…compelled to take her in his arms and offer her any kind of comfort beyond words. But with Julia—he didn't think he could stop himself from touching her.

Maybe he felt guilty at causing her pain. Or maybe he was reacting to some base, dormant, male need bred into him by genes, but awakened by the press of Julia's soft, sexy, womanly curves against his harder shape. The utterly feminine mound of a breast flattened against his chest. The bright scent of her teased his nose. And the absolute softness of her skin and hair teased his fingertips and made him remember the lessons his mother and father had taught him.

Respect a woman.

Treasure her.

Those same values had stopped him that night. He'd sent that bully Wozniak running with a few succinct threats and some serious intimidation. Then he'd draped his jacket around Julia's shoulders and walked her home.

He'd treated her far better that night than he had since she'd come back into his life yesterday morning.

To repay a favor.

''I'm not a hero, Jules.'' He apologized in a raspy whisper against her temple. ''I'm just a man. I'm not even very good at that anymore. You don't owe me anything.''

''That's not true.''

She flattened her palms against his shoulders and squirmed in his lap, trying to push away. But her attempt to escape, to ease his guilt, had an immediate effect on his body.

Mac held her still, closing his eyes and enjoying the rush of awareness between his thighs. This woman blew his cool reticence, his need to think before he acted, right out of the water.

He wished he could see her expression now, wished he could know if she was feeling any of the same emotional and physical response he was feeling. Without thinking, he moved his fingertips to her face and began to explore.

He tried to picture that frightened teenager she'd once been, but quickly lost himself in the delightful sensations of the grown woman. Smooth, cool skin. Freckled, she'd said.

"Funny," he murmured his thoughts out loud, tracing his fingers across hills and hollows of her face from sculpted brows down to the tiny dent beneath her nose, "I can't feel freckles."

"Mac—" He smiled with the delight of discovery as he felt heat creep into her cheeks. He let his thumbs join the exploration. Her soft gasp matched his own when he found her lips, soft and full, with no trace of braces to mar their beauty now.

Maybe he *could* see her expression. Maybe he *could* know her reaction to him. He could certainly feel it. He could identify different sounds and interpret how they reflected her mood. He could absorb her scent and let its freshness heal his troubled soul.

The only way he hadn't discovered her was through taste.

An instant hunger sparked in his mind and tightened deep in his belly. He desperately wanted to taste her. To complete the picture of his grown-up Julia, he rationalized. He needed just one little taste.

With the corners of her mouth framed between his

thumbs, he pressed his lips to hers. It was just a touch, really. Not even a nibble. A chance for their breaths to mingle. An opportunity for the ultrasensitive skin of his lips to learn the goddesslike contours of her sultry, pliant mouth.

A moment for every nerve ending in his body to sit up and take notice of the beautiful woman he held in his arms.

"What do you think you're doing?" she whispered, moving her lips against his as she spoke, rewarding him with an unintentional caress. She curled her fingers into the front of his shirt. But she pushed with her fists, sending a mixed message that echoed his own turbulent thoughts.

"Well, if I haven't lost my faculties completely, I think I'm kissing you."

"Mac—"

"Shh." He pressed the pad of his thumb against the quivering arc of her bottom lip. "And I think I'm going to do it again."

Chapter Seven

"You shouldn'—"

Julia's protest was cut short beneath the heady persuasion of Mac's mouth.

He shouldn't be kissing her, she thought, as the pad of his thumb abraded a gentle trail from the fullest part of her lower lip to the dimple at one corner. His lips followed the same path, embarking on a leisurely mission to drive her mad.

She was the healer here. She shouldn't attach any significance to the warmth pouring into her body through the touch of his hands and mouth. She shouldn't notice how those hurtful memories scattered and faded and were absorbed into the solid strength of his broad shoulders and the unhesitating sense of purpose in his kiss.

She caught her breath at each foray of his tongue, each gentle nip. She didn't know whether to breathe in or out, and it was suddenly very hard to hear herself think above the sound of her heart pounding in her throat.

And then his tongue dipped inside the seam of her lips and stroked the moist heat there, asking for something she wasn't sure she could give. She breathed his name on a fearful sigh, but her doubts were lost in the wonderful demand of his mouth opening over hers.

Julia lost all sense of herself as she dared to meet the

soft friction of Mac's tongue mingling with her own. He slid his hands around to cup her head and tilt her face to an angle that allowed him to claim her completely. The tips of his long, dextrous fingers sifted through her hair and held her a willing prisoner to the plundering force of his mouth.

Comfort had long evolved beyond curious interest into a blazing passion that pulsed between her legs and left her fingers clutching handfuls of soft cotton sweatshirt and the hard muscle beneath.

Patients didn't kiss their nurses like this. Old family friends didn't kiss like this.

She didn't kiss like this.

She should make him stop. But she didn't want him to.

This was way better than any schoolgirl fantasy. Warmer than her pillow. More responsive than the back of her hand.

This was real.

This was Mac.

Cradled in his hands. Cherished by his mouth.

And Julia answered back in every way she knew how. She unclenched her fingers and pressed her hands into the hard strength of his chest. Her palms tingled at the heat and shape that made him so uniquely male. With a curiosity of her own to match the scientist's himself, she skimmed her hands along his chest, down his arms, across his flanks.

The raspy moan in his throat touched off an echoing vibration in her own vocal cords. The vibration shivered down her chest, making her breasts hot and achy and heavy with want. Her body yearned for something she couldn't name. She wanted to touch his face, to explore his mouth as he had hers, but with the position of his arms and the angle of their bodies, she couldn't reach him. Frustrated by the lack of contact, her body compensated.

She simply leaned into him. Her nipples puckered and hardened into tight, tiny beads as his heat seared through her. The almost painful friction sank like a heavy weight deep in her most feminine core. She curled her hands up behind his back and latched on to his shoulders. She was falling. Falling too fast beneath the awakening gift of his mouth and hands.

"Jules—"

His long thighs shifted beneath her bottom, tilting her off balance. A tiny whimper of despair escaped as she fell away from his mouth. But with something like a heavy gasp for air himself, he snaked his arm around her waist and caught her.

Splaying those long fingers across her bottom, he lifted, somehow making her feel light and graceful before she could give a second thought as to whether she might be too heavy for him.

He leaned back in the chair and let gravity carry her into him. Julia slid down to the juncture of his thighs and discovered his most masculine response to the kiss just as he reclaimed her mouth. He stole inside and stole her grown-up woman's heart.

She tumbled down a vortex of sensation. Heat and hardness. Man and magic.

Ray Wozniak's brutal kiss hadn't been like this. Anthony Cardello's practiced finesse hadn't been like this. No man in between her first and last kiss had ever been like this.

"So responsive."

Mac whispered the praise against her mouth, then left a trail of damp heat along her jawline as he followed it to the sensitive skin beneath her earlobe. She hitched her shoulders against the erotic tickle of his lips and teeth and tongue as he tested the spot again and again. He seemed to delight in the discovery of that flashpoint that had her digging her fingers into his shoulders and squirming in his lap. Something almost like laughter rumbled in his throat.

"Very responsive." He stroked his tongue there one more time. "Very beautiful."

That one word mocked her, ringing in her mind with the jarring disharmony of a cymbal crash. She turned her ear away from the next sweep of his tongue. His lips scudded across her cheek and moved to her mouth again. But the first shot of reality had already sunk its nasty confidence-robbing teeth into this little bit of heaven.

"Mac—"

His touch had drained her of her strength, thrown her completely off balance.

She tried to pull away, but he leaned forward and caught her lips again, stealing the protest right from her mouth.

Julia turned her clutching fingers into fists and pushed at his chest. "Mac—"

A melodic ding-dong rang through the house, in strident discord to the panic playing inside her head.

But the sound of the doorbell was enough to finally distract Mac and break the spell. Though his arms were still wrapped around her, he tipped his head back and muttered a raspy curse. His nostrils flared as he breathed in deeply through his nose. His lips parted as he blew out the cleansing air on a sigh.

"Lousy timing, huh?"

Yes. She knew he meant the doorbell, but it was always a bad time for her to drop her guard and make herself vulnerable to a man. Humiliation always seemed to be the next step for her. And while she didn't believe Mac would intentionally hurt her, she'd be hurt all the same.

The instant she felt his grip on her relax, she scooted off his lap and tried to stand. But her legs had lost their strength and coordination. She tangled one foot in the chair leg in her haste and pitched forward.

But two strong hands seized her by the waist. "Steady." Mac's husky voice still danced with the desire that had erupted between them. "Someone might think you're anxious to get away from me."

For a brief, traitorous moment she was glad he couldn't see. She didn't think she had it in her right now to cover up the wide-eyed embarrassment she knew must be written across her face.

But there was something psychic in those eyes that couldn't see. Suddenly, the tender warmth in his steadying grasp became coolly impersonal and he released her. "Jules? You trying to get away from me?"

She backed up several steps. She needed space. She needed strength. She needed a better way to say this.

"Don't feel any guilt or regret." She clasped her fingers together, then pulled at them, then clasped them again. "I know that kiss didn't mean anything. You were comforting me, and it got out of hand. I understand how things work."

With his fingertips braced on the tabletop, Mac slowly stood. With unerring accuracy, he turned his head and faced her. "You'd better explain that."

Julia had to look away from the harsh suspicion stealing over his expression. "It's just that you've been injured and hospitalized. Your body hasn't been able to act on its natural drives. And now that it can—"

"So I'm some washed-up invalid getting frisky with his nurse because I can't get it anywhere else?"

"No. That's not what I meant." The doorbell rang a second time, followed by a polite knock. Julia looked toward the living room as a means of escape, but knew she had to finish this conversation. She tucked her olive T-shirt back into her jeans and straightened the placket of her matching shirt. It was all a stall to put off admitting that horrible truth she believed in her heart.

She was no one special.

"I'm a woman. And I was available."

A deadly pall of silence answered. She didn't want him to try to make up some kind of feelings for her when he'd only reacted on the spur of the moment. He'd kissed her out of kindness. And that had triggered a hormone. Or perhaps a recluse's need to hold and be held and feel alive again. He would understand a logical explanation like that, if he'd only listen.

"Mac—"

"Go answer the door."

"But—" He turned away, and by the cold set of his shoulders, she could tell there would be no further discussion, no chance to explain that her rejection of his touch really wasn't a rejection at all. But he didn't want to hear about self-preservation and shredded pride and aching wounds that had no chance to heal if she allowed herself to be hurt again.

"I should finish wrapping your eyes."

That wasn't going to happen, either.

He leaned over the table, knocking things aside and onto the floor until he found his dark glasses. He stood up straight, put them on and shut her out.

"I'm sorry." She offered the apology even if he didn't want to hear it. "This is my fault. I should have stopped it sooner. I just don't want you to be disappointed in me."

"Detective Taylor?" The concerned male voice at the door wasn't as deep or loud as Wade Osterman's. The difference was enough of a distraction to allow her to walk away from Mac.

She might as well start getting used to the idea.

Because, eventually, once she was no longer needed, he would walk away from her.

MERLE BANNING WAS every bit the electronics and computer expert his cousin Mitch had promised him to be, thought Mac.

Two months ago, he could have run these same scans, taken the hardware apart, made the same evaluations himself. But now he was no more than a consultant. And he doubted Banning even needed him for that.

The kid might be soft-spoken, but he knew what he was talking about. In a lot of ways, Banning reminded Mac of the man Jeff Ringlein should have been. Bright. Promising. But whereas Jeff had been a little too eager to please, Merle simply did the job asked of him. While Jeff's attention was easily scattered—by his beautiful young wife or a possible promotion or an exciting new case—Merle Banning was able to focus on the task at hand.

No wonder Mac's sister-in-law, Detective Ginny Taylor, couldn't say enough about Banning. The kid was, after all, Ginny's partner.

Merle typed something into the laptop computer he'd brought with him. He drummed his fingers against the plastic casing, waiting the few seconds it took for the screen to boot up the information he wanted.

"Just as we suspected," Merle reported, reading something from his screen, then turning to talk to Mac who stood beside him at the desk. "The listening device from your phone and the one I found in your CD player are both government issue. The lot numbers match a surplus batch sold to KCPD earlier this year."

Mac really needed to stop thinking of Banning as "the kid." He was a natural for this kind of investigative work. "Any chance of them being issued to Internal Affairs?"

Banning typed another command into his computer and drummed his fingers. Julia had said Eli Masterson was snooping around his shelves when I.A. had paid their first visit to the house. The connection couldn't be that simple, could it? A police plant to dig up information on Jeff's death and the trail of missing evidence?

Wade Osterman had been in the house unobserved, as had Eli's partner, Joe Niederhaus. Hell. Even Melanie Ringlein had had access to the house.

About the only person he wouldn't suspect of planting listening devices and the hidden microcamera Merle had found above the front porch was his mother. Martha Taylor preferred the surprise visit approach to keep an eye on his activities.

"No, sir." Then again, the kid made Mac feel like old news when it came to figuring out who was spying on him. "Vice squad. They were used in a casino sting on some bookies who were taking in more than their fair share of the profits."

"Let me guess," Mac queried. "They ended up in an evidence locker in my lab."

A series of clicks told him Banning was scrolling down the computer screen. "Case Number 1193. Exhibit F."

"Can you log into the D.A.'s records with that thing?" Mac wasn't sure he had the right to pursue this hunch. He didn't want to get the young detective into any trouble with Internal Affairs or Mitch. But since Banning seemed willing…

"Give me a second." Mac listened to more typing, then waited in silence.

When he heard Merle's fingers stop drumming, he asked. "What's the status of 1193?"

"Dismissed. The assistant D.A. couldn't prove his case."

"Why not?"

Mac didn't think he was going to like the answer. "Stolen evidence."

Stolen evidence? The irony of it made Mac's icy blood boil.

He could guess the answer to his next question. "Who put together the samples for the trial?"

"Jeff Ringlein."

An hour later, after a cross-referenced search of the crime lab and district attorney's databases, a disturbing trend began to reveal itself.

In the past year alone, eleven cases had been dismissed or pleaded down to a lesser charge because the circumstantial evidence wasn't there. He'd prided himself on running a clean lab. On average, three or four cases fell through the cracks each year because evidence went missing or was too damaged at the scene or in transport to be deemed irrefutable in a court of law.

Eleven botched cases was a high number.

And of those eleven cases, Jeff Ringlein had worked on eight.

"The next logical step is to check Jeff's bank accounts. See if he was taking any kind of payoff." But Internal Affairs had already beat him to the punch on that one, too. He couldn't get that kind of information unless he had his badge and a judge's order behind him.

"Maybe the guy was incompetent," suggested Merle. "You said he caused the explosion that killed him."

For a moment, Mac considered the young detective's blind faith in his word. I.A. didn't believe his story; they suspected him of some sort of collusion or coercion, if not actually covering up his own mistakes by staging Jeff's death.

"You know, Banning…" Mac thought it only fair to warn off the young detective. "You could get into trouble for helping me."

"Captain Taylor says you're family, and to treat you with the same respect I would him." Mac wished he could read the expression on the young man's face. But judging by the deliberate way he shifted in his chair, Merle had already evaluated the risk he was taking by providing Mac with information. "That's a daunting order, sir. I have no intentions of disappointing the old man."

Mac nearly laughed. Mitch was only three years older than he. No wonder Merle kept calling him "sir." "I appreciate the family loyalty. I'll put in a good word for you with Mitch."

"Thanks."

"In the meantime, find out what you can about Melanie Ringlein. If she comes from a moneyed background, her tastes might have been more than Jeff could afford on a cop's salary."

"Will do."

No way could Mitch be disappointed in this kid.

Disappointed.

As keys clacked and fingers drummed, Mac turned toward the front door where Julia had gone outside with a cup of coffee to chat with Wade Osterman.

I just don't want you to be disappointed in me.

Julia's last words crept into his mind despite his best efforts to block the memory of that totally unexpected kiss. She was right. His original intent had been to comfort her, to make amends for dredging up that horrible story about Ray Wozniak.

But something had gotten out of hand.

Maybe it was her fresh, cleansing scent that filled his brain and made him see sunshine and hope. Maybe it was the discovery of that sweet, luscious mouth of hers—or the short, curly hair that caught and sprung around his fingers like a dozen silky caresses. Maybe it was finally getting the chance to explore those voluptuous, womanly curves. Rounded hips. Heavy breasts. A real woman's figure. A fantasy figure.

And with all that velvety soft skin stretched out across

all those curves—his fingertips tingled and his breathing went shallow just remembering the divine feel of her.

I don't want to disappoint you.

That statement bothered him more than anything.

He couldn't stop replaying that conversation in his mind. He couldn't stop trying to figure out where he'd gone wrong. Had he somehow made her think he wasn't incredibly turned on by her? Maybe if he'd said something, done something more, she wouldn't have been so eager to get away from him.

True, he wasn't the playboy of the family. His youngest brother Josh enjoyed that title. His older brother Brett had been the consummate flirt before meeting his wife. Even Gideon, the so-called quiet one of the family, had maintained a serious relationship with a woman for nearly two years. The fact that the two had split up suddenly still remained a mystery—women usually fell all over themselves for that solid, dependable type. And Cole, well, he had that whole dark, brooding thing going for him—an intriguing turnaround from the all-American kid he'd been growing up.

But Mac?

Studious. Logical. Workaholic. Scarred. Blind.

None of those words leaped to mind when it came to charming women.

He had no business kissing Julia like that, no business wanting to do more than kiss her. Maybe he had somehow reminded her of that Wozniak bastard who had tried to use her to promote his own status.

He thought he had shown her how wrong that high-school jock had been about her. He remembered seeing the promise in her then, even at age fifteen, of the woman she would become. The braces would go. The angular muscles would turn into softer curves. The freckles would keep her eternally young.

And her eyes had been so expressive, revealing her fear, her strength, her intelligence. And ultimately, her tears and laughter. They'd been such a unique shade of...

"Damn."

"Sir?" Detective Banning interrupted the pointless wandering of Mac's thoughts. "I've got a profile on Mrs. Ringlein started, but I need to get outside and relieve Officer Osterman. Is there anything else you want me to check in the meantime?"

Frustrated by his inability to ferret out any kind of truth, Mac slipped his thumb and middle finger up beneath his glasses and began to rub at the itchy new skin. But the thought of Julia's stern reprimand, the thought of ruining his chances of ever being a normal, sighted man again, had him curling his fingers into a fist and pressing it to the bridge of his nose.

"No." Mac didn't even try to locate Merle's position. "Don't let me keep you from doing your job."

"Yes, sir."

A surprisingly warm breeze swept over Mac as the front door opened and closed. Maybe he should get outside and enjoy the sunny day. He should take a walk. Some fresh air and exercise might clear his clogged-up brain.

Of course, he might get lost just going down the front walk to his mailbox. Lost in his own front yard. Oh yeah, that'd be the way to show the world he was still a man in control of his own space, his own destiny.

Mac's wry laugh echoed in the empty house. Some man.

His reputation could be destroyed by the Internal Affairs investigation. Hell. He could end up in prison if Niederhaus and Masterson made their case against him. Would one of them sink so low as to set him up? Or were they simply jumping on the easy trail arranged by someone else?

If he wanted to find out who'd been blackmailing Jeff, he'd have to do it himself.

Fat chance.

And what about Julia?

"Hell."

There she was again, sidetracking his thoughts when she had no business being there. She was the nurse. He was the patient. Nothing more. He should tell her the debt with Wozniak had been paid and send her on her way.

Then he wouldn't have to bother with being polite. He wouldn't need to work to make himself presentable. He wouldn't keep obsessing about that soft waver in her voice when she worried about disappointing *him*.

Mac oriented himself in the living room and stalked down the hallway toward his bedroom. He'd leave the fresh air to someone who could handle it.

"Dammit, Detective! I'm fine."

Mac halted at Wade Osterman's loud voice. Even through the closed door, he could hear the uniformed officer arguing with Merle Banning. "It's time for you to go home, Osterman."

"Hey, hey, hey, guys. I'm not used to grown men fighting over me." That was Jules, making a joke, trying to defuse the tension. "Can't we work something out?"

Before he could question the futility of his resolution to ignore her, Mac spun around and hurried to the front door, arms outstretched to save himself from damage as he traversed the living room in record time.

Merle Banning lifted his voice a notch to do battle with Osterman. "I'm not pulling rank, I'm following orders."

"*I'm* following orders."

Mac swung the door open.

"C'mon, Wade. You've been here nearly twenty-four hours straight." Jules. She'd grown up in a lot of ways. Maybe she didn't need rescuing anymore. Certainly not by him. "That's your fifth cup of coffee today. You can use the break."

"Maybe I want to hang around for more of your home-cooking." Mac bristled at the flirtatious inflection in the big man's voice.

"Flattery will—"

Merle interrupted Julia's response. "That won't be happening, ma'am. Officer Osterman is already over the limit for his overtime hours."

"I need the money."

"You need to quit calling your bookie."

He heard the crunch of gravel on concrete beneath crepe-soled shoes. Instinct pushed Mac forward a moment before the tell-tale thump and string of curses told him that Osterman had shoved the younger man.

"Hey!" That was Jules. Great. She didn't need to get caught in the middle of this.

A thud of muscle hitting muscle and the shuffling of feet on concrete and grass told him Merle had shoved back.

"Stop it, guys!"

With arms out, Mac lurched down the sidewalk. He smacked into someone's back, reached out to catch his unfortunate target so they wouldn't fall. Solid. Soft. Julia.

"You're a snot-nosed punk who doesn't know what he's talking about." Wade's good-natured persona had been replaced by this defensive bully.

The instant Mac made the recognition, Julia pulled away.

"Wade, it's not that big a deal," she pleaded. "Just go."

But Mac wouldn't let her escape entirely. He hooked his hand through her elbow and shifted to her side. She strained against even this most impersonal contact, but he tugged her closer, refusing to be cast aside.

In the next breath her muscles relaxed as she accepted the request for her help. Ironic. She never refused him medical or therapeutic help. Just the personal stuff. Maybe it was for the best.

With the two officers trading words and physical threats, this was certainly not the time to work through their differences.

"Back off. Back off!" *Tell him, kid,* Mac cheered Banning's decisive voice. "It's common knowledge around the precinct that you're losing money betting on the games again. I know you got busted down from sergeant and that you need to keep your nose squeaky clean or you'll lose your badge entirely."

"That's *my* business, not yours, you son of a—"

"You're relieved of duty, Osterman." Mac issued the command in a stern voice that sounded cold and foreign on his rusty vocal cords.

In the sudden silence, Mac heard the heavy breaths from Wade's chest, and felt the big man's glare boring down on him. The warmth of the afternoon, the man's exertion, and the round-the-clock duty made Osterman's pores open up and ooze the scent of sweat and nerves.

But that didn't stop his bravado. "You're not really a cop, anymore, Taylor."

"I'll be back on the force before you know it." The vow came from some determined place deep inside Mac, speaking aloud the wish before he could censor the foolishness of it. "And believe me. I never forget a face. Or a voice. Or a smell. I won't forget yours."

Now the big man shifted on his feet, deciding whether to keep playing it tough or back away. The tremor in his bass voice told Mac he had chosen somewhere in between. "Like that's a real threat coming from you. I hear you screwed up, and now Arnie Sanchez is gonna walk."

Bad news traveled fast. Did anyone *not* know that evidence from the Sanchez case had turned up at his house?

One advantage to a lanky build was that Mac could make his six-three height seem even taller when he sucked it in and steeled his spine against unjust accusations. An absence of emotion aided the intimidation factor. "Leave now, or you're on report."

Osterman's defiant curse rumbled deep in his chest. But, fortunately, dirty looks had no effect on a blind man. Mac imagined Wade was using up his meager brainpower debating the wisdom of striking out at a superior officer.

In the end, ice won out over the big man's fiery temper. "I'm outta here." Mac imagined him tipping his hat to Julia. "Ma'am."

"Bye, Wade."

He didn't feel the tension in her relax until a car door slammed and the powerful hum of the police cruiser's engine started.

Mac dipped his head to ask if she was all right when his sensitive ears picked up the sound of Wade's voice. He must have rolled down the car window. "...called in his own man..." He missed the next few words as the tires ground against asphalt and he pulled into traffic. "...you still gotta pay me..."

And then Osterman was gone.

"Everybody okay?" Mac asked.

"Sorry about that, sir."

"You handled him fine." Osterman had been a little too weird for Mac's taste. He was just glad to have him gone. "You know what set him off?"

Julia answered. "Wade and I were having some coffee, and I was listening to him talk about his ex-wife, how he was going to win her back when he got on his financial feet again."

"Which is never going to happen unless he gets help with his gambling problem," added Merle.

Julia turned within Mac's grip, but didn't pull away. "When Detective Banning came out, Wade jumped to attention and asked what the two of you had been talking about inside. He said he needed to be kept apprised since he was involved with the case."

Merle finished the report. "I told him what Captain Taylor said to me, that no one, unless it was directly approved by him, was to work with you."

"Mitch suspects something's going on in his department. He doesn't know who to trust." But his cousin's hands were tied by Internal Affairs. "You sure you want to be a part of this, Banning? It might get uglier before we find out the truth."

"What do you mean by that?" asked Julia, her concerned voice hushed but steady.

Hell. Should he be reassuring her instead of letting her hear the truth? He decided it was already too late to amend his words.

"If I take the fall for whoever blackmailed Jeff, anyone associated with me might come under suspicion as well."

If his other senses hadn't fine-tuned themselves to compensate for his blindness, Mac might not have felt the subtle bunching of muscles in Julia's forearm. Now if his brain could just interpret what her reaction meant.

"I wouldn't blame either one of you if you wanted to leave."

Merle answered quickly. "I'm just doing my job."

"Me, too."

From the angle of her voice, Mac could tell Julia was looking right up into his face. Would he see resignation stamped there? Professional concern?

He took mixed comfort in Julia's promise to stay with him. He breathed in deeply, feeling inexplicably calmed and more confident with her at his side. She might not be staying for the reasons he wanted, but at least she was staying.

His thank you was drowned out by the screeching sound of rubber spinning on asphalt and the monstrous roar of an engine picking up speed.

Tugging Julia along with him, Mac instinctively retreated from the sound.

"Mac?"

"Get down!"

A volley of gunshots thundered through the quiet neighborhood as Merle shouted the command.

Mac threw his arms around Julia and dove for the ground as a chip of the sidewalk flew up and nipped him in the leg. They landed with a thud in the dirt. He kept moving, crawling toward cover—he hoped—with Julia in tow.

The sounds came too fast and too full of purpose for Mac to clearly map the nightmare crashing down all around them.

Two guns, he thought. Two shooters? Or was Banning returning fire? Seven? Eight shots? Some muffled in the dirt or swallowed by the house. Others hitting metal and ricocheting. Others…

The car screeched to life on the pavement again, kicking up dirt and gravel, clipping the corner of a parked vehicle, finding traction and speeding away.

Then all was still.

Chapter Eight

"Are you hurt?"

Mac growled the harsh question right in Julia's ear.

"No." Suffocated between the Mac's hard weight and the even harder ground, Julia was already checking his face, his shoulders, running her hands down his arms—anything she could reach. "Are you?"

"I think my leg's cut. Nothing serious."

In her emergency-room experience, a man's idea of "nothing serious" could mean a severed artery. She wedged her elbows between them and pushed, shoving him off her. She drank in reviving air and filed away her fears as he rolled away.

"Let me look."

She knelt beside him and pushed aside the neat tear in his jeans that was turning dark red with blood. "It looks clean." The short, wide gash in his calf was the wrong shape to be a bullet hole or graze. He'd been hit by debris. "You'll need a couple of stitches." She pushed herself up. "I'll get the first-aid supplies."

"No." Mac grabbed her arm and pulled her back to her knees before she ever reached her feet. "He might come back."

"Dammit, Mac. This is what I do. Let me go." She

jerked her arm from his grip and shot to her feet. And froze. "Oh my God."

"What is it?"

"Merle!" Mac stumbled after her as she dashed to the man lying on the front sidewalk, curled up in a spreading pool of blood.

His eyes were open. Alert. He darted a glance her way before squeezing them shut and grimacing as he tried to speak.

"Shh." Julia talked to him in a soothing voice while she spread open the front of his jacket and shirt. She found the neat little entry hole where a bullet had struck the upper right side of his chest. She circled behind him and checked him gently. She kept the bad news to herself as she laid him flat on the ground.

No exit wound.

A bullet had struck a bone in his leg as well, but, thankfully, had missed the femoral artery. It might be the more painful wound, but the unknown damage inside his chest was what worried her.

She took the weight of Mac's hand on her shoulder as he knelt beside her. "Banning?"

She shushed the young man as his lips formed an "O" and he tried to speak. Julia turned her head and whispered to Mac. "He's got a bullet in his chest. I think it's lodged in the soft tissue, but there's no way to tell if it hit anything else inside."

Mac shifted his grip to Merle's shoulder. "Hang in there, kid."

Julia stripped off her big over-shirt and packed it against Merle's wound to staunch the flow of blood. She wrapped her belt around his thigh to control the bleeding there. She tuned out the sounds of people coming out of their houses, the curious mumble of questions being asked, a vehicle crashing into a solid object. She even tuned out the terminal blare of a horn that indicated the solid object had refused to budge.

"He may have hit the shooter. Banning, did you get a look at him?"

She was only marginally aware of Mac's observations about the crime. Though Merle nodded his head, she didn't relay the message to Mac. Right now, her patient was her entire world.

Julia grabbed Mac's hand and slid it beneath the weight of her own on Merle's chest. "Can you feel how hard I'm pressing down?" Mac nodded. "I need you to maintain the same pressure. No more, no less. I don't want him to lose any more blood."

"Got it." Mac scooted over to take her place as she moved away. "Where are you going?"

She was already running toward the house. "To get more compresses and a phone."

Since she had no trauma cart and nothing resembling sterilization, she improvised. She tore through the house grabbing anything that looked useful, including the afghan off the back of the couch, clean towels from the laundry basket and a handful of ties from Mac's closet. She snatched her phone from her bag on the way back out and punched in a number. She prayed this delay was the right choice to make.

"Hello?"

"Mom." Later, she'd think of a way to apologize for scaring her mother so. "Call Mitch Taylor. Tell him Merle Banning's been shot."

"Who?"

"No one else, Mom. Only Mitch. He'll understand."

"Julia. What—?"

Before she ended the connection, she added. "I love you."

She ran out the door and dialed 911. Chances were a

neighbor had already called in the gunshots. But, then, she wasn't much of one for taking chances.

"Here." She butted Mac aside, took over his job and placed the phone in his hands. "It's the dispatcher. Tell her our situation and location, then give it back to me so I can report his vitals."

Mac's calm, sure tone threaded its way through Julia's veins, creating a pocket of normalcy amidst the crazy world where her hospital bed was dirt and concrete, and her state-of-the-art equipment was little more than her own two hands. She packed off Merle's chest and leg with the towels and secured them with her belt and the ties.

"Here." Mac's fingers groped for her shoulder, then slid straight up her neck. "You talk. I'll hold it."

Cupping his other hand around the shell of her ear, he held the phone in place while she reported the visible signs and suspected extent of Merle's injuries, freeing her hands to elevate Merle's feet and tuck the afghan around him for warmth.

"I can hear him trying to say something." Mac bent low over Merle and turned his ear to the young detective's mouth. "O? No? Go?"

"He's nodding." Julia stayed on the line with the dispatcher while she marked Merle's response to Mac. "Go?" Another nod. "He wants us to go." She shook her head. "I'm not leaving you, pal."

While she reported the fluctuations in Merle's pulse, Mac slowly lifted his head and turned it in another direction, toward the uneven sound creeping up behind them.

"I'm sorry. I have to do this."

With a jolt, Julia turned, shivering at the odd inflection in that familiar basso profundo voice. Wade Osterman staggered through the hedgerow, bleeding from the cut across his forehead and from somewhere beneath the bright red stain on the shoulder of his pale blue shirt. "They'll make me pay. I have to do it."

He lurched forward on unsteady feet, his gun held between two shaking hands.

Julia stared into the deadly void of the black steel barrel and sat up straighter. But she didn't move from Merle's side. "Wade? What's going on?"

From the corner of her eye, she saw Mac push up onto his hands and knees, angling his ear toward their would-be assassin. Wade might have seen the movement, too, but his perception was impaired. He swung his gun to the left, beyond Mac, then back at her.

Keep him talking, she thought. "Did you shoot Detective Banning?"

"I had to." The big man was nearly in tears. "I can't pay."

"Can't pay who?"

Mac threw himself at Wade's legs. The two men tumbled to the ground. A wild shot rang out and Julia leaned over Merle's body to protect him.

She prayed for a miracle, and hoped her mother had understood her message, and that Mitch had dispatched someone he trusted to help them.

Mac had his hand on Wade's gun now. The two men rolled in a tangle of legs and fists. Wade might be injured, but his size and vision still gave him an advantage over Mac.

Julia felt a gentle nudge against her thigh. Merle. She angled herself to see his face. Sirens wailed in the distance now, so she moved closer to hear him.

His lips moved against the pain and his hand slid from under the afghan. "My gun."

Of course. They needed a weapon to fight Wade.

Julia spun around on her hands and knees, and found Merle's compact weapon beneath a pile of leaves. "I don't know how to use it." Mac sailed backward and landed, still, in the grass. "Mac!" Oh God. A wave of panic started at her toes and shimmied up through her body. She hurried back to Merle's side. "I've never fired a gun."

Wade found his own gun, then climbed up on his feet with a series of jerks.

Merle's fingers splayed beside his hip. His eyes guided Julia to the subtle movement there.

Mac began to move. He was stunned, disoriented. But alive. Healthy.

For now.

Wade lifted his gun.

Julia wrapped Merle's fingers around his weapon.

"I'm sorry, Mr. Taylor." Wade squeezed the trigger as he apologized.

A shot exploded in Julia's ears.

Wade crumpled to the ground and Merle's hand fell to his side.

"Jules?" Mac's hoarse cry cut through the shock of seeing a man shot to death right before her eyes. With his right arm outstretched, he crawled toward her.

She met him halfway. "I'm here. I'm all right."

When their fingers touched, he grabbed her and pulled her to him. He framed her face in his hands and looked down as if he could really see. She winced at the swelling around his left eye.

"You're hurt."

"I'm fine." His hands were quick and hard as they swept across her body, verifying what his vision could not see. She caught his hands in a prayerlike grasp between them. "Merle shot Wade. He tried to kill you."

Mac squeezed his eyes shut and shook his head, as dumbfounded by these last few minutes of hell as she was. "I wish I knew what was going on." But in the next breath, he was in control again. "Get me Osterman's gun.

I want to find out if it matches the slug in Banning's chest.''

"How?"

"Just do it."

Julia scrambled off to do his bidding. She pressed two fingers against Wade's throat and searched for a pulse that wasn't there.

"Jules?"

She didn't fully understand, but she obeyed Mac's need to hurry. Choking down the urge to retch, she pulled the gun from Wade's still-warm fingers. Useless tears stung the back of her eyes. The big doofus shouldn't have died. He shouldn't have been mixed up in any of this. "Why, Wade?"

She pleaded with a senseless world for answers, but found none. She swiped the back of her hand across her eyes and turned back to Mac. One awful night fifteen years ago, he had made sense of all the madness. He found a way to make everything right again.

But could even Mac Taylor make sense of this?

Mac tucked Wade's gun into the back of his jeans when she handed it to him. He had crouched beside Merle and held the younger man's hand. Held it tight. "Hang in there, Banning. Help's on the way."

"Go." Merle's chest heaved with the effort to speak that one word.

The sirens grew louder as they rounded the corner. Julia found the strength to offer him a smile. "The ambulance is almost here." She brushed a lock of hair off his forehead. "You saved our lives. Now you be quiet and save your own."

But his continued agitation concerned her. "I'll go meet the ambulance."

"No." Mac caught her ankle as she stepped away, tackling her to the ground. "It could be the police."

Julia pushed at the weight of his body on her legs. "Then I'll meet the police."

"What if it's Masterson and Niederhaus?"

Julia slumped back on her elbows and buttocks. She was feeling tired. Beyond tired. Too weary to fight anymore, she sank into the hard-packed dirt as her adrenaline wore off and her patience wore thin. "What are you saying?"

Mac loomed over her, his bruised and battered face lined with the same frustration she was feeling. "I have two downed cops on my lawn and my bloody fingerprints all over everything. I don't think they'll be interested in any explanation."

"But they're cops. They're the good guys, right? They have to—"

"Didn't you hear what Wade said? *Can't pay.* He shot at us because someone forced him to."

A glimmer of understanding relit the fire in her veins. "Blackmail?"

"Blackmail." Mac sat back on his heels and pulled Julia up to a sitting position. "Another cop on the take dies while I'm around. I'm starting to feel guilty myself."

"You're not." She reached out and cupped the side of Mac's jaw. "You need to leave. That's what Merle meant. You need to go someplace safe until we can find out who's behind all this."

He covered her hand with his, linking them in a quick caress. But just as quickly, he wrapped his fingers through hers and clutched them against his heart. "You've been a trooper. I can't thank you enough for all you've done. But I want you to stay with Banning. Make sure he pulls through."

Julia looked about as he released her hand. The sirens had now taken on an ominous tone, like great predators hunting down their prey. "Where will you go?"

"I'll figure that out later." Mac was already half crawling, half limping toward the front door. "Just answer anything they ask as honestly as you can. Don't get caught in any lies."

"But you're hurt." He hit the front step and pitched forward, catching himself on the frame. "Dammit, Mac. You can't do this on your own."

Julia picked up her phone and bolted to her feet. Even though he had given her the order to stay, she knew in her heart she had no choice. How did a blind man try to hide? Or watch his back? She caught Mac's left hand and slipped it through the crook of her arm, pulling him up and into the house behind her. As they dashed through, she grabbed her bag, their jackets and Mac's antibiotic drops from the kitchen.

As the ambulance spun into the driveway, they ran out the back door into the alley behind Mac's house.

While the paramedics tended to Merle, she tossed their things into the back seat of her car and Mac climbed in.

And when the unmarked police car skidded up onto the curb in front of the house, Julia slammed her car into gear and sped away.

"YEAH, JOSH, WE'RE FINE." Mac had taken a chance on contacting a cop he could trust. His youngest brother. He already felt guilty as the criminal I.A. believed him to be for getting Julia involved in this mess. He didn't want anyone else in trouble or danger on his behalf. But regret and pride had given way to practicality. "But we need some help."

With one ear to the phone, he could still hear Julia puttering about the office of the abandoned warehouse where they planned to hole up for the night. Busy again. She was moving some furniture around, and cleaning things off, judging by the cloud of dust tickling his nose. Other than the ancient creaks and moans of the building settling around them, she made the only sounds in this derelict neighborhood between the old stockyards and the Missouri River.

Josh's bright, teasing voice took on an unusually serious tone. "Word around the station house is that I.A. wants to bring you in for questioning."

"I.A. wants to put me away permanently." He expelled an angry, frustrated sigh and bent his mouth closer to the phone. "I can't find answers from a jail cell, Josh. And nobody else is asking the right questions. They're convinced I'm behind the trail of missing evidence. Or that I discovered it and now I'm covering it up to make my department look clean."

"Did you kill Ringlein?"

"No."

"Did you steal that evidence?"

Damn. Did even his own brother doubt him? "No."

Josh laughed, and his rich, robust tone almost gave Mac hope. "Then I'm not aiding and abetting a felon. I'm taking care of my big brother."

As a big brother, Mac felt compelled to remind Josh just how serious this situation was. "If this turns out badly, you could lose your badge for helping us."

"Understood. Now tell me what you need."

Mac ticked off a list of items—fresh clothes, toiletries, cash. While they talked, he became aware of the sudden silence in the room. For the barest instant of panic, he thought Julia had left. And then he heard her sudden catch of breath. It was a shivery sigh that seemed to shudder through her all the way from her shoulders down to the floor.

"Jules?" Mac stretched out his arm, blindly seeking contact, silently asking for her hand.

She didn't disappoint. She hadn't yet.

Her fingers touched his in a timid grasp.

Her skin was like ice. And he didn't think it was solely due to the lack of heat in the building. Had she just now realized what they were up against? Was she thinking of the blood she had stopped to wash off her hands more than once that day?

Alarmed, concerned, Mac turned his head away from the phone, wishing he could read her face. But he couldn't, of course. So he did the only thing he could think of. Treat the symptom. Even if he didn't fully understand the cause.

He tugged her into his chest and wrapped his arm around her shoulders. She folded her hands between them, to seek warmth or to form a barrier of protest, he couldn't tell.

Mac squeezed her tighter, and dipped his nose into the stale smells of dirt and stress that tarnished her beautiful hair. Her hands never snuck around his waist or clung to the front of his jacket, but at least she didn't pull away. She might not want to be intimate with him, but, thankfully, she'd accept whatever human comfort he could give her. He owed her that much. And more, so much more.

"Mac? You still there?" Josh's voice summoned him across the line.

Keeping Julia close, Mac answered. "I'm here."

They arranged a time and meeting place for the next morning. Josh promised to find and hide Julia's car where they had abandoned it in a suburban mall parking lot before switching to a public transport bus to ride back downtown.

Finally, Josh asked, "What about Jules? She need anything?"

Mac felt like a total jerk. He hadn't thought to ask if she had any particular requests. He could feel her shifting in his hold, raising her face toward his.

"Did you hear that?" he asked.

Her ear brushed against his shoulder as she nodded. "Some shampoo? I feel pretty gritty."

Shampoo. Yes. Definitely. He wanted her to wash away those horrible memories from the day. "Shampoo, Josh." He closed his eyes and thought of his first impression of the grown-up Julia. "Something simple and clean. Nothing perfumey."

"Got it. You sure you don't want me to bring it out tonight? I can do it on the sly."

"No." Mac thanked his brother. "I want to lie low for a few hours. See if anyone shows their hand. I'm going to do this on my own, Josh." Correction. He nuzzled his cheek against the crown of Julia's hair. "*We're* going to do this. I don't want anyone else getting hurt."

"I'll let you call the shots on this one, Mac. But take care of yourself. I'll have a hell of a time explaining it to Ma if you get hurt again. Or something worse."

"I will." He felt a sudden tension creep into Julia's shoulder and automatically began to massage it, kneading in a smidgeon of the warmth she reluctantly took from him. She must have heard Josh's last comment. "One more request."

"Sure."

"I don't suppose you could get me something to drive?"

"And put a blind man behind the wheel? I guess it couldn't be much worse than some of the other folks I've pulled over." Mac shook his head. Josh could find something humorous in the entire world coming to an end.

But fortunately—and to his chagrin—Julia saw the humor in it, too. He could hear the hushed giggle in her throat, and feel the rhythmic rise and fall of her chest as she tried to hide her amusement at the silly comment. He stilled his fingers as she finally relaxed.

Mac felt a relaxing bit of relief himself now that her

fears had eased. But then he was broadsided by an emotion completely foreign to him.

Jealousy.

Josh had made her feel better. Josh had made her laugh. *He* could only get her killed.

But common sense demanded that he set that stabbing feeling of betrayal aside. Josh was his brother, not his competition. Hell. Julia wasn't even interested in him. She'd made that clear this morning with her packed bag and her rejection of his kiss. She was here to repay that stupid favor. Nothing more. He should appreciate whatever it took to help her get through all this.

He just wished he'd been the one to make her laugh.

Mac crushed his emotions beneath his sternest big-brother voice. "Work with me here."

"Okay." Josh's laughter finally subsided. "What does Jules like to drive?"

Her giggles stopped more abruptly, as if she was surprised to be asked. "Nothing too big," she said, after a thoughtful moment. "Nothing with a stick shift."

"Did you hear that?" Mac asked.

"Got it. I'll have her carriage delivered first thing in the morning. See you then." Josh caught his breath then, and for a moment, was deadly serious. "You take care of yourself. And tell Jules good-night."

Mac quietly answered both requests. "I will."

He disconnected the call, and he and Julia were alone again. She took the phone and stepped away. The chill in the stark, silent air washed over him as she left him to pack it in her bag.

He paused to consider for a moment the quick, intense emotional reactions this suddenly shy woman caused in him.

By simply being herself—practical and efficient, sassy

and stubborn, cool under pressure yet somehow unsure of herself—she made him more aware of himself as a man.

He'd always considered himself a scientist. First, as a student. Then as a forensic cop. He'd always enjoyed the challenges of learning, the thrills of discovery. The triumph of ascertaining an exact answer to the questions posed to him throughout his life. But he could see now that he'd neglected to train his heart in the same way he'd developed his mind.

He loved his family. Shared a bond with his brothers and sister that he'd trade for no other. He'd dated a respectable number of women, and had liked them, had cared for them on some level.

But no one turned him inside out and worked him over the way Julia did.

He just didn't understand it.

But understanding would come with time and study. And just like any other mystery, he was determined to solve it. Just not tonight.

He didn't have the answers to any questions tonight.

"Tired?" he asked, feeling a need to break the silence. She was busy again. Whether she had a legitimate purpose, or was simply working through the same nervous energy he was feeling, he couldn't tell.

"Exhausted." The busy sounds stopped for a moment. "Here's a bite to eat. I always keep something in my bag for emergencies."

She handed him a small square package wrapped in paper. He sniffed at the open end and discovered half of a chocolate bar. "We'll be thirsty if we eat this sugar." He took a bite, anyway, as his stomach and taste buds overruled his reason.

"I have a bottle of water in my bag, too."

Mac smiled. No wonder her bag was so heavy. She

wasn't just prepared for emergencies, she was prepared for everything. "Anything that's not in there?"

"A miracle."

A rustle of denim told him she had settled onto the floor. The momentary buoyancy of his mood sank along with her. He didn't want her to be discouraged, but he didn't want to lie to her, either.

"Where are you?" he had to ask.

"About four steps straight in front on you."

Mac took two steps, then sat on the floor facing her. "I don't necessarily believe in miracles, Jules. I believe in hard facts. Things I can prove or disprove."

"I know." She handed him the water bottle. "I just wish I knew what we needed to do, so we could go home. So I could feel safe again."

Safe? Hell. He'd taken that from her, too. Mac kept his damning curses to himself. He really knew how to show a lady a good time. This was the first she'd mentioned how she felt, and it was more like dropping a hint. He doubted she'd ever complain outright. He didn't intend to give her any reason to.

"I've got a scenario in mind as to what's going on. I just need to figure out who's behind it." Mac took a drink and passed the water back to her. "Someone blackmailed Jeff into compromising or destroying evidence in order to throw cases. Someone blackmailed Osterman into trying to kill me—probably to keep my curiosity in check."

"Or someone thought you were on to them."

"Exactly." He polished off the last of the candy bar, wadded the foil wrapper and stuffed it into his pocket. "If people are being blackmailed, then someone is doing the blackmailing. They're trying to make it look like it's me. I'm going to prove who's behind this. I'm going to find out who's benefiting from this whole mess."

Julia's energy seemed to rise as she caught on to his

line of thinking. "Melanie Ringlein sure seems to be in the money. Or do you think it's Arnie Sanchez? Maybe the earlier thefts were just a cover so he'd look less suspicious when his case gets dismissed."

"*If* it gets dismissed. Dwight Powers doesn't take him to trial until Monday."

"That's only seventy-two hours away, Mac. Can you figure it all out by then?"

"I'll have to." He took another swallow of water and listened to her pack it away in her bag. And rearrange the contents. Busy again. He reached out and found her arm. He trailed his fingers down to her hand and stopped their nervous quest. "But not tonight. You've been through enough already today."

"No. If there's something—"

Her yawn betrayed her and he smiled. "Tonight we need to rest." He released her and stood up, bracing himself for her protest, having his own argument ready. "You say there's just the one cot in here?"

She stood up and brushed something off her clothes. "That and some file cabinets and a three-legged desk."

"Then we'll have to sleep together on the cot."

Here it came. Fast and furious in that husky, helpful voice of hers. "You take the cot. I can lean against the wall or curl up on the floor in my jacket."

"There's no heat in this building, no blankets, and it's going to get down to freezing tonight." Mac splayed his fingers at his waist and tamped down his temper. She couldn't argue with solid, unemotional logic. "You're the health expert. Shouldn't we combine our body temperatures so we don't risk hypothermia?"

"Yes. But—"

"I promise to keep my hands to myself." He held them up in mock surrender, showing proof that she needn't fear another encounter like they had that morning. ''We'll just cuddle enough to be practical.''

''Okay.''

Her ready acceptance of his hands-off offer stung his ego. But then, his ego wasn't the most important thing at stake here.

She'd sacrificed enough already, just by being here with him. She'd witnessed a man's death and saved the life of another. She'd fled a crime scene with a suspected felon. She'd put up with his moods and demands.

She didn't have to risk her health on top of all that.

With his hands in front of him, Mac walked in the general direction of the cot. He bumped it with his knee, braced his hand on the wall behind the cot, then turned and sat. The canvas stretched and creaked beneath his weight, but held fast. He moved slowly, afraid that she'd doubt his word if he made any sudden movements. He took off his leather jacket and then lay down. He made himself as comfortable as a length of canvas three inches shorter than his body allowed.

He held his breath as he held out his hand to her. ''C'mon. Your turn.''

With equally careful, controlled movements, she lay down beside him. The cot was so narrow, they had to lie on their sides, spoon-fashion. Mac bit down on his lip in an effort to ignore his body's feverish reaction to the soft curve of her bottom nestled against his groin. Instead, he focused on more tender feelings, and covered them both with his jacket, tucking the collar up beneath her chin.

Then he leaned back against the wall. He had his left arm folded up beneath his head to use as his pillow. But his right hand...

He tried laying his arm straight down his side. But that put a hitch in his shoulder. He let it slide down behind him, but the old concrete wall was cold. He let it hover in the air, wondering if he could rest it on her shoulder. But no, his elbow would cramp at that angle. Her hip? Too intimate.

"Ah, the hell with this."

Mac curled his arm around Julia's waist. She stiffened immediately inside the hug, even though his hand rested on the edge of the cot, and didn't touch one of her inviting curves.

"For warmth." He growled the excuse into her ear when she started to speak. She caught her breath and chose silence instead of protest.

Maybe he had spoken a tad harshly, but, dammit all, he was tired. She was tired. And he'd kept his promise and hadn't touched her with his hand.

Despite the fact that he could pull her closer and they could conserve more body heat if he touched her. Despite the fact his hand itched to learn more about her feminine shape. Despite the fact he'd found strength and comfort in even the simplest of embraces with this woman.

He'd kept his word.

Still, it seemed like an eternity passed before she relaxed, and the even sound of her breathing filled his ears.

He followed her into sleep soon after.

Chapter Nine

The first thing Julia noticed as the sunlight filtered through the single greasy, dust-caked window of the office was how cold her nose was.

In the drowsy stage of half sleeping, half waking, she automatically wrapped her fingers around the tip of her nose and tried to warm it.

The second thing she noticed was the heat burning beneath the gentle pressure on her breast.

She snapped her eyes open as sleep abandoned her and consciousness rushed in. Cautiously, moving nothing but her eyes, she looked down to see Mac's hand cupping her breast inside the gaping front of her jacket. Through her T-shirt, he caught the taut, distended nipple between two long, strong fingers.

Forcing herself to breathe normally, in through her nose, out through her mouth, she tried to scoot away from the sinful temptation of his possessive hand.

She realized her mistake when her hip pushed against the bulge at the front of his jeans. Julia's heart skipped a beat and her skin flushed with embarrassment. Even asleep, he made her body come alive. He made her want things she was never destined to have. Things it hurt too much to want.

She wanted to slip away before he awoke, before he felt

compelled to apologize for his body's instinctive response to a warm body. He'd promised no hands last night. She didn't want him to feel guilty for going back on his word. He was asleep, after all. A man couldn't consciously control his actions when he was asleep.

She was tired of men apologizing. Tired of men using her, seeing her as some kind of challenge to be overcome, some kind of bet to be won. Not seeing her as a woman. Or worse, not seeing her at all.

Too big. Too plain. Too shy. Too frank. Too old. Too inexperienced.

In her hurry to escape the paralyzing rush of self-doubts, she rolled forward. Her breast pressed into the waiting warmth of his hand, and she nearly moaned aloud at the sweet torture of his unknowing touch.

If only he could really...

The hand at her breast squeezed. "Shh. It's okay."

Julia's rampaging heartbeat slammed in her chest. "I didn't mean to wake you."

"Believe me, this is the way to wake up." She froze as his soothing words mocked her. He whispered against her ear in his raspy, sleepy, impossibly sexy voice. "He would have lost, you know."

He? Lost what? Julia scrambled out of his grasp and jumped to her feet. The room spun around her with the speed at which she stood, but she braced her hand over her eyes and staggered to the wall behind the desk.

"What are you talking about?" She adjusted her bra, her shirt, her jacket, but found no relief from the blazing awareness of Mac's touch still sending aftershocks throughout her body.

"Ray Wozniak. Thinking he could win that dogfight with you."

With a deliberate ease, Mac swung his feet to the floor and sat up on the edge of the cot. His legs veed out in

that most basic of masculine stances, and her body
throbbed with the female need to answer the call of his.
His gray eyes, as implacable as granite, stared in her general direction.

But she felt the impact of his husky whisper clear across
the room. ''You're too pretty a woman for that.''

Julia huddled in the corner beside a dented filing cabinet
while Mac excused himself to use the toilet down the hall.
For a moment, she paused to wonder at the likelihood of
the water still being turned on in parts of the building.
True, the water in the sink ran in cold, colder, or coldest,
and she would never drink the rusty brown stuff. But there
it was. Real. Something they desperately needed.

Then she wondered at the likelihood of Mac paying her
a compliment. He'd been simple. Direct. Lacking the gran-
diose charm with which Anthony Cardello had finally
earned and shattered her trust. It was a compliment she
desperately wanted to believe.

Mac had never lied to her. He was as honest with his
moods and needs as he was with the facts of the case he
pursued. Real.

You're too pretty.

That Pandora's box that guarded her heart tried to spring
open and seize the wonderment of Mac's matter-of-fact
words.

Could he really see her like that? See *her?* Want *her?*

By the time Mac returned, she had that little bud of
wishful hope firmly under control with a simple explanation.

Pretty to a blind man might not be pretty at all.

MAC SWALLOWED THE last two bites of his bacon and
licked his fingers. His arteries were screaming in protest
at the fatty combination of fried eggs and bacon with buttered toast on the side, but his stomach was happy. It was

the first real meal in nearly twenty-four hours for him and Julia. They'd need their strength. And who knew when they'd get a chance to eat again.

Josh sat at the breakfast counter beside him sipping his coffee. Julia sat on Mac's left, eating an English muffin.

The diner at Kansas City's downtown bus terminal might not serve five-star cuisine, but it did offer a diverse number of people of various ages, gender, and ethnic and economic backgrounds. With the morning rush of changing buses and temporary layovers, a blind man, a curvy nurse and a hulking blond heartbreaker could easily lose themselves in the crowd.

"Everything you asked for is in the green Ford pickup parked out south on the street. Should I tell you I packed them in a University of Kansas duffel bag?"

Mac managed a smile. "Traitor."

They'd had a lot of fun over the years, having attended rival colleges in Missouri and Kansas. Josh used the Mizzou T-shirt Mac had given him to wash his car. Josh's gift of a jar with a Kansas Jayhawk emblazoned on it sat on the desk in Mac's office with an insect specimen inside.

That Josh would think of the old joke now reminded him of how close a family the Taylors were. They'd grown up poor, in a tough neighborhood. But they'd flourished. They were stronger for it.

Mac drew on some of that familial strength.

"I probably shouldn't have gotten you involved with this. I.A. could come down on you, too."

"Are you kidding?" Josh's easy strength and abundant energy were almost contagious. "I always thought you were an old stick-in-the-mud. This is probably the coolest thing you've ever done."

"Running from the scene of a crime is not cool. It's illegal."

"And necessary, from the sound of things." His coffee

mug hit the counter with a decisive thunk. "Ma wrapped up some sandwiches for the two of you, and Mrs. Dalton packed some things for Jules. Here." The rattle of crisp paper unfolding caught Mac's attention. "It's the address of a lab you can use. It's all the way over in the Thirteenth Precinct, but Mitch said the guy in charge was a man you could trust. I don't know what you want it for, but we figured between Ginny and me, we could get you in."

Mac handed the paper on to Julia. His mother. Barbara Dalton. His brothers. Brett's wife, Ginny. Merle Banning. Julia. If it were just him, he wouldn't quit until he'd uncovered the truth. But he had others to consider now. "Too many people are putting their neck on the line for me. Maybe I should turn myself in and let the investigation run its course."

"Mac—"

"You're kidding, right?"

With objections coming from both sides, Mac pushed his plate back and leaned his elbows on the counter. He surrendered to the chain of events already set into motion. "I want to check the bullets in Wade Osterman's gun against the slug in Merle Banning's chest before that evidence disappears, too. Osterman was somebody's hired gun. I'd like to cross-reference his ballistics and see if he's responsible for any other unsolved shootings. Maybe I can establish a pattern of some kind. Link those incidents to cases that have been thrown out of court."

"How *is* Merle?" Julia's soft voice asked the question behind his back, and Mac felt like a heel for not asking about the kid himself.

"He came through surgery fine last night," answered Josh. "But they're going to have to rebuild his knee. Ginny and Brett are at the hospital with him this morning. She'll deliver the slug."

"Does he have any family?" Again, Julia was asking the questions he should be asking.

"All I know is his mom's there with him."

"He's a good kid. I'm glad he's going to make it." Mac wished he could convey the message in person. But he understood that time was a critical factor, and that his expertise lay in uncovering facts, not offering comfort. He sat up straight, taking charge the way he would have six weeks ago. "Banning was working on a profile of Melanie Ringlein at the house. Plus, I wanted him to find out if Arnie Sanchez has a connection to either of the Ringleins. Any way you can get your hands on his laptop?"

Josh's cringing sigh told him no before he spoke. "I.A. cleaned out everything after you left. Even Ma and Mrs. D. I guess they drove over right after Jules called her mom."

Julia wrapped her fingers around Mac's knee, transmitting the sudden alarm he felt. "They didn't hurt them, did they?"

He covered her hand with his, waiting for Josh's answer.

"Nah. From what I hear, Ma made old Niederhaus take his stogie outside and put it out."

Mac laughed with a bit of pride. He supposed he'd always appreciated strong women. "That sounds like Ma, all right."

"I'll see what I can do about tracking down that information. In the meantime…" A telltale jingle of metal on metal, and the warmth of Josh's arm reaching in front of him told Mac his brother was handing a set of keys to Julia. "Compliments of Cole. He swears the plates on that truck are legit, and are registered to a Fred and LaVerne Anderson."

Plastic ID cards came next. "Hi, Fred. Hi, Verne. But you know you'll always be Jules to me, Verne."

Julia snickered. "Jules Verne? Your jokes haven't improved any over the years."

"Maybe not. But I have."

That annoying surge of jealousy attacked Mac again as Julia laughed outright at Josh's goofy flirtation. Her attempt to stifle her laughter only pointed out the fact that Josh had succeeded where he had failed.

Did Josh lust after Jules the way he did? Was he drawn to her vulnerability? Did he want to solve the complex mysteries that made her sweet and tender and hot to the touch one moment, and cold and distant and even outright afraid the next?

No. Mac squeezed his eyes shut and tapped into his powers of observation. Josh and Julia teased each other like brother and sister. His brother's idle flirtations were part of the jokes they shared. Julia understood that and gave it right back. Friendly, yet superficial. He could hear the genuine liking in their voices, and nothing more.

But with him, she was different. Was it still that damned debt? The obligation she felt existed between them?

He rubbed at the skin beside his eyes and concentrated harder, replaying the words surrounding their kiss, the truth he'd shared when he woke up that morning.

He narrowed his sightless gaze as his mind seized upon a theory.

It was the intimacy that scared her. It was the notion that he *did* find her attractive that sent her into a state of panic.

But why? Was he really so repulsive to look at?

Would she really curl up in bed beside a monster?

He felt her hand still on his knee, silently including him in her conversation with Josh.

And then he knew the answer.

Did Ray Wozniak's cruel joke still have influence over

her today? Or had something more recent happened to cause her to doubt the true extent of her beauty?

He turned toward her laughter. Couldn't she see it? Couldn't she see what a blind man so clearly could?

"What?" Her mood changed abruptly. Self-consciously. He must have a frightening countenance when he frowned—raw skin and ragged angles and blank, staring eyes. "What's wrong?"

He turned his hand and laced his fingers through hers. He might have a theory, but how did he go about testing it?

Josh's vinyl stool creaked behind him, alerting Mac to the change in his demeanor. Normally a big, easygoing man, his brother's sudden stillness set off instant warning bells inside Mac's head.

"Heads up, boys and girls." Josh's hushed warning confirmed the danger. "I think we've got trouble."

Mac tightened his grip on Julia. "What is it?"

"A blue suit walked in. He's scanning the crowd."

A uniformed patrol officer looking for someone. Not good.

The temperature dropped in Julia's skin. She hunched closer to Mac. "Is he looking for us?"

"I can't tell. It could just be a routine patrol. But even if he's here for someone else, your descriptions are out on the wire." Josh stood and moved behind them, using his big frame to partially hide them. "One last thing. Here."

Josh tapped an object against Mac's chest. Mac discovered he'd handed him a pair of sunglasses. They were still warm with the heat from Josh's body. He traced the long, narrow shape with his fingertips, noting how the curves raced around the corner and blended in with the earpiece. He recognized the ultracool dimensions. "These are yours. I can't take them."

Josh shoved them back when he would have handed them over. "They're yours now."

"He's moving this way." Julia's warning made their goodbyes short and sweet.

Mac snatched his brother's hand in a heartfelt handshake. "I owe you."

"I won't forget. Call me or Mitch or Ginny if you need anything. I'll lose this guy and meet you at the lab this afternoon."

"You be careful, little brother."

"*You* be careful." Josh leaned in and Mac heard something that sounded like a kiss. "Keep an eye on him, Jules."

"I will."

After Josh slipped away, Mac felt exposed and alone. The crowd was an unintelligible buzz of white noise that closed in on him. Any one of them could be the enemy and he wouldn't know it. An undercover cop or bounty hunter tracking them. He didn't even know which direction to run. Where to find the door.

But he had Julia to protect. He had to stay free until he could find out the truth. That meant he had to think clearly. Panic was not an option.

He concentrated on how Julia's hand fit so perfectly within his, the sense of calm her touch empowered him with. With the calm came rational thought. He tilted his nose toward her unique scent. "Am I looking right at you?"

She hesitated. "Yeah."

"I mean right into your eyes. Does it look like I can see you?"

"I get it." Julia's voice filled with that familiar sense of purpose he admired. "He's looking for a blind man."

Her cool fingers touched his chin, lifting his face to a different angle. "That's it." She slid her hand along his jaw until she was cupping his face. Smart move. She played the charade of an everyday loving couple to blend in with the crowd, and obscured his face at the same time.

Fighting the urge to rub his cheek against her tender touch, Mac focused on the business at hand. "Am I more convincing with or without the glasses?"

Her fingers danced across his face like a lover's caress, analyzing the web of scars at his temple and forehead, studying the blank eyes in between. "With."

He put on the glasses and kept his sightless eyes pointed toward hers. "Where's Josh?"

"He's with the officer now, showing him his badge. They're talking. He has him turned toward the door now."

The urgency in her voice prompted him to move. "Let's go."

She slipped off her stool and pulled Mac along with her. "C'mon. We can get in line and go out through the loading dock."

In a movement that had quickly become a habit, Julia took his hand and hooked it through her arm.

"No, wait." She was clearly puzzled, impatient to know why he'd stopped. He purposefully switched their positions, drawing her hand through his arm and holding it tight. "Don't want to look like a blind man."

"Right."

The trick was, now he had to lead the way. While he concentrated on the sounds of the people around them to avoid bumping into them, she nudged him along. "Another two steps. We're at the turnstile."

He butted his hip against the windmill-shaped device and pushed his way through as if he knew exactly where he was going.

"Stop." Julia tugged at his arm and he obeyed. "We're in line for the bus to Tulsa."

"I've always heard Tulsa's a nice city." He added that for effect, then asked about Josh.

Julia moved in front of him and turned so she could look behind them without drawing attention. Without warning, her fingers sank like claws into his forearm. She buried her face in his chest and whispered harshly. "He's looking right at us!"

Though she still had the gumption to move them along with the line, her fear was a palpable thing. She peeked again.

"He's walking this way."

Strangely enough, as Julia's pulse rate quickened beneath his fingertips, a sense of calm stole over Mac. He knew what he had to do. He framed her face and tipped it up, then dropped his forehead to touch hers. "If he comes after me," he whispered, brushing his nose against hers, "I want you to lose yourself in the crowd. You're not part of this."

Her hands tugged at his wrists. "No. I'm not leaving you."

"Your debt has been more than paid."

"This isn't about—" Her rapid breathing caught, then slowed in a conscious effort to report everything clearly. "Josh is leading him away. They're questioning someone else. Let's get out of here. Now. Please."

A part of him knew he'd pay for her choice somewhere down the line. Pay dearly, no doubt. The laws of science dictated that their actions today would have equal and *opposite* reactions tomorrow. But at this moment he was selfishly glad she was willing to stay with him.

"Lead the way."

With a brief excuse to the ticket-taker about changing their minds, Julia grabbed Mac's hand and led him out a pair of glass doors. They dashed across the asphalt driveway and down a set of cracked concrete steps to an uneven sidewalk. When Mac caught his toe and tripped, she slowed their pace to a walk and slipped his hand through her elbow as she had before.

"There's a wall here that blocks us from view."

"Do you see the green truck?"

With a tangible task to keep her busy, Julia's breathing slowed to a healthy rate. He could still feel the tension in her muscles, though. It was the same tension that tied his own into knots.

"There."

He was getting so good at reading the movements of her body that he stopped when she did. He even backed up a step with her.

"It's across the street. There's a curb. Step down, six inches."

Her concise directions allowed him to move easily at her side. When they were on the opposite sidewalk, she fished the keys from her pocket and unlocked the passenger door. She moved aside to let Mac climb in, but he grabbed her by the waist and lifted her up into the cab ahead of him. "Let's just get out of here."

They'd escaped detection thus far, but time and the city's police force were not on their side. Josh could way-lay one cop for a few minutes. Mitch could block action for a day or so. Ginny could pocket a bit of evidence and deliver it to him before the misappropriation was discovered. Their mothers could even nag Internal Affairs and buy them a few minutes of time.

But, ultimately, Mac knew the clock was ticking.

Julia inserted the key into the ignition and turned it over. The hum of the truck's engine spoke of power, while the new smell of the upholstery told him Cole had spared no expense in furnishing them a vehicle.

A lot of people believed in his innocence.

A lot of people had given him their trust.

The germ of an idea took root and stood poised on the brink of numerous possibilities. He mulled it around for a moment or two, but then set it aside. He had other priorities he had to take care of first.

"Where do I go? Back to the warehouse?" Julia pulled smoothly into traffic.

"No. We're Fred and LaVerne Anderson now. Let's find a motel.

"I need a quiet place to think."

THOUGH A HOT SHOWER with plenty of soap and shampoo had gone a long way toward restoring her opinion of the world, Julia still lingered at the motel's bathroom mirror, touching up the neutral tint of her lipstick.

Lord knew it wasn't vanity or a lack of energy or even her worries about Mac's investigation that kept her hidden behind the wall that divided the bathroom area from the king-size bed in the next room.

How was she going to spend another night in the same room with him? In the same bed? And not make a fool of herself like she had that morning?

Anthony Cardello had taken her to a hotel. A posher one than this. He'd booked them in a suite and ordered room service.

I've never done it with a virgin before.

Julia shut her eyes against the memory of Anthony's gleeful rejoinder, but couldn't stop the painful flashbacks from rushing in.

She hadn't realized all the sight-seeing and dining, the fine wines and expensive gifts, the stolen kisses and the clever words had all been about getting her into that hotel room. It had taken a month of phone calls before she accepted that first date. Two weeks more before their first kiss. She hadn't necessarily been saving herself for marriage, but she'd been saving herself for a man she really wanted to be with. A man who wanted to be with her. After six months, she thought Anthony was the one.

He was the one, all right.

The one who made her understand just how foolish she could be. The one who let her know that thirty-year-old virgins were a rare breed. He'd thanked her for the challenge of seducing her. Said she had made it a worthwhile game.

She'd summoned the courage to confront him about it in his office the following Monday. She had to understand that there wasn't a relationship between them anymore, he'd told her. The thrill had gone for him. But if it was any consolation, she wasn't half-bad in bed.

She'd slapped his face and walked out. But the damage had been done. She'd only had to overhear one conversation in the hospital lounge about Dr. Casanova's latest conquest for her to sit down and write out her resignation. Four weeks later she was home.

And face to face with Mac.

How could she be so competent in every other aspect of her life, but so completely clueless when it came to men?

A cramp in her hand brought Julia back to the present. She eased her grip on the vanity counter and gathered her composure by repacking only the most necessary items in her black leather bag.

Ray Wozniak had taken her self-confidence. Anthony Cardello had robbed her of her pride.

But Mac Taylor could steal her heart.

And what kept Julia at the sink, packing and repacking her bag, was the fear that he already had.

This wasn't about a schoolgirl's heart. In the past few days, her teenage crush had turned into the real thing. He wasn't just the hero who'd stepped out of the night and saved her dignity and protected her from more physical abuse. She'd gotten to know the real man. Honest and temperamental. Tender and passionate. Brilliant and brave.

If she wasn't careful, Mac could hurt her in a way that Ray and Dr. Casanova never could.

Deciding that she couldn't stall any longer, Julia slung her bag over her shoulder and stepped around the corner.

A hopeless smile spread across her face.

It didn't help that Mac Taylor was the sexiest man on the planet. And that he didn't even know it.

She watched him pace back and forth along a memorized path, counting out something on his fingers and talking to himself.

He stood tall and lean in jeans that hugged his long legs and cupped his firm butt with each stride. Josh had packed him a black Henley shirt that clung to the broad points of his shoulders and hung loosely at his trim waist.

With no desire to repeat their first night together, she hadn't offered to help him shave. And now a golden scruff of beard shaded the sharp angles of his jaw and faded down his neck to the unbuttoned V of his collar.

As if he sensed her stare, Mac stopped pacing and turned. Just like the man, his smile was succinct and sincere. "Ready to go?"

Julia nodded as if he could see. "Sure."

He put on Josh's sunglasses and picked up his leather jacket from the bed. But he hesitated a moment, as if she had made some small sound or comment to draw his attention. "Is everything all right?"

Careful, Jules, she warned herself.

She fixed a smile on her face, hoping her sarcasm would reflect in her voice. "What could be wrong? I'm about to break into a police lab with a wanted blind man so he can fire off a gun."

A question flitted across his face before he answered in

a similar tone. "You're shooting the gun. I'm the look-out."

Her laughter burst out before she could stop herself. And without her conscious permission, those shaky walls that guarded her heart crumbled into dust.

"I CAN'T DO THIS."

Julia pulled off the earphones that were meant to block the sound, and let them hang around her neck. She turned the pistol over in her hand and hefted its weight. It seemed so big, so heavy. So deadly.

"I keep thinking about Wade and Merle Banning."

Mac closed in behind her, and placed his hands on her shoulders, kneading the tension that had settled there. "You want me to do it?"

"You can't."

They had a twenty-minute window of opportunity to retrieve a spent bullet, compare its markings under a microscope to the one from Merle's wound, and then run a check through the computer to find any unsolved crime-scene matches.

Mac bent his head close to her ear, keeping his voice low. "All the technicians are working a scene, or attending a seminar until four o'clock. Nobody's getting past Josh on the other side of that door until then. Take all the time you need. But take it quickly."

Julia nodded. She worked her lower lip between her teeth. This part should be a piece of cake compared to getting into the Thirteenth Precinct building. Newer and bigger than the facility in her old neighborhood, the Thirteenth had a state-of-the-art entry system. But their fake ID's had passed inspection and they'd been issued visitors passes. Josh's sweet talk and a back stairwell had gotten them past a receptionist and taken them down to the lab in the basement.

"C'mon, Jules." Mac's lips brushed against her neck, sending a tickle of sensation all the way down her spine and disrupting her thoughts. "I know you can do it."

With his hands still resting on her shoulders, Julia put the earphones back on, took aim through the hole in the Plexiglas shield, squinted her eyes and pulled the trigger.

The recoil from the explosion in her hands pushed her back into Mac. For less than a heartbeat she sagged against him and savored his strength. But he pressed a kiss to that sensitive spot behind her ear and thanked her. A dozen nerve endings that had been paralyzed with fear tingled to life and boosted her into action. "Good girl. Now let's get to work."

She stepped away from that wicked mouth and those tempting hands and did as he asked.

Mac talked her through the process of comparing the bullets beneath the microscope. A set of markings unique to each gun were carved into the bullets as they spun through the firing chamber. If the carvings matched, it proved they came from the same weapon.

The carvings matched.

Forensics confirmed what Merle had reported. Wade had driven by the house and shot at them. Merle had gotten off a few shots himself, wounding Wade in the arm. After losing control of his cruiser, he'd come back to finish the job.

Unfortunately, the markings didn't tell them anything about his motive.

"Over here." Mac tapped on the computer monitor across the room and pulled out the chair in front of it. "This is the real test." After she sat down, he knelt behind the chair and talked her through the access codes that got her into the necessary program. "How much time do we have?"

Julia checked her watch. "Just under ten minutes."

"Feed the picture into the scanner."

When his hand reached around her and hovered over the keyboard, she understood his impatience. The old Mac could have gotten this job done in twenty minutes. He snatched his fingers back into an anxious fist. She was slowing him down.

"Now tell it to run the check for any matches."

She read the message on the screen. "It's searching. But you know what you're going to find, don't you?" she asked.

"Maybe." He brushed his fingers through her hair as he pulled them back. The energy in the room suddenly tightened like the twisting strand of a web. "This is the part I always hated."

"What's that?"

"Waiting."

Julia rocked back and forth in the chair and checked her watch again. "Will it be done in time?"

Mac pushed to his feet. "It has to be."

She spun in her chair and watched him trail his hand along one of the stainless steel counters, stroking it like a favored pet. "You really miss your work, don't you?"

He picked up an empty specimen tray and studied its contours with his fingertips. "It's all I ever wanted to do."

"If the transplant operation doesn't restore your sight, what will you do then?"

"I don't know."

The wistful sadness in his raspy voice tugged at her heartstrings. She heard a tinge of anger there, too. She was angry for him. A senseless accident had robbed him not only of his sight, but of his life's work, and maybe even that driving sense of confidence and satisfaction so many men took from their jobs.

It wasn't fair. Mac shouldn't have to hurt like this. He shouldn't have to suffer.

But instead of pounding her fist against the chair, she got up and put the gun away in her bag. And then she began cleaning. Though they wore plastic gloves to keep from leaving any fingerprints, she found a rag and wiped down the counters and equipment they'd used, anyway.

"Busy again?"

Julia stopped with her hand on the open cabinet door and the microscope in her hand. "Excuse me?"

Mac leaned his hip against the counter where he stood and smiled. "Whenever you're nervous or afraid, you get busy. The world's a cleaner place when you're upset."

She overlooked the obvious teasing and went straight to defending herself. "Our time's limited, right? I want to have this place straightened up as soon as that printer spits out the information we want."

She set one microscope on the shelf and reached for the second one.

"Do I make you nervous?"

Chapter Ten

Through a feat of gymnastic contortion, Julia saved the microscope from crashing to the floor. Mac was behind her in a second, giving her no time to recover from her startled reaction.

"Easy there." Somehow, he had his hand over hers on the microscope and he lifted it, stretching his body along the length of her back and hips, pinning her to the counter. "Where am I going with this?"

Through the stuttered gasps of her breathing, she stretched along with him. "A little higher," she directed. She guided him to the top shelf where he deposited the microscope and closed the cabinet door.

But he didn't move away.

She tried to focus on the hard surfaces of steel and wood in front of her, but all she really noticed was the steely warmth of Mac's chest pressed into her back, and how her bottom nestled against the hard trunks of his thighs.

When the long arm that had stretched above her came down and wrapped around her waist, she knew she was lost.

She tried to push away the thumb that had settled beneath her left breast, but his hand refused to budge. The web of tension in the room twisted in a new dimension, and she ended up clasping her hands together over his forearm and surrendering to the pools of frustrated heat gathering at the tips of her breasts and deep inside at her most feminine core.

With the threat of discovery making every charged moment alone a precious gift, Julia decided not to waste her time denying this contact. She didn't understand what the rush of images, past and future, playing through her mind meant.

Mac, tall and dangerous, coming up behind Ray Wozniak's shoulder and asking if she wanted to be there. Mac, scarred and bruised, throwing her to the ground and demanding she stay safe. Mac, bronzed and naked, rising above her and claiming her body as well as her heart.

Mac, calm and rational, telling her how grateful he was for her help, then telling her goodbye.

She must have shivered as she fought off that last inevitable image, because Mac's hold on her tightened imperceptibly and his lips whispered against the nape of her neck. "Shh. Don't be afraid of me. It's all right."

"You don't know what I'm like, Mac." The confession came out on an anguished sob. He should know about her shortcomings. Even if he couldn't see them, he had the right to know. Her hands clutched tighter, willing him to free her, begging him not to let her go.

"I'm not pretty like you said. I've never dated very much. I've only had sex once, and he said..." Her hands flew to her mouth when she realized what she had just admitted out loud.

Julia curled into herself, self-consciously trying to hide from her mistake. But Mac's shoulders seemed to fold around hers in a protective embrace. He brought his left arm up across her chest and cradled her cheek and jaw in his broad, sheltering hand.

"I can't speak for the other men in the world who are too *blind* to see your beauty. But let me tell you what I know.'' His lips created a moist, seductive ripple along the bundle of nerves beneath her ear. ''I love your hair short like this.''

''Are you kidding? It's practical for the hours I used to work. But it looks mannish, I think.''

His lips grazed a path along her nape and lingered on that particular spot that sent tremors along the surface of her skin. ''It gives me access to your long, beautiful neck.''

Julia's shaky voice made a mockery of her protest. ''It's not that long.''

His frustrated sigh was like a hot wind across her ear. He spread his arms out wide and stepped back, leaving her cold, bereft. Unprotected. Her knees threatened to buckle as the chilly air from the lab swept over her feverish skin. She grabbed on to the counter to hold herself upright.

''I don't know all the pretty words, Jules, to make you believe me.''

His hoarse whisper held no trace of anger. And it wasn't a plea. It was more—a statement of fact. She attuned her ears to that ruined voice, willing to hear more, wanting to believe.

''When a man gives you a compliment—when *I* give you a compliment, just say thank you. I haven't lied to you yet, have I? Why would I lie about the wonderful things I'm discovering about you after all these years?''

She tried to come up with an argument. It wasn't like he'd compared her to a summer's day, or mentioned how she reminded him of a popular cover model. He hadn't praised her charms or exalted her virtues. Her breathing slowed to a normal rate and rational thought found its way past the irrational emotions protecting that Pandora's box inside her.

"So I have a practical haircut that allows you access to my neck."

"Not exactly." His fingers touched the back of her head. "You have beautiful hair." He tunnelled his fingers down to her scalp and branded her with their heat. Then he fanned them out and sifted them through her curls, playing with them, mussing them. "It's soft to the touch. Springy. It catches in my fingers and teases my skin." The temperature rose as he leaned in behind her and buried his nose in a handful of hair. "And it's the cleanest, sweetest thing I've ever smelled in my entire life. Believe me, this nose knows."

She couldn't help giggling at his age-old pun. He truly didn't know about those pretty words that men like Anthony Cardello used like loaded weapons. She was glad. And whether she knew it or not, she believed him.

Needing one more step to complete the lesson, he pulled away. "Now, what do you say?"

She slowly turned, bracing her hands on the counter behind her, taking the risk—for Mac. "Thank you."

The lazy grin that softened his expression was worth the risk. He reached out to her, with fingertips only, and found her chin. She held her breath as he tilted her face up to his. "You're welcome."

With his thumbs he traced the width of her mouth, finding her, holding her. She watched with awe as her hero's mouth descended toward hers. He kissed her once, just a light bit of pressure to test her response. He kissed her again, sealing her thanks beneath his lips.

And then, because logic said she must, and because a tiny part of her really believed Mac's words, she made herself an equal partner in this embrace. She wound her fingers into the front of Mac's shirt and pulled herself up on tiptoe. Pulled herself closer to Mac. Pulled herself into his kiss.

With her permission granted, her invitation issued, his mouth opened over hers and her tender hero became a passionate man, claiming what had always been his. His hands swept into her hair, skimmed along her back, squeezed her bottom and lifted. She was floating on air, pinned between the counter and Mac's strength, bound together by their hands and mouths, and a liquid electricity that flowed between them.

The Pandora's box around her heart sprung open, and passion, need—love—flowed through her. Uncensored. Unjudged. Unencumbered by second-guessing or self-doubts.

She looped her arms around his neck and held on as her body exploded with the glorious friction of man against woman. Hard angles and softer curves. Needy hands and needier mouths. Tender strength and gentle demands.

''Jules—'' She granted his unspoken request with a breathy moan and he slipped his hands beneath her shirt, searing her skin with his possessive touch. Like the delicate sandpapery rasp of his voice teased her ear, his eloquent fingers skimmed across her skin, tracing her spine, stroking her flanks, cradling her breasts. She cried out his name when they slipped beneath the strap of her bra and sizzled against the delicate skin there.

A storm was building inside her. Jolt after jolt of sensation turned her liquid. Turned her hot.

She drank the salty sheen of perspiration at his throat. Rubbed her lips against the sexy stubble of his beard. Clung to his shoulders and waited for the storm to overtake her. ''Mac?'' she called to him. ''Mac?'' she begged.

Beeeeep.

A breaker switch stopped her cold.

Mac's hands stilled. His wet, wonderful mouth blew hot, steadying breaths against her ear.

Beeeeep.

Julia buried her face in the juncture between his neck and shoulder and fought her way back to the real world. "What's that?"

Mac straightened her bra strap and pulled down her shirt. "It's the printer. The computer's finished its search."

"Oh." She fell a million miles as he set her back on the floor.

A sharp rap at the door jerked her firmly back to the Thirteenth Precinct Crime Lab and the danger at hand.

"Your twenty minutes are up, boys and girls." Josh opened the door, ran his gaze from the top of Mac's ruffled hair to his brother's hands still resting at the sides of her waist. And then the son of a gun smiled and winked. "You can do that on your own time."

Mac turned his head toward the door and frowned. "Remind me to put you in your place sometime." When Julia would have scooted away, Mac ran his hands up her sides until he found her jaw. He pinpointed her mouth with the tips of his thumbs and dropped a hard, quick kiss on her lips. "We're not finished with this conversation."

"Today, folks." Josh's warning spurred them apart.

Mac picked up their jackets from a nearby stool while Julia tore off the printout from the computer, stuffed it into her bag and turned off the equipment.

"Hurry." Mac had his hand on her hip, steering her toward the door while she shrugged into her jacket.

He moved his hand to her shoulder and they hugged the wall as they followed behind Josh down the hallway toward the service stairs.

As they rounded the corner, she smacked into Josh's broad back. Mac plowed into her before she realized that Josh had stopped to listen to something.

But Mac heard it, too. "Someone's coming."

Like dominoes in reverse, Josh pushed them back

around the corner they way they'd come. "Coming down the stairs. We can't wait for the elevator." He skirted around them both and shoved open the door to the men's room. "In here."

They scuttled back toward the empty stalls, her body still pulsing from Mac's powerful kiss, her nerve endings shooting wild sparks like broken electrical relays.

But in a stunning moment of clarity, Julia halted in her tracks and changed course. "I left the picture in the scanner."

She dropped her bag and rushed out the door.

"Jules!" But Mac's hoarse warning and outstretched hands couldn't stop her.

She glanced over her shoulder and dashed down the hall, mentally trying to calculate the distance of the footsteps on the stairs behind her and the amount of time she had to retrieve the picture and hide herself.

Her calculations got lost in the instinctive need to move as quickly as humanly possible, to simply survive without getting caught.

She grabbed the picture and started to bolt. But a light in the hallway flipped on, and the image of her unknown pursuer silhouetted itself in the smoked glass of the door.

Too late to run.

She spun around but saw nothing bigger than a cabinet, nothing more closed in than a cart.

No place to hide.

This was an emergency.

Julia knew how to think in emergencies.

After a two-second search, she found what she wanted. She pulled a manila envelope out of the trash just as the door opened, and stuffed the picture inside.

"Who are you?"

This short, unassuming, middle-aged man in a plain brown suit could be her worst enemy if she wasn't careful.

"Courier."

When he adjusted his black-framed glasses to get a better look, Julia flipped up the collar of her jacket and looked down at his shoes. "We send our packets to the front office to be delivered."

She started chomping on an imaginary piece of gum and shrugged her shoulders. "I know. But it wasn't there. They said to check back here. But nobody's here to help me. So—hey, you don't know anything about some printouts headed for the D.A.'s office, do you? No? Well, thanks, anyway. I'll just go back to the office and call in. Thanks."

Without giving the man a chance to speak, she scooted past him and out the door. She resisted the urge to stop and catch her breath and made herself walk—not run— down the hallway. The door never opened and she never looked back.

When she turned the corner, a pair of hands grabbed her and shoved her into the wall. "Don't you ever do that again."

She stifled a yelp and glared up at Mac's harsh growl. The glasses might mask his eyes, but they didn't hide the grim set of his mouth.

And they could never see the fear quaking through every cell of her body.

"Here's your stupid picture." She shoved the envelope at his chest, shoved him away, and stalked on past. She took the stairs two at a time, letting Josh and Mac follow more slowly behind.

By the time Mac climbed into the green truck beside her, she could almost listen to reason again.

"I'm sorry." His quiet rasp was a far cry from the aching fury he'd used a moment ago.

Her only answer was her measured breathing as she consciously tried to take charge of her fears.

And then he reached out, with an open hand across the

seat. Palm up. A gentle beseechment for her to either accept or ignore.

She stared down at his hand. Noted the elegant length of fingers and thumb. The sinewed strength. The calloused tips.

The fine little tremors that echoed her own.

Unable to resist his silent request, she reached across the seat and laid her palm over his.

He folded his hand around hers, squeezed it tight, and repeated, "I'm sorry."

"READ THAT AGAIN."

Mac paced the length of the room and paused at the foot of the bed. He knew exactly where he was. He'd memorized the number of steps an hour ago.

Plus, he had Julia's presence to steer by. Her sunny scent had imprinted itself on his brain the first day she walked into his house. She was sitting in the middle of the bed right now, surrounded by the papers they'd confiscated from the crime lab.

"Lawrence Munoz. Forty-two-year-old Hispanic male. Dead on scene. 42100 North Walnut. Up All Night Liquor Store holdup. Cause of death—"

"Skip that part." Mac stuck his thumb and index finger up beneath his glasses and rubbed at his eyes. "I know that name." He scanned his memory like a computer database, cross-checking and backtracking until...

He snapped his fingers and pointed toward Julia. "Sanchez's chauffeur."

"Arnie Sanchez?"

"He was supposed to be a prosecutorial witness in the trial. Sanchez used him as an alibi for the night his son was kidnapped."

"I was in Chicago during the kidnapping. Don't you mean a defense witness?"

Mac shook his head, seeing the story in his mind as if he was reading it straight from the headlines. "Arnie Sanchez said he went for a drive in the country to 'think' after his import deal with Caracas Industries fell through. But his chauffeur said he was changing the oil in the limo that night."

The mattress shifted and papers crunched atop the bedspread as Julia moved. Sitting up higher on the bed, on her knees, perhaps, according to the change in her vocal position. "But then Munoz was killed in the crossfire at that holdup."

"Lucky for Sanchez, his man was in the wrong place at the wrong time."

"Before the D.A. could subpoena him to testify against his boss."

"And the officer who owned the gun that shot him was...?"

"Wade Osterman."

Man, he loved it when answers clicked together.

Mac sat on the edge of the bed. Bouncing ideas off Julia was almost as efficient as cataloguing and analyzing them on his own. And it was a hell of a lot more interesting. Doing anything with Julia made his life more interesting.

With her, his world was less about cold, hard facts, and more about warm, soft laughter. Though finding the link between the missing evidence and Jeff Ringlein's death was imperative to his freedom, he was equally, if not more, interested in solving the mystery surrounding Julia.

How could she kiss him like that in the lab, let him kiss her like that, and not think she was pretty? Gorgeous? Dynamite?

She was a catalyst to his dormant male sex drive. No woman had ever excited him the way his science did. Until now. Until Julia Dalton walked through his door with her ample curves and velvet skin and state-of-the-art hands and refused to let him sulk in his room and wallow in his guilt.

But something had happened to her in Chicago. Something that put her back in that alley with Ray Wozniak. Something that kept her from believing in him. Something that kept her from believing in herself.

Mac pushed himself back onto his feet. He didn't belong in the same bed with Julia. Not yet. Maybe not ever. Even if he could break through her self-doubts, even if she was willing to explore their feelings for each other, he had no business being there.

He had to prove his innocence and regain his sight before he dared to pursue any kind of permanent relationship with Julia.

And she was too special, too fragile to settle for anything less.

His wandering thoughts must have registered with Julia. ''You're not still apologizing for what happened at the lab, are you?''

It took a second for his thoughts to move beyond that explosive kiss. ''The only thing I'm apologizing for is scaring you to death, and that was only because you scared me.''

''I didn't want to leave any trail. We don't want anyone to find us until you're ready to present your case.''

''You're right.'' He resumed his pacing, needing an outlet for his restless energy. ''We'll have to figure out something so that doesn't happen again. Since I can't keep an eye on you, though, I—''

''What if we were connected by sound?''

Mac stopped. His other senses had sharpened since losing his vision, but, ''My hearing's not *that* good.''

''No.'' He *could* hear her rearrange papers and slide off the edge of the bed. ''I mean electronically. Don't the police have listening devices? Little transmitters we could wear in our ears and microphones you clip on your collar or stick in your pocket?''

"Yeah." He wondered if she wore the same expectant look on her face that she conveyed in her voice. "Good idea. I'll call Josh."

He turned toward the curtained windows and headed for Julia's bag and the phone inside. Since they couldn't tell who might be watching or reporting, he didn't want to use the motel's line.

"I want to call him anyway and tell him about the two unsolved shootings that match the ballistics from Osterman's gun."

"And Lawrence Munoz," she reminded him.

"Right."

At first, Mac ignored the soft tapping sound, thinking Julia had gone into the rest-room area for something.

But he stopped when he heard it a second time. Julia was behind him. The tapping was straight ahead.

A bolt of panic swept through him, energized him, put him on guard. "Someone's at the door."

Julia was at his elbow in a heartbeat. "Do we answer it?"

He answered her in the same low-pitched whisper. "The motel staff would have announced themselves."

"Maybe it's Josh."

"He said he'd show up in person only if there was an emergency."

Her fingers curled slowly around his bicep. "Do you think…?"

He covered her hand with his, reassuring her, trying to reassure himself. Another five taps.

"I'll go look." She slipped away, and he knew he couldn't stop her. Shouldn't stop her.

Damn. *He* should be the one on the front line. The one protecting *her* from potential danger.

"Oh my God."

"The police?" He knew better. They would have announced themselves as well. "Have Niederhaus and Masterson tracked us down?"

"It's our mothers."

"What?" Absolute surprise quickly gave way to a sense of relief. But he had moved on to anger by the time he opened the door and dragged in Martha Taylor and Barbara Dalton from the balcony sidewalk.

He hoped Julia took long enough to check behind them before closing and locking the door.

With his hands gripping her shoulders, he glared down toward the Taylor matriarch. "Ma. What the hell are you doing here? You could have been followed."

"But we weren't. Barbara kept a lookout. And this is the third motel we stopped at, just in case we needed to throw anyone off our trail."

"We certainly surprised that gentleman when we knocked on his door at the Holiday Inn," Barbara added.

It was Julia's turn to be surprised. "Mom. You didn't."

"We did." A thunk on the table and the slide of a zipper made Mac wonder what kind of container she was opening. But the mouth-watering scents of fresh-baked bread, ham and some kind of vegetable told him it was a cooler filled with homemade food. "We gave him a package of the same cookies we brought you. They should still be warm."

"Josh said we couldn't come straight here," answered Martha. "He said Internal Affairs could put a tail on any one of us in the family."

"Exactly." When he bent to hug her, he realized she carried something heavy with her. He slipped his hand down her arm, found an overnight bag and took it from her. He set it on the bed before turning back to her. "I don't want you to be pestered or hurt on my account."

"MacKinley." He stood up straighter at that stern maternal voice. "You are my son. If there's anything I can do to help you when you're in trouble like this, I will. A little pestering from that rude Joe Niederhaus isn't going to stop me. I've met men like him before. He just wants to tie up all his loose ends before he retires. If the man took the time to do his job right, you wouldn't be in this mess."

Like the front line of invading troops, the two mothers were a determined force to be reckoned with. They set the table, served food, rearranged the furniture, and had Mac and Julia sitting down together over a delicious, filling meal before they explained the real purpose of their surprise visit.

"Obviously, we don't want to stay too long." Martha went to the bed and opened the tiny suitcase she'd brought with her. "We know you have work to do."

Mac stuffed the last bite of biscuit into his mouth and joined his mother. He heard something suspicious in her voice. The same kind of irresistible baiting she had used when he was a child and she'd make him deduce through easy clues what kind of birthday present she'd made for him before he opened the package.

"What else did you bring?" he asked, already curious.

"It's something from your house."

"I thought my house had been sealed off by the police."

"I was in there for a few minutes before they asked me to leave."

Julia interrupted to ask her mother a question. "Were you there, too, Mom?"

"Yes. We probably did something we shouldn't."

"What?"

He heard Barbara moving closer to Julia. "We visited Detective Banning in the hospital. He's a very nice young man. I think I've met his mother before, as a substitute in one of my bridge groups."

Mac schooled his patience. This was his mother and her dearest cohort in crime he was talking to, after all. "Why did you talk to Merle Banning?"

"So we would know what we needed to do with this." She took his hand and placed a flat, square piece of plastic in it. A computer disk. "I borrowed a laptop computer from Mitch. I have no idea how it works, but he said it would run the files on that disk."

"What files?"

"Something about background checks?"

"Ma!"

Score one for the meddling mothers. Mac grasped Martha by the shoulders and zeroed in on her cheek to give her a kiss.

"You just saved us a ton of time in research."

Martha's skin warmed with a blend of pride and embarrassment. "We just wanted to help out."

"Barbara?" Mac turned, found Julia's mother, and kissed her as well. "Thank you."

She patted his shoulder and whispered into his ear. "You just take care of my little girl."

"I will." She didn't have to ask, but it was a promise he intended to keep.

"Well, Barb, we don't want to overstay our welcome." The room surrendered to another attack of mothers, packing everything they needed to take with them, and folding and fluffing almost everything else left behind.

Julia checked the balcony and parking lot before letting them out the door, and after a flurry of hugs, they were on their way.

Mac tripped all three locks that were on the door and smiled as he leaned against the steel partition and listened to them heading down the stairs.

"He's feeling better," Martha insisted.

"He should be," Barbara answered. "Julia's here."

He *did* feel better with Julia around. Healthier. More alive. More interested in being alive.

Barbara continued. "You know, I should be concerned that your son has my daughter locked away in a motel room. But I'm not. You know why?"

"Why?"

"Because I've always thought that your son and my daughter would make a wonderful couple. Of course, I didn't know which of your sons it would be."

As their voices faded into the distance, Mac realized Julia was standing beside him, listening to the same conversation.

"How'd we end up with two mothers like that?" she asked.

"Just lucky, I guess."

"Do you want to finish eating, or turn on the computer first?"

Julia's eagerness fed into his own. This was better than his birthday.

"Both."

ACCORDING TO Merle Banning's research, Melanie and Jeff Ringlein were living way beyond a police chemist's means. Melanie had expensive tastes, developed in her pampered childhood as the daughter of a wealthy, third-generation banker. Julia's instincts about her had been right. Jeff's widow was used to getting her way, and with Jeff gone, she had turned to Mac for help.

Was Jeff financing Melanie's spending habits by taking bribes to alter or destroy case evidence? Did Melanie know about her husband's illegal activities? Perhaps even encourage them? Was she the one trying to pin the crimes on Mac in order to cover up her own collusion?

Julia shifted in her chair again. It was the third or fourth time in as many minutes. A sign that she was growing fatigued. How long had they been at this? Mac wondered. With his own internal clock gone haywire, they could have worked straight through the night and he wouldn't know it.

"Tired?" he asked.

"A little."

He suspected her answer was a concession to her innate honesty, despite her refusal to complain about the less than ideal hours she'd been forced to work as his nurse.

"Maybe we should call it a night," he suggested.

That king-size bed sat there in the middle of the room, beckoning them to sleep. But Mac doubted there'd be much rest involved if he crawled onto that mattress with Julia.

He would have made love to her on the counter of the lab this afternoon, if Josh hadn't knocked on the door. He had a sense of incompletion, a memory of almost-heaven imprinted onto four of his senses. It would only take a spark—a touch, a smell, a taste, and he'd want her like that all over again.

But, fortunately, Julia could be sensible.

"I'm stiff, more than anything." When her chair creaked again, he knew that she'd gotten up. "Do you really think Wade was a hit man? I know Merle's records show he had problems with his gambling—but to kill someone in exchange for paying off his debt? He seemed like a nice guy. I kind of felt sorry for him. I mean, the man broke into your house to steal food."

"Maybe he broke in to plant that evidence from the Sanchez case."

Her heavy sigh filled the room with a frustration that matched his own.

"So is Sanchez paying off everybody?"

Mac shook his head. "Then why try to kill me? If I'm alive, he has a fall guy so his case will be dismissed. There has to be something else that ties this all together."

"This is making my head hurt. If it's okay to take a break for a few minutes, I think I will jump into the shower and run some hot water over my achy muscles."

"You go ahead."

Mac leaned back in his chair and closed his eyes to listen to the concise sounds of Julia sorting through her toiletries and preparing for her shower.

The instant the sounds stopped, he turned his head, waiting for the spray of running water and all the fantasies that could create. He heard Julia's voice instead.

"For what it's worth, I'm glad you're still alive."

Mac tipped his head and wondered if the longing note he heard in her voice was an accurate observation, or part of his suddenly wishful imagination.

A timeless moment later, he heard the sound of her footsteps in the tub, and the sudden gush of water as it worked its way through the pipes before settling into a rhythmic, pulsating spray.

His body pulsed with a matching rhythm, and a groan of desire rasped inside his throat.

There must be some logical way to fight this. Some way to put his physical needs on hold until he could prove his innocence. Until he could prove to Julia that her perception of herself held many intrinsic fallacies.

He rubbed the skin at his temples and dragged his hand down his weary face. The scratch of a two-day stubble on his jaw and neck gave him an idea.

He couldn't clear his name tonight. In the morning, they'd pay a visit to the district attorney's office and take a look at the D.A.'s dismissed cases. He had a theory he hadn't yet shared with anyone else. A theory he hoped he couldn't prove true.

But there was one thing he could do. He might not be the best man for the job, but he'd be damned if he'd let anyone else do it.

Mac stood and pulled his shirt off over his head. He'd kicked off his shoes and socks when they first sat down at the computer. He unsnapped the top button of his jeans as he crossed the room on the now-familiar path. He didn't need any lights to find a towel or the disposable plastic razor that Josh had bought him.

With his hand on the doorknob to the shower room, Mac hesitated.

I've only had sex once, and he said... If the bastard hadn't told Julia she was the most caring, giving, innocently sensuous creature that God ever put on the face of the earth, then the man should be lined up in front of Wade Osterman's hired gun.

But Mac had a sick feeling the man's words had been less than flattering, that the man hadn't taken into account Julia's past and the misconceptions about herself she carried with her as a result.

She needed to understand that she was more than a resourceful thinker, more than a good friend, more than an excellent nurse.

She was a desirable woman.

He could do that for her. If she'd let him.

He needed to do it for himself.

Mac pushed open the bathroom door. "Jules?"

"What?" He'd startled her. Good. He had a better chance of proving his point if she didn't have those defensive walls locked into place. He heard the scrape of metal and rattle of plastic that indicated she'd turned off the water and stuck her head around the edge of the shower curtain. "Did you need something?"

He held the towel open between his outstretched arms. "For what it's worth, I'm glad you're alive, too."

Chapter Eleven

"Can you see me?"

"Jules." And then he realized she was serious. Mac closed his eyes and gave her a serious answer. "In my mind's eye, yes. And I like what I see."

"How?"

"Touch. Sound. Scent. Taste." He could hear the plastic curtain rattle as she shivered, and he reminded himself to go slowly. And explain everything thoroughly so she had no reason to second-guess anything. "I could tell you that I extrapolate the data I gather through those four senses and create a theory about what you look like, but mostly I just enjoy the discovery process."

"Oh."

"Come here." He gave the towel a tiny *el toro* shake. "Before you catch a cold and I have to tell your mother how it happened."

She laughed at that one. Good. Laughter was good.

"Okay."

As she stepped out, he swore he could hear the sound of water running off her body. Streaming down her legs. Catching in that dimple beside her mouth. Dripping off the tips of her breasts.

A switch turned on in his body, sending a rush of flaming heat straight to his groin and to the itchy tips of his fingers and toes.

Too fast, too fast, he warned himself. This was all about Julia, remember?

She turned her back to him and reached for the ends of the towel, but he took the opportunity to wrap her up in it himself, tucking the ends beneath her arms and folding his arms beneath her breasts. He lifted her a fraction, catching her up close to his chest. He buried his nose in the wet curls behind her ear and drank in her raw scent. He hugged his body around her, letting her warmth, her smell, her softness ease the frantic charges stabbing his body with instant desire.

He held her close, with her arms clutched over his, her temple turned in to the rasping caress of his cheek, until the electrons in his body hummed at a rapid, but even and controllable rate.

Only then did he let her heels hit the floor. Only then did he allow her to tuck the ends of the towel more securely around her. Only then did he dangle the razor in front of her face.

"Will you do the honors?"

Her nervous laugh was his only answer. But she took the razor from his grasp and pushed at his shoulder. "Sit."

When she got busy sorting through the toiletries for the shaving cream, and running the water until it was hot in the sink, he knew she was nervous. Mac smiled. He hoped he could find another way to channel that nervous energy.

He knew when she returned. Her skin still radiated the heat from her hot shower.

But his instinct to reach out and touch that skin was put on hold when she pressed a hot washcloth to his face and neck. "Ow!"

He leaned back, away from the sudden, overwhelming

heat, but Julia stayed with it, stepping between his legs and holding the washcloth in place.

Gradually, the initial shock wore off and Mac sat up straight. But Julia was right there, and he would have knocked her backward if he hadn't reached out and grabbed her. As his hands settled at her waist, he decided this was nice, after all, and that active brain behind those blind eyes started rebuilding a steaming heat that meandered slowly, but surely, through his veins.

He closed his eyes and let her work. The minty smell of the shaving cream tickled his nose, but it was nothing like the wonder of Julia's hands gliding over his face, sliding down his neck, caressing every pore, and stoking the furnace burning inside him.

She worked quickly, gently, efficiently, until his face was clean. But when she wanted to get a towel to dry him, he stopped her. "Wait."

"But you're dripping." With the flick of a finger, she wiped away a trickle of water from the tip of his pectoral muscle.

Mac's breath hissed through his teeth at the unintended caress.

And then Julia's body went completely still.

He could feel the pull and slack of the towel beneath his hands as she breathed in and out, but nothing more.

And that was when he knew she understood exactly what he wanted.

"Mac—"

He knew a brief moment of doubt himself. Were the scars on his body too much for her to bear? Too numerous for her to touch?

"I don't know what to do." Her hushed admission was the only reassurance he needed.

"Then let me."

He fanned out his fingers and turned his hands so they

could reach down and cup her bottom. Her squeezed her gently, loving her womanly dimensions. She set the razor and washcloth down behind him and braced her hands lightly on his shoulders as he pulled her a step closer. And closer still.

He leaned forward and nuzzled his nose in the towel that carried her scent and held her warmth. But it wasn't enough.

Giving her a moment to rescind her permission, Mac untucked the ends of her towel and let it fall to the floor. He moved his face close, but didn't yet touch. He felt the heat of her on his skin; he let the musky, clean scent of a beautiful woman fill his nose and give new fuel to the growing hum of power inside him.

And then he pressed a kiss to her belly. Her muscles clenched, drawing her away from him. He gave her a chance to breathe, a chance to get used to his touch on her bare skin, and then he kissed her again. And again.

He trailed kisses from the soft curve of her belly to the harder strength of her sternum. And then his nose was nestled between the twin globes that bespoke her femininity so uniquely, that touted her fertility so completely.

Thousands of electrons were zapping each cell of his body every moment that he held her this close, that he touched her this intimately. But still he held back. He wanted Julia to know the beauty of every part of her body the same way he did.

He slipped one hand behind her bottom, so she couldn't bolt. So the same trapped energy building inside of him built inside her, too.

He palmed his right hand over her breast and felt her fingers dig into his shoulders. "You like that?" He squeezed her gently and felt her flinch.

"Yes."

He cradled the generous weight inside his palm. He

stroked the nipple with his thumb, rolled it to a nubby bead between his fingers.

Her buttocks squeezed together beneath his hand. Her breath caught on a ragged gasp and her breast pushed into his hand, seeking more, seeking him.

He pressed his lips the swelling curve, let his tongue moisten a trail toward the straining tip.

"Mac, please."

She skimmed her fingers up his neck, traced around the shell of his ear. And then she clasped his head firmly between her hands and guided his mouth to her engorged nipple.

Her relieved gasp was short-lived. Her shy demands bombarded his will with the need to take her, to claim her, to make her his in every sense of the word.

He stroked her with his tongue, heard her cry out in that soft, husky voice. He shifted his attentions to the other breast, laving its tip with his tongue, suckling the energy from her tinderlike body with his hot, wet mouth.

Her fingers clenched into fists, fanned out, clutched at him. Her breathing quickened, stuttered, matched pace with his own ragged gasps for air. She twisted in his grasp and Mac knew the only thing keeping her standing was the support of his hand.

"Jules."

This time he cried her name on a hoarse whisper, needing her closer, needing her touch, needing her.

He pulled her down into his lap, just as he had wanted to those few nights ago. He spread her legs so that she straddled him. He lifted her by her bottom and pulled her close, so close that his denim brushed against her, so close he could feel her most intense heat next to his.

His body throbbed in response. "Touch me," he begged. "I need to feel you touch me."

And she did.

She hugged her arms around his shoulders as he claimed her mouth. Her breasts branded his chest like tiny electric jolts, feeding the power that coiled ever more tightly inside him. She slid those magic hands down his back. She dipped her fingers in the waistband of his jeans. She smoothed them along his flanks and created sparks when her thumbs found his flat male nipples and tormented them beneath her touch.

Their tongues linked, parted, tasted, and reconnected to create a heady circuit of sensation that shot with painful precision down to that most male part of him.

"Jules." He pushed her up, back to her feet, but caught her lips time and again beneath his to reassure her, to tell her this was wisdom, not rejection. He stood in front of her, gripped her shoulders, slid his hands down her back, and rubbed himself against her with almost shameful need. He rested his forehead against hers, breathed in as she breathed out to steady them both. "I can't see to carry you. But I want you in bed. I want you now."

"I know."

Knew what? What did she know? Did she want him, too? That's what she should have said if she really believed in their desire.

But before he could form the rational words to challenge her, she slid her fingers down his arms and took his hands. He followed mindlessly, willingly, as she backed out toward the bedroom.

When she broke the contact between them to pull back the covers, Mac stripped off his jeans and shorts, and stood before her, as potent and vulnerable as a man could make himself.

Those moments apart gave him the time he needed to think. To ask. "It's obvious I want you, isn't it? That it's *you* I want?"

He closed his eyes and breathed deeply. If she thought

this was all about latent hormones, and that he was this aroused, this needy, just because she was available to him, he'd stop. It might kill him to prove his point, but he'd stop.

Julia huddled in the center of the bed, her muscles turned to liquid by the power of Mac's loving hands and mouth. Mac stood beside her, naked and tall and glorious in his aroused state.

"I know."

"Say it." His quiet demand vibrated through the very heart of her.

She knew what he was asking. She knew what he needed to hear. A feeling of unique feminine power settled over her like a calming caress. Maybe she did believe.

"It's me you want."

She rose up on her knees and reached for him then, pulling him down beside her on the bed.

"I do want you, Julia Dalton." He whispered the husky vow as he gathered her in his arms and rekindled the flame inside her with his burning touch.

She rose to the needy stamp of his mouth, tried to touch him in every electric, intimate way he was touching her. She cried out his name and clutched at his shoulders when the palm of his hand found that primed core between her legs. Then his long, wondrous fingers pressed their way inside her swollen feminine heat.

"Mac. Mac—"

When his touch was almost too much, when she could feel herself buckling, squeezing, almost flying apart, Mac rose above her. Just like in her dreams. He entered her in one swift, perfect stroke.

"It's you I want, Jules. Only you."

His crushing mouth swallowed her reply. His hips rocked. A jillion megawatts of voltage tore her apart as he made her his.

She had never belonged to anyone else like this.

She never would.

When the world returned to her and she knew herself again, Julia led Mac into the shower where they washed each other's hair and cleansed their bodies and the scarred scientist made her his all over again.

Afterward, feeling more exhausted, more replete, and more frightened for her future than she had ever been in her entire life, she and Mac fell asleep together.

They cuddled as close in the king-size bed as they had on that short, skinny cot the night before.

"CAN YOU HEAR ME?"

Julia spoke into the tiny microphone that was pinned beneath the collar of her teal-green turtleneck.

Mac answered in that calm, raspy tone that was becoming as much a comfort to her as holding his hand. "Talk in your regular voice. No need to shout." He was somewhere down the hall, hidden safely out of sight in the custodian's closet, while she forged ahead down the deserted marble hallway into the wing of offices that housed the assistant district attorneys.

She heard a moment of static, then Mac spoke again. "How about you, Josh?"

Josh sat in his truck, somewhere outside, keeping an eye out for anyone entering or leaving the county court building. Mac's sister-in-law, Ginny Taylor, was out there, too, along with his cousin Mitch, captain of the Fourth Precinct.

Located in the heart of downtown Kansas City, the historic limestone structure might have a small-town-sized replica of a domed and columned courthouse built atop a thirty-story tower, but the building and its annexes still took up most of a city block. Two intrepid detectives scouting out the D.A.'s case files on the eighth floor had a lot of ground to cover if they wanted to watch their backs.

"Loud and clear. Sunday afternoon's pretty quiet down here. You shouldn't have any trouble."

"Be sure to watch out for the cleaning crew." Mitch's clipped voice came across the transmitter in her ear. She jumped at the gruff sound of authority. "Are you sure you don't want us in there with you?"

Mac laughed, reminding Julia that Mitch's bark was a lot worse than his bite. "You're not running the show today. This way, if something happens, you guys can drive away."

If something happens.

Julia leaned her back against the solid walnut door bearing the name Dwight Powers, and shuddered.

Josh had given her a crash course in how to use the lock-picking tools that she gripped tightly in her fist. Her job was simple. Break into Dwight Powers's office, access his computer, and print out any data relating to cases that had been dismissed due to tainted or missing evidence from the Fourth Precinct CSI unit. Mac's unit.

She exhaled a deep breath that echoed and turned into steam in the cold, cavernous hallway. The ongoing conversation in her ear provided a small, but distant, realm of normalcy for her to cling to. She knelt in front of the door, wiped her sweaty palm on her pantleg and set about picking her first lock.

"May I remind you," Mitch went on, "that I'm responsible for my precinct. If I've got a cover-up in my department, I want to know about it. I will not drive away."

"But if there is a cover-up," Mac argued in his coolly unemotional way, "then you could be implicated in it if Internal Affairs finds out you're helping us. That goes for you and Ginny, too, Josh."

"I know the risks." Ginny's voice was rich and commanding for a woman, a unique contrast to her small stature and delicate Nordic looks. She herself was a surprising contrast to her husband, Brett. Mac's older brother was as dark as Ginny was fair, as big and brawny as she was petite. Yet when she'd met her in person that morning, Julia had been impressed by how well she held her own with the other Taylors. And how much she loved her husband. "You went out of your way to help me find my sister's killer last spring. Don't think I'm not going to pay you back."

"Focus, people," Mac reminded everyone.

Something clicked in the lock and the door sprang open in front of Julia. "I'm in."

"Good girl."

That small bit of success was enough to refuel her energy and put her fears aside. The buzz of communication in her ear fell silent, and she knew everyone was listening to her now.

"How do I know which desk is his?" she asked, looking at the double row of cubicles through the dusky light of tall, narrow windows.

Mac answered. "Those are *his* assistants in the front room. His office is in the back."

She put the stainless-steel tools she'd used inside the pocket of her denim jacket and crept through the office. The place was eerie in its silence. Each desk she passed looked as if its owner had been whisked away in the midst of some project. A cold, half-drunk mug of coffee sat on the blotter of one desk; a stack of letters with a pen to sign them lay on another. She tiptoed on past as if the place was inhabited by ghosts who would wake at any minute if she made the slightest of sounds.

Another walnut door loomed ahead of her. "I see it," she whispered.

"Everything all right?"

"It's just creepy." She knew if he got worried about her, he'd leave his hiding place and come after her. "I'm fine."

She could envision Mac hurrying down the hallway, trailing his fingers along the cold, unforgiving marble. He might take a wrong turn and get lost before she could find him. Or worse, he might run into someone who recognized him. Someone who'd call the police. Someone who could take him away from her.

The old bronze knob rotated a quarter turn, then stopped. "This is locked, too."

"Easy, Jules," Mac coaxed her. "You can do it."

Breaking through the second door proved easier than the first. "What other bad habits can I learn from you, Josh?"

But, surprisingly, Mac's affable little brother didn't laugh. "You just be careful."

"Now you tell me."

Julia closed and locked the door behind her. She debated whether or not to turn on the overhead light, since the morning sun barely penetrated the row of high windows running along the west wall of the assistant D.A.'s office. Instead, she opted to turn on the green-shaded desk lamp.

Unlike the desks in the first room, Dwight Powers's things were arranged in meticulous order. No doubt the attorney knew exactly where each pencil and paper clip sat, and if she moved anything even a millimeter out of place, he'd know an intruder had broken into his office.

Keeping that in mind, she noted the angle and distance of his black leather chair from his desk before pulling it out and sitting in front of his computer. She turned it on and jumped as the loud tone clanged in her ears and bounced off the cold walls.

"Jules?" Mac again.

"I just got startled."

Her heart might be racing in her chest, but knowing Mac was there for her allowed her to think clearly. He'd been there for her last night, too. Not just physically—Anthony Cardello's version of making love seemed a pale comparison to the raw, overwhelming need Mac had revealed in her—but emotionally, as well. He'd given her a precious gift.

A different perception of herself.

She'd seen herself through his eyes.

And she wasn't half bad.

Mild praise, she knew. But she had fifteen years of a negative self-image to overcome. She needed time.

"Jules? Is the computer up and running yet?"

But time seemed to be in short supply.

"Yes. It's asking for his password."

"Vendetta."

"How do you know that?"

"Trust me. It fits him."

She should never have doubted Mac's intellectual capabilities. She typed in the word, and moments later the screen gave her access to Dwight Powers's files.

She had fallen into the habit of explaining her actions out loud over the past few days, so that Mac could follow her and navigate his own way around the world. So it was easy enough to chat out loud as she searched through the files. Mac's sure, steady voice guided her through glitches, narrowed her search, and finally took her to the screen she wanted.

Josh's voice intruded over the line. "You're at fifteen minutes, Jules. You'd better wrap it up."

"I'm...just now there." Her rapid pulse gave her voice a stutter.

"Calm down." That was Mac. She breathed in deeply

through her nose and tried to picture his hand reaching out to hers, sharing his calm, resolute strength.

Julia scrolled through the document before her, looking for the key words Mac had suggested.

Ginny reported in. "I've got three members of the cleaning crew out the back door. They're lighting up cigarettes. It looks like break time."

"According to the manifest, there's a crew of thirty," Mitch reminded them.

Julia gave a shaky laugh. "Thirty seemed kind of intimidating. But I can handle twenty-seven."

"The file?" Once again, Mac brought her back to the task at hand.

"Bingo." She read through the list of names a second time, wondering if her eyes had deceived her. They hadn't. "Oh my God. Oh my God, Mac, you're right. Let me check the next file."

She clicked on the print icon and looked at the next case on the screen. "It's on this one, too."

Success gave her a heady rush of adrenaline that propelled her quickly from one command to the next. She printed and searched and printed again. A horrible pattern started to repeat itself. "It's in every file, Mac."

"Twenty minutes, Jules." Josh had appointed himself timekeeper.

"Time to close up shop, sweetheart."

"I've got one more name to run through."

"We've got enough. Let's go."

But she had already typed the name in the next file. She clicked on Search and waited for the computer to scroll through the information.

"Jules." Mac's sharp gasp never registered. She was scanning the names for herself. "There's someone in the hallway."

"Yes." Julia pumped her fists and hit print for the last time. "We have everything we need. We have our proof!"

"It won't stand up in a court of law." Mac's ruined voice was barely audible at that low pitch. "It's just the bait we need. Now get out of there!"

"I'm going, I'm going."

The printer wasn't.

"I think the printer's jammed."

Mac's colorful curse was echoed by Mitch and Josh. "Just turn it off. Get out of there. Go."

Julia punched the power button on the printer and tore the paper from the output tray. She rolled it up and stuffed it inside her jacket, but it unrolled itself and fanned out like an accordion onto the floor.

"Darn it. I need my bag."

"Jules." The impatience in Mac's voice finally hit her, reminding her that success didn't necessarily mean safety.

"I know. I'm going."

She turned her attention to the computer itself, logged out and turned off the machine.

Without the constant hum of the computer's fan to blanket the noise, she finally heard it. The distinctive rasp of metal sliding against metal. The tumble and click of a key in a lock.

Julia froze. Her rush of victory sat like a lump in her throat. She had to force the words past it.

"Someone's in the outer office."

She killed the light and rose to her feet as the outside door opened and closed.

If she used such words, she would have cursed. "Mac?" It was barely more than a breath. Not enough to carry through the walnut door.

She heard footsteps, too muffled on the carpeting to guess their direction, but from the even purpose in every stride, she knew the intruder wasn't there to clean the place.

Her heart rate pounded in her neck, drowning out the sound of rational thought. "What do I do?"

"Try the side door."

Of course. Julia tilted her head back, able to breathe again. She dashed to the second exit and tried the knob. "It's locked."

She reached inside her pocket for Josh's lock pick, but a key rattled in the other door.

"Jules?"

She glanced about the room. Windows on the eighth floor weren't an option. They were too high to reach, anyway. That left hiding.

"Jules?"

Hugging the printout inside her jacket, she dove for the floor and crawled beneath the heavy walnut desk.

As the doorknob turned, she pulled the chair to its original position and held her breath.

The light came on. For one horrible instant, she thought she cast a shadow. But no. Of course not. She was hidden beneath the desk. In her earpiece she heard a different door slam. She pressed her hand over her mouth to stifle the bubble of hysteria that threatened to rise from her throat.

The intruder took two more of those powerful strides and then stopped.

Please be hanging up a coat, she pleaded in her mind. *Hang up your coat and go away.*

Of course, why would someone do that? Why would someone bother to come into a deserted office on a Sunday morning and do nothing more than hang up his coat?

The intruder moved again. Intruder? Ha! She was the one who didn't belong here. She wondered if it was safe to breathe, or if she should just go ahead and pass out.

Unconscious people were pretty quiet. And quiet was good.

Her mind was babbling.

Thirty years old with a college degree in one of the most challenging fields on the planet—and she was babbling.

The intruder moved again. He crossed over to the second door and shook the knob. He knew she'd been there. He knew!

Though he walked more slowly, she could still detect the deliberate placing of each foot. He circled the desk now. He stopped behind the chair, giving her a glimpse of expensive leather loafers and tailored wool slacks.

And while her mind catalogued the idea that this man made good money and had even better taste, the chair moved.

No. It flew.

Almost quicker than the events could register, the man swooped down, snatched Julia by the arms, pulled her up onto her feet and had her slammed against a wall and pinned at the neck by a meaty forearm.

Brooks Brothers suit aside, this man didn't spend all his time behind a desk. He was big. Though not quite as tall as Mac, he was muscular. And angry. Not that out-of-control fury that turned a man's cheeks red. This was cold anger. Heartless anger. The glare in this man's gray-green eyes told her he had no heart.

"Who are you?" The man's voice held the same chill as his eyes.

The pressure on her neck eased only enough for her to answer. "Julia Dalton." She had to think of something to say, some excuse to defend herself. But all she could manage beneath his unforgiving glare was, "I'm a nurse."

The room began to spin and she found she had to make an effort to breathe. If he was aware of her discomfort, he didn't care. He pushed a little harder with his forearm, lifting her onto her toes, though he still wasn't suffocating her. She flattened herself against the wall, avoiding the brush of his hand as he reached inside her jacket and pulled out the paper. "What are you doing with these, Nurse Dalton?"

"I, um—"

"Jules?" Mac's sharp rasp cut through the fog of fear, and she knew he was coming for her.

"No. Stay away."

"I won't hurt you," the man said, misinterpreting her plea. "But breaking and entering is a crime. A serious one in the D.A.'s office. You're not going anywhere. Give me one good reason why I shouldn't call the police right now."

Mac shouted a command into her ear, his voice sounding impossibly close. "Tell him you're with me."

"I—"

"Tell him you're with me!"

"I'm a friend of Mac Taylor's," she stammered, more afraid of what Mac had in mind than what this man could do to her.

All at once he released her. Her feet hit the floor with an embarrassing thud and her knees started to crumple. But he put a hand on her arm and steadied her. "This should be interesting."

"I don't understand." Why the abrupt change in his demeanor?

"I've been waiting for Taylor to show his face. I want to ask him myself why he feels the need to blow the biggest trial of the year for me."

"It's not like that," she pleaded, following him back to his desk when she should be running away. "He's not like that. He's been set up."

That coldhearted beast sat back in his chair as if he

didn't have the power to ruin Mac's life and destroy hers in the process.

"Then let him prove it."

The office door swung open with a wild slam.

There stood Mac, tall and scarred and impossibly brave.

"Let her go, Dwight. And I will."

Chapter Twelve

"Are you sure we can trust Dwight Powers?" Julia asked, pulling Mac's hand through the crook of her elbow as they left the green truck and headed toward the Independence Center Mall complex, a sprawling, bustling, three-story yellow brick testament to shopping and entertainment.

Mac gave her arm a reassuring squeeze. He'd touched her like that a lot today. Putting an arm around her shoulder, squeezing her hand, linking his arm through hers. It was as if he didn't want to let her out of his sight, or, in a blind man's own way, he didn't want to let her out of his touch.

"What Dwight Powers lacks in personality he makes up for in integrity. Believe me, he wants to nail this guy as badly as we do."

After explaining the facts she and Mac had uncovered—the trail of missing evidence and conveniently dead witnesses, the cases that were dismissed as a result, the names that showed up repeatedly in each situation—Dwight Powers was more than willing to place a phone call regarding the Arnie Sanchez trial.

He'd set up a meeting for Mac to supposedly make a deal. Mac would get his name cleared off Internal Affairs's most-wanted list in exchange for testifying that the fibers I.A. had confiscated from his house had been mislabeled, and that they'd come from the Sanchez house, not their murdered son's burial site.

"But why here?" she asked. Independence Center was located in a suburb a good twenty miles east of their home neighborhood near downtown Kansas City. Julia couldn't help but survey the parking lot around them, wondering in which one of the thousands of parked cars sat their blackmailer.

"Chances are, the cops here won't recognize me on sight, so they won't interfere with the sting."

"And Josh and Mitch and Ginny are here, right?"

He leaned over and pressed a kiss to her temple. "A good plan always includes backup. All I have to do is get the offer out of this guy. Mitch will get it on tape, and then one of them can make the arrest."

"You make it sound so simple." Julia opened one of the entrance doors to the mall, and as was his habit, Mac held it for her to proceed first. They linked arms again when they were through the second set of doors. "But none of this has been simple, has it?"

"No. But I promise this will be over soon."

Mac's words were meant to calm her anxious nerves. But instead of allaying her fears for his safety, they set her mind on the unsure course of her future.

Mac cared for her. Of that, she had no doubt. He found her reasonably attractive. Last night had given her proof of that.

But Mac seemed content to live in the moment. He had made no mention of any kind of future together. What if this was all one grand, glorious adventure on his part? An investigation like any other he might obsess over? She was merely his partner for this one particular journey. Would he have any use for her—as his eyes, his nurse, his companion—his lover—when all this was over?

Or would he give her another one of those blood-searing

kisses, tell her again that her debt to him had been repaid, and then send her back to her old lonely life?

She had given up pretending she felt anything less than love for Mac. And she knew in her heart that she would never love another man.

But was she woman enough for a man to commit his whole life to? Or was she, as Dr. Casanova had said, only good for a fling? Anthony hadn't wanted anything more from her once she'd served his purpose. Would Mac cast her aside once her usefulness to him had ended?

"It's been a lot of years since I've been out here." Mac interrupted the depressing self-assassination of her confidence with a grim, all-business expression on his face. "Why don't you walk me around and orient me to the place. We have time, don't we?"

Julia checked her watch. They had a full forty-five minutes before their contact was supposed to show.

She buried her misgivings about a future with Mac and applied herself to the very real threat of simply surviving the present.

She walked him down ramps and across catwalks, all the while identifying stores and the scents or sounds he could associate with them. She walked him through the maze of chairs and tables at the center of the food court, and took him by the children's play area with its snack carts and two-story carousel. She answered every question about this security booth or that power relay grid, about the escalators and stairs and the indoor rock garden.

With the same patience she had always shown, she answered everything he asked. By the time five o'clock rolled around, she had her microphone and transmitter in place, sore feet, and a very real fear that a blind man couldn't find his way around this mall—much less trap the crooked cop who wanted him dead.

MAC GRIPPED THE rail of the catwalk where he stood and waited for the vertigo to pass. When the dizziness faded, he relaxed the clench of his jaw and opened his eyes.

He hadn't had an attack like this since—since before Julia. She'd forced him out into the real world again. Forced him to do something about his guilt instead of wallowing in it. She'd shown him there was a hell of a lot more to life than test tubes and badges and finding the truth.

He definitely had to make time for a personal life once all this was over. He had to make time for a trip to the hospital and his eye surgery. Time to recover. Time to regain his strength.

Time for Julia.

But he had to survive these next few minutes first.

Running an undercover sting wasn't exactly his forte. He flourished behind the scenes, after the fact. But knowing she was out there somewhere, watching over him, expecting the best from him, made the deception a little bit easier.

"Are you sure you don't want me there with you?" Julia's clear voice washed over him, taking away his dizziness and making him feel normal. Strong.

"Yes. If this gets ugly, I don't want you in the way." Knowing she was safely out of harm's way, serving only as another lookout, helped, too.

"But I feel so helpless just standing here watching you."

He grinned. "Now you can get a taste of what it was like for me when you were in Powers's office."

"But you suspected Powers would be our ally, didn't you? I doubt—"

"He's here." Josh's voice clipped over the line, cancelling out the personal conversation and getting them down to the business at hand.

"Everybody ready?" asked Mac.

"You bet." That was Josh.

"The tape's ready when you are." Mitch had that under control.

"I've got the main entrance covered." Ginny had come, too.

"Okay, Jules." Mac briefly turned his attention back to her. "Give me a visual of what's going on."

"I see Arnie Sanchez, suit, overcoat. He's with another man. Taller, a bit plump. The second man's carrying a black leather briefcase." Her calm, measured voice made it easy for him to turn and meet his guests. "They're coming from the east, just passing the leather shop now. About twenty paces from you."

Mac adjusted his dark glasses over his eyes, then tucked his hand inside the pocket of his black leather jacket and fingered the plastic evidence bag he'd brought with him.

"Ten paces." He waited for the exact moment. "Four."

"Gentlemen," Mac greeted them. "I'm glad you could make it."

"Mr. Taylor." He recognized Arnie Sanchez's voice from the numerous television reports that had aired earlier in the year during the kidnapping investigation. "I thought you were blind."

Tactless, but rich and desperate. "I got better."

"This is my lawyer, Marvin Lee."

Mac didn't consider shaking hands. "Shall we get down to business?"

He pulled out the evidence bag that held a thread from the black shirt he'd worn yesterday, and held it up, tauntingly, between two fingers.

Sanchez didn't waste any time. He knocked Mac's hand down, and Mac smiled as he stuffed the bag back into his pocket. "I paid very good money to have that evidence disappear, Mr. Taylor. I was not pleased when Marvin called and said the district attorney was introducing a second sample that could implicate me in my stepson's death. When your call came, it wasn't the one I expected."

Mac shrugged as if he didn't care about the D.A.'s case. "I'll bet not. I just wanted a piece of the action. After all, my career's been pretty well shot to hell. I might as well get something out of it."

"How much?"

"How much did you pay Joe Niederhaus?"

Sanchez's lawyer tried to hush him. "Arnie, don't say anything more."

Julia reported Sanchez's reaction. "He's waving him off. The man looks pretty impatient to me. Be careful."

Mac nodded, acknowledging her comment and goading Sanchez at the same time. This was the connection he needed Sanchez to make.

Arnie took the bait. "If I match Niederhaus's price, that fiber sample winds up in a fire or a vat of acid?"

"Done." So that smoky old I.A. bastard had been responsible for Jeff Ringlein's death. And Lawrence Munoz's. And in an indirect way, Wade Osterman's. "Did you pay him to kill me, too?"

"That was his idea." Sanchez was getting hot now. A trace of his old-world accent shaded his polished voice. "He thought you were getting too curious for your own good."

"He's done work for you before, hasn't he?"

Julia again. "His lawyer's pulling him back a step."

Mac could hear the heated whispers, but couldn't make out the words. He was going to lose them if he wasn't careful. But Sanchez had one more accusation to make. "This is sounding more like a setup than a business meeting. I'll make the same arrangements with you that I did with Niederhaus. A generous deposit will be funded into your retirement account. And then I don't want to hear from you again.''

Vindication sent a surge of victory through Mac's veins. He flipped out his badge. ''I'm a long way from retiring, Sanchez. You're under arrest for attempting to bribe a police officer.''

''You're on leave,'' the lawyer reminded him.

''A citizen's arrest, then.'' Mac pocketed his badge, and took a step forward, sensing Sanchez's retreat. ''Numerous counts of bribing a police officer and tampering with the judicial process. I'll get around to the fact you killed your stepson some other day.''

''Why you—''

''Arnie, don't make it worse.''

''Josh is right behind them.'' He could hear Julia's sigh of relief over the transmitter. His chest expanded with one of his own.

''Will my badge do, gentlemen?'' Josh took entirely too much pleasure in his work, thought Mac. He listened for the definitive rachet sound of handcuffs closing over Arnie Sanchez's wrists. ''Nice going, big brother.''

''Thanks.''

''I'm on my way up.'' Julia's breathless excitement skittered along his nerve endings. With his hand guiding him along the railing, he turned to his left and walked toward the ramp that led down to her lookout position to meet her halfway.

''Hold it right there, Taylor.''

''Mac?'' He heard the low, steady voice the same time Julia saw the man behind him. ''It's Eli Masterson.''

Mac halted in his tracks. He had a feeling…

''He's got a gun.''

Mac could hear Julia's breathless panic. ''Stay where you are,'' he warned her.

''But—''

"Stay put. Mitch, Ginny—find Niederhaus. He's got to be here somewhere."

And then he turned around. His first impression of Masterson was that he was an honest cop. Fair. He prayed his assumption was right.

"Do you know where your partner is?" asked Mac.

"He came in the back way to cut you off, in case you tried to escape. I hate to cuff a blind man, but in your case I'll make an exception. Funny how a man who can't find his way around the house can make himself disappear in a big city."

"I had help."

He heard the creak of leather, the solid clack of metal on metal. Eli had holstered his weapon and pulled out his handcuffs.

"I'll be interested in meeting them, too. But first, I want to know how a decent cop like you could sell out to Sanchez. Wrists, please."

"Why don't you ask your partner."

Julia spoke again. "Mac, don't let him take you. Tell him the truth. Tell him how Joe Niederhaus has been blackmailing other cops. How he used his I.A. connections to know which cops were in trouble and could be coerced into helping him."

"Hold it right there, lady."

Mac's blood turned to ice in his veins.

In his ear Mac heard the metallic double click of a bullet being loaded into the firing chamber of a semiautomatic gun.

Then he heard Joe Niederhaus's breathy voice whisper right into Julia's ear. "We've gotta find your boyfriend and convince him to turn himself in. Tell him to confess to taking the bribes and destroying all that evidence himself."

"Jules!"

Cold metal hit his wrist as Eli locked one arm into the cuffs. "Now, Taylor."

"Your partner is guilty of taking bribes. Arnie Sanchez just confirmed it on tape."

"That's desperation talking."

"He's holding my girlfriend hostage."

"He's bringing in your accomplice."

"With a gun to her head?" Mac was beyond reason now.

"I won't do it!" Julia grunted as if she'd stifled a yelp of pain.

"There!" Mac backed away from Eli and pointed over the railing. Julia was down there somewhere, and Niederhaus better hope to hell he didn't hurt her.

"If you resist arrest, Taylor..." Eli advanced.

Julia shouted. "He sees us."

"Joe?"

Taking advantage of Masterson's startled assessment of the situation, Mac swung out. The handcuffs had only been locked on to his right wrist, and the loose metal flew out and clipped Eli in the side of the head, knocking him to the ground.

"Jules!"

Mac whirled around and took off running. He plowed into someone, knocked them down, tripped over them and rolled. He apologized and cursed his handicap all at the same time. And then he was rolling down. Down the ramp. He rose to his hands and knees and crawled to the edge. If he could find the railing, he could orient himself. He could get down to the first level and help Julia.

Hell. She might not even be there anymore.

More people streamed by, blocking his path. But he crawled on, until his shoulder hit the plexiglas side beneath the railing. He pulled himself up onto his feet.

"Josh? Mitch? Ginny?"

"We're on it." That was Mitch.

"Can you see her?"

"No, I'm on the wrong level. I'm working my way down now."

"I'm coming." That was Josh. "Ginny has Sanchez. Where are you?"

"Bottom of the catwalk ramp. She was in the food court with Niederhaus."

"I'm there now," said Josh. "I don't see her."

"Find me," he commanded.

Mac stood in place, helplessly lost in a spinning world of noise and crowds and…

"Taylor!"

Mac swung around toward the voice. Apparently, Eli Masterson didn't appreciate being smacked in the head.

"Got ya, bro."

Josh snatched his arm the same moment Eli reached him. Josh was on the other cop in a heartbeat. "Back off."

"I'm doing my job," argued Eli. Josh was a big man, but Eli had the strength to shove him back a step into Mac.

Not to be outdone, Josh shoved back. "Your job is to bring in crooked cops. Start with your partner."

"Enough." Josh's defense, his absolute trust, made him proud as hell, but he didn't have time to thank him. "We have to find Julia."

And then in his ear he heard it. Mac squeezed his eyes shut and concentrated on the sound. He tuned out the harping noise of curious onlookers passing by. He tuned out the sounds of laughter and conversation from the food court below him. He tuned out Josh and Eli arguing over the evidence piled up against Joe. He even tuned out the sound of Julia's shallow, rapid breaths as Niederhaus pushed her along to some unknown destination.

Carnival music.

"The carousel." Mac clutched at the sleeve of Josh's coat. "He has her at the carousel."

"You coming?" Josh dared Eli.

"If you're wrong about this, I will have the badge of every one of you Taylors."

"Done." At this point, Mac would agree to anything.

He latched on to Josh's arm and followed his brother toward the sound. "Jules, can you hear me?"

"Yes." If his hearing hadn't been sharp, he would have missed her breathy reply.

"Don't make any sudden moves. We're coming for you, sweetheart."

"Okay."

"Who are you talking to?"

"Damn."

But it was too late. "Give that to me!"

He heard the struggle. He heard Julia scream. He heard the shouts of people scattering around them.

"Jules!"

Then he heard Joe Niederhaus's voice, loud and wild right in his ear. "You stay away from me, Taylor. Or your little sweet-assed girlfriend is gonna take it right in the head. You understand?"

Mac winced at the high-pitched squeal in his ear. He snatched the transmitter out of his ear. There was nothing to hear now but static.

Josh and Mitch were still connected, though.

"We've got more trouble," warned Josh. "Mall security spotted Niederhaus's gun. They're swarming down in the children's area."

"Evacuate it," Mac warned. "Get everyone out of there."

"Mitch is on it."

"Good." If Mitch Taylor couldn't take charge and control a potential riot, no one could. "But how the hell are we going to find her now?"

Niederhaus could simply pocket his gun and walk out, undetected, with Julia and the rest of the crowd.

"I'll circle around and come down by the escalators." Could Eli's offer be trusted? "I don't want anybody to get hurt. And I want to hear Joe's side of the story before I decide who I believe. He's been the best there is at a thankless job for over forty years."

Mac appreciated the honesty of Eli's request. "Maybe he finally decided he wanted some thanks."

"Maybe."

When Eli left, Josh and Mac hurried on down to the first level. The chaos he'd heard over Julia's microphone was nothing like the real thing. The movement of people. Nervous mothers shouting for their children. Children crying for their mothers. Mall security giving commands.

"And a desperate man with a gun in the middle of all this."

He could feel Josh's movements as he scanned the crowd. "You're the idea man, big brother. What do you want to do?"

Mac closed his eyes and thought of Julia's clear, patient voice, with just enough huskiness to its tone to make it irresistibly sexy. He thought of her clean, sweet scent and how she'd brought sunshine into his dark world.

His eyes popped open.

"Seal off all the ramps and stairwells. I want to funnel people onto the escalators."

"Okay." The hesitancy in Josh's voice was clear. "You've heard of a stampede?"

"There'll be a few seconds of shock first. That's all I need." He waited the few seconds it took for Josh to call the directions in to Mitch. "Now take me to the power relay grid."

Josh might not have Julia's patience, but after a few missteps and cuss words he followed Mac's directions to the letter.

"Now."

Josh threw the switch at Mac's direction, and suddenly the Independence Center Mall came grinding to a halt. Escalators became frozen steps. Elevators became suspended boxes. Music stopped. Games stopped. People stopped. Mac recognized the sudden blackout by the one stunned moment of absolute silence.

"Generators are kicking on," said Josh.

"Now. Get me there now."

It was a simple plan really. Throw everyone into a state of panic. But one man would panic more than anyone else.

Mac kept pace with Josh's running jog.

"I see him!" shouted Josh. "He's breaking through the crowd on the escalator now."

"Coming up toward us?"

"Going down."

"No!"

"I lost him."

And then plans didn't matter. Mac shoved his way into the crowd, with Josh a step behind. He didn't need to see to pull his way past people. They were all facing forward, climbing up the stairs. He was going down.

"Julia!"

"Mac!"

He was closer. He could hear her.

His foot left the hard metal stair and hit soft carpet.

"Jules!"

"Stay away!"

He could smell him now. Stale cigar smoke. Boozy breath.

Mac shifted directions. His world spun on its own axis,

made no sense. But it didn't matter. He wasn't functioning in the world like anyone else around him.

"Mac! Ow!" Julia's yelp of pain turned him to his right.

"Get your hands off her!"

Sunshine. Crisp autumn sunshine.

Mac sniffed the air as he shoved his way past people who had already been shoved aside.

He was close.

"Jules!"

The path cleared. Mac's momentum pitched him forward, but he caught himself with an extra step.

"That's far enough, Taylor."

Mac tilted his nose. Niederhaus was to his left. He tilted his face to the right. Julia. Clean. Sweet. Fresh. Frightened. Gutsy enough to be on her feet from the sound of her voice.

"Mac, don't let him hurt you."

Niederhaus inhaled a wheezy gasp of air into his lungs. "I know this place is swarming with cops. But I'm walking out of here, understand?"

"I don't think so."

"I'm the one with the gun, lab boy. I'm the real cop here. You're the one with the girlfriend who's gonna die."

"Jeff Ringlein and Wade Osterman died for you already, Niederhaus." Mac's voice was as cold and devoid of emotion as it had ever been. "I think that's enough."

And then he heard it. The shift of crepe soles, the steadying breath of air.

Mac threw himself at the rancid smell of Joe Niederhaus. He hit his soft belly and they went down with a thud as his gun went off.

Niederhaus was too out of shape and Mac was too angry for it to be much of a fight. Mac shook the gun from Joe's hand and turned him onto his stomach. He took the man's own handcuffs from his belt and anchored them around Niederhaus's wrists.

When he fell back onto his knees, Julia was there, hugging him from behind. He turned and gathered her into his arms, holding her close, running his sensitive fingers along every part of her he could reach without letting her go. "Are you all right? Did he hurt you?"

"I'm fine."

"But I heard you with him."

"Maybe a few bruises. They'll go away."

Mac smoothed back her hair and tried to look at her face. "Anyone else?"

"No." She covered his hands with her own. "His shot hit the carousel."

"I love you, Julia Dalton."

He gathered her close again, burying his nose in the sweet smell of her hair that had led him straight to her time and again.

It didn't bother him that she hadn't said the words back to him. For now it was enough to know that she was safe.

Chapter Thirteen

The next two weeks passed by in a blur for Julia.

Eli Masterson took over the sad duty of arresting his own partner, and a system-wide investigation of all of Joe Niederhaus's contacts ensued. A man with forty-plus years of experience on the police force knew a lot of people on both sides of the law, and as retirement approached he'd come up with a foolproof plan to walk away with a lot more than a gold watch.

Fortunately, Mac was no fool. By piecing the seemingly unconnected clues together, and testing his theory against the dismissed cases in Dwight Powers's office, he'd figured out Niederhaus's system. He'd taken money from criminals, and used the talents of cops in trouble with Internal Affairs—Jeff Ringlein's lab connection, Wade Osterman's muscle, countless others—to destroy cases that good cops and the district attorney's office had built against them.

Like Mac, she'd been interviewed time and again by the police, though she avoided contact with the media. She let Captain Mitch Taylor handle the public relations on this one. She was content to stand back and let others deal with the spotlight.

And she was out of a job again. Almost as soon as they

got home, Mac received a call from his doctor. They were ready for his lens transplant—if he was.

At the hospital there were other nurses who saw to his daily care. And his wonderful family was always there with him, if not en masse, then his mother or father, or a brother, his sister Jessie, or cousin Mitch. And then there were friends to support him. Fellow cops who wanted to thank him for getting the bad cop out of their hair. The chief of CSI who promised Mac a job would be waiting for him when, not if, his sight returned. Dwight Powers stopped by, and in his terse, cold way thanked Mac for making his job a lot easier.

Mac, uninterested in staying in his bed the entire recuperative period, visited Merle Banning every day. Julia did, too. There didn't seem to be enough ways she could thank the young detective for saving their lives.

She was searching for a lot of ways to keep busy.

She was slowly, intentionally, distancing herself from Mac. He had so much to look forward to, so many people who loved and needed him. He didn't seem to need her the way he had those few days they were on the run for their lives.

Why would he?

She was that plain Jane tomboy who'd lived across the street. The one with no common sense where men were concerned. The one a blind man thought was pretty.

But when Mac regained his sight…

Julia hugged her arms in front of her chest and looked out across the Kansas City skyline from the waiting room on the tenth floor of St. Luke's Hospital. Autumn had its grip on the city now. The leaves along the trees in the Plaza had turned from golds and reds to a dull brown and were ready to fall to the ground. The sky itself was a dingy gray at twilight.

And though she had prayed, in almost every waking

moment, for Mac's surgery to be a success, there was a tiny selfish part of her, where that Pandora's box around her heart used to be, that wanted things to stay the same. She didn't think she could stand it if Mac opened his eyes and a flash of disappointment crossed his face. He wouldn't be cruel to her, like Ray or Anthony. But she'd disappoint him all the same.

The possibility sat like a crushing weight deep in her heart.

"I flew in from the coast for this unveiling. What are you doing out here? You'll miss the whole show."

She turned her face to the dark-haired man who'd come up beside her. "Cole!"

Julia threw her arms around his neck and was swallowed up in a crushing bear hug by one of her favorite childhood friends. When he set her back on the floor, she stepped back and took a good look at him. Part of her couldn't help but feel better. He'd matured into a handsome man, taller and broader than she remembered, but with the same killer smile. The extra lines beside his eyes worried her a tad, but he was still her best buddy.

"When did you get here?"

"This morning."

She reached behind him and flicked the long ponytail that hung down his back. "And what's this?"

"Fifteen years of hard living." He captured her hand between both of his. "Don't change the subject. They're about to take off Mac's bandages. Don't you want to be there?"

Her gaze flitted out the window and back to Cole. She had no way to explain how torn she was, no way to make him understand the depths of her feelings for his brother, no way to tell him how badly she could be hurt.

"He's asking for you."

With that, something flip-flopped inside her heart. If Mac needed her, she couldn't stay away.

MAC KNEW THE instant Julia entered the room. It wasn't the sound of the door opening and closing, or the hushed welcomes and good wishes as his family greeted Cole.

It was sunshine. Pure and simple.

Mac breathed in deeply and felt a sense of calm sweep through him. Today was the day. He'd find out if the transplant was a success. One eye couldn't be saved, but maybe—maybe there'd be enough of a man left among all the scars for Julia to love.

"You ready, Mac?"

Mac liked Dr. Perulakhar. The man didn't mince words, and he knew his business. He'd made it clear from the beginning that the lens transplant wasn't a guaranteed success. And though the surgery had gone well, there was a possibility that his body could still reject or refuse to adapt to the new eye.

"I'm ready."

"I'll have to ask everyone to leave." His family lined up for hugs and handshakes and prayers and then filed out of the room.

"Wait." Mac reached out his hand. He couldn't do this alone. He needed Julia. Sight or no, he needed her.

"It's not customary to have an audience for this. Sometimes their reactions can affect a patient's recovery."

"She's a registered nurse."

"Very well."

His hand seemed to hover in the air for an eternity. Mac frowned. An unexpected sense of loss sabotaged his preparation for this last step of the operation. Had she left despite the doctor's approval?

"I'm here." Julia's fingers touched his. He turned his hand and gripped hers tight, pulling her to his side at the edge of the hospital bed. He breathed in deeply, calmly. All was right with his world again.

"I'm ready now."

"I'll just dim the lights."

Mac held his breath. He pumped his hand around Julia's, then held her with both hands.

The doctor cut the bandages from his eyes. "Keep them closed for a moment." He dabbed at his eyelid with a cool compress of some kind, did the kind of checking that doctors do. "All right. Open them slowly. Slowly."

Mac was terrified of what he might or might not see. But with Julia there beside him, he could face anything. With that thought in his heart, he opened his eyes.

"I see a light." His voice was breathless, hopeful. "Do you have dark hair, Dr. Perulakhar?"

"Black as pitch."

Mac squeezed his eyes shut and nearly wept. "I have one thing, more than any other, that I am dying to see."

He turned toward Julia's warmth, her heady scent, and opened his eyes again.

They were green. No, brown. No, a wonderful combination of green and gold.

"Hazel."

"Excuse me?" asked the doctor.

Mac's wide smile almost hurt his face. "She has hazel eyes."

"You can see me?" He saw her smile match his. "You can see me!" Julia released his hand and hugged him tight. "That's wonderful."

Mac swung his legs off the edge of the bed and pulled her right up between them. This was better. Much better. He buried his nose in the fresh scent of her soft brown hair.

The doctor, who understood the type of recovery his

patient needed at that moment, excused himself from the room.

Mac framed her face between his hands and drank in all the details with his miraculous eye. Her face was a delicate oval with flawless skin dotted with tan freckles that would keep her looking young her entire life. She had slightly tilted brows over wide, almond-shaped eyes. A straight, proud nose. A full, beautiful goddess's mouth with a dimple at one side.

And then because there was nothing more fitting to do, he kissed her. Gently, longingly, reminding himself of her taste and her shape and her touch while he memorized the sight of her as well.

But suddenly, that heaven of discovery was torn away from him.

In a breathless gulp of panic, Julia flattened her hands on his shoulders and pushed herself away. She would have left him entirely if he'd released his hold on her waist.

"You can see me?" The first time, the question had been full of joy, full of thanks. This time, he heard the old Julia's voice. The one who thought she wasn't pretty.

But he had a plan in mind for such a contingency. She might not believe the emotions of his heart. Yet. But the woman couldn't argue with logic.

"Jules. What do you find attractive about me?"

She frowned. "What?"

Mac smiled gently. He needed to push her a little, but not push her away. "I'm not fishing for compliments. I'm proving a point."

Her shoulders lifted in an confused shrug, and that bottom lip pouted out in a tempting curve as she searched for a thoughtful answer.

"Your mind. It's so powerful. That kind of power is sexy." Her magic fingers played nervously at his shoulders as she continued. "And your heart. I love how you stick with a thing until it's done. That determination to know the truth. And your devotion to your family. It shows your kindness, your caring. That's all attractive, I suppose."

Mac felt his skin heat beneath her flattering words. "Thank you." She'd given him more than he expected, more than he had hoped for. But he was making a point, so he continued. "My tight butt didn't even make the top three on your list."

"Mac." Julia blushed, and he couldn't resist lifting his fingers to her cheek to feel the rise in temperature there. "That's different—"

"How?" He had her now. He looked straight into those eyes of verdant gold and dared her to deny his logic. "How can you see me that way, but I'm not allowed to perceive you in the same way?"

She was floundering in self-doubt now. He could feel her desire to believe in the clutch of her fingers on his shirt.

"Why can't I love your mind? Your gentleness? Your stubborn, hardheaded determination to do what needs to be done, even when it's unpleasant or hard or dangerous. But because you believe in it, you do it."

"Mac—"

"I can tell you about your sexy hair and soft skin. And your body…" He exhaled deeply, steeling himself on this one. It was beyond his imagining for her to think her body was unattractive. "You're not a stick figure." He leaned back to look at her, and let the awe he felt shine through his eyes. "You have these wonderful curves for a man to hold, to fantasize about…" He stopped there, feeling his body heat with the fantasies he was already imagining.

He leaned forward then, cupped her chin in his hand and spoke gently. "And your eyes are more beautiful than I could have imagined."

"Mac—"

He should have noticed the change in her hold on him, how her hands had slipped behind his neck. How she'd pressed herself closer to the edge of the bed.

"Have I ever lied to you?"

"No."

"Then believe this." Cool, calm, rational Mac Taylor shut off his mind and spoke with his heart. "Your beauty is in here," he touched her forehead, "and here," he touched her heart.

"And here."

He brought his hand back and touched his own heart.

"I love you, Julia Dalton. But I want you to love yourself. I want you to see yourself the way your parents and friends do. The way I do. I want you— no, I need you— to believe that I love you for who you are."

She stood there, silent. Thinking. He'd wanted her to think, right? But it was so long, and she was so quiet, and he began to wonder if maybe logic wasn't the way for a man to declare his love to the woman he wanted to spend the rest of his life with.

"Do you really think I have pretty eyes?"

Mac laughed out loud with relief. "Out of all I said, that's what you heard?"

Julia started to snuggle and Mac started to hope. "I heard that…you love me. And I believe you. You're a man of honor, Mac. I don't think it's in you to lie."

His heart soared. But he caught himself before celebrating. This was so important to him. "So you believe me when I say you're beautiful?"

She climbed up into the bed beside him, hugging herself close, pressing all those wonderful curves against him. "To be honest, 'beautiful' may take some getting used to. But I do feel awfully sexy when you're around."

Mac grinned. He wrapped her in his arms and fell back

onto the bed with Julia draped on top of him. "I like sexy."

He kissed her then. Passionately. Earth-shakingly. He closed his eyes and savored the feel of her in his hands. He opened his eyes and drank in the sight of her subtle, wonderful beauty.

And then he realized he might have broken through her false image of herself, but he had yet to hear the one thing he needed to hear most.

He rolled onto his side, keeping her close, but reluctantly ending the kiss. "So—you think you could learn to love me?"

Julia circled her arms around his neck and gave him the earth goddess of all smiles. "You know, for a smart guy, I'm surprised you never figured it out."

"What?"

"That I've always loved you, Mac Taylor."

Epilogue

Three Months Later

Julia looked at her reflection in the full-length mirror and smoothed the sheer neckline of her ivory wedding gown. For just an instant she saw herself as she was fifteen years ago—a freckle-faced plain Jane with shiny braces and frizzy hair. The way she'd mistakenly viewed herself for so many years.

And then she saw herself the way Mac did.

The way she saw herself now.

Barbara Dalton put the last pin into the crown of ribbons and silk roses that adorned her daughter's hair. "What's that smug look all about?" she asked, hugging Julia from behind.

Julia covered her mother's hand where it rested on her shoulder and gave it a squeeze. "I'm glad you didn't let me quit, Mom. I wanted to run home and hide from the things that hurt me. But now I realize that facing them made me stronger."

Barbara adjusted the veil. "You'd have figured that out soon enough."

Matching pairs of hazel eyes met in the mirror. "Did

you know that Mac was my hero when you sent me to work for him?'' asked Julia.

Her mother's cheeks flushed. She and Martha Taylor made no bones about conspiring to help her and Mac get together, but Julia doubted she'd ever hear the whole story behind their motivation. "I knew something had happened when you were in high school. And that you always felt indebted to him. I thought that obligation would motivate you to stick by his side." Her mother's gaze sank to the floor. "I had no idea I was putting you in danger."

Julia turned and hugged her. "You aren't responsible for anything Joe Niederhaus did. Maybe by the time Dwight Powers gets done prosecuting him for bribery and conspiracy to commit murder and everything else he did, he'll understand how many people he's hurt." Julia pulled away, pinpointing her mother's gaze, making sure she understood that neither she nor Mac blamed her for those perilous days they'd survived on the run together. "I can never thank you enough for believing in me even when I didn't." Her face softened into a serene smile. "Thanks for raising me to be strong." Then she remembered the purpose of this day and her happiness bubbled up into full-blown laughter. "And thanks for moving across the street from the Taylors when I was in third grade."

Her mother's laughter matched her own. "I knew you'd trip up one of those Taylor boys, eventually."

"I always knew the one I wanted." Julia sobered at the love for Mac that filled her heart and made her soul complete. "I'm a lucky woman."

Barbara handed her her bouquet of pink and ivory roses. She blinked back the telltale tears that glistened in her eyes. "*He's* a lucky man."

Minutes later, Julia walked down the aisle of the small,

historic chapel. She clung tightly to her father's arm and smiled at the friends and family gathered to share this crisp winter afternoon.

Mitch Taylor, staunch leader of the Fourth Precinct, stood at the back of the church, cradling his brand new baby boy, Mitchell Taylor III, on his broad shoulder. Little Mitch had his mother's red hair and his father's bellowing voice. But Julia didn't mind the infant's tired cries. In moments, he quieted with a pint-sized yawn and fell asleep, secure in his father's arms. As secure in the love of a good Taylor man as she was.

She spotted Merle Banning's metal crutches leaning against a pew and stopped to take his hand and give it a heartfelt squeeze. Without his brave sacrifice, neither she nor Mac would be here. The pain in his rebuilt leg was evident in his deep green eyes, though he returned Julia's smile. Over the past few months, he'd become more than a welcome friend to the Taylors. He'd been adopted as an honorary brother into the family, and Mac had promised him a position on his forensic team if he was interested in the job when he returned to work.

Beside him sat his partner, fair-haired Ginny Taylor. Her husband, Brett, would be at the altar, standing up as Mac's best man.

Josh and his devilish grin came next. Julia prayed he'd been kind to Mac's truck, and that there'd be no surprises beyond a few tin cans and a Just Married sign. She crossed her fingers against her father's arm.

Then there was Gideon Taylor, and Mac's sister, Jessie.

Julia let her gaze drift to the front of the chapel. Cole stood to the left of the minister, looking handsome and mysterious in his black tuxedo. His smile softened the dangerous cut of his expression as he reached out for her bouquet.

''You're sure you're okay with this best man for the bride thing?'' Julia raised her eyebrows in an apologetic grimace.

But Cole had no qualms about his unusual role in the wedding. He kissed her cheek after Julia's father joined her mother in the front pew. ''I wouldn't be anywhere else today, old pal. You just make him happy, okay?''

''I'll do my best,'' she promised.

''Mind if *I* kiss the bride today?'' Mac's raspy voice sang along her nerves like a secret caress. He reached for her as he always had. Needing her. Wanting her. Loving her.

Julia laced her fingers through his and joined him at the altar. She looked up into his eyes, shining down on her like silver behind the gold rims of his glasses. She silently mourned the loss of his full vision, but sent up a prayer of thanks for the miracle that restored sight to his right eye. And the miracle of love that had brought them together.

''I love you, Mac.''

''I love you, Jules.''

He bent down and pressed his lips to hers, claiming what she had always longed to give him. Praising her and loving her and thanking her with the wonderful heaven of his kiss.

The minister cleared his throat. Twice. ''Shall we take care of business first?''

With a grudging reluctance that made her laugh, Mac stepped back. But he never released her hand. She never released his.

"By all means. I can't wait to make this woman my wife."

MARTHA TAYLOR pressed her hand to her mouth, and tried not to cry again as she watched her son bend down to kiss his new wife as they waltzed by. Imagine. Mac dancing. Enjoying life, no, loving life once more. "I never thought I'd see the day. Mac is so happy."

Barbara Dalton stood beside her friend with her hand pressed over *her* mouth, wondering if she'd ever seen her daughter so happy. "He's so romantic with her. So attentive."

"He's never loved anyone else."

"She's never loved anyone else."

Martha nodded, pleased with herself, pleased for their children. "I knew she was perfect for him."

"He's just the man she needed."

Martha and Barbara's shoulders lifted in unison. Their wistful sighs were drowned out by the laughter and music and conversation from the wedding reception around them. Then Martha's lips curved into a maternally satisfied smile. She stuck out her right hand. "Mission accomplished?"

Barbara laughed and shook her hand. "Mission accomplished. If we hadn't have helped, those two might never have found each other."

"They were destined to be together. We just gave them the opportunity they needed to discover that for themselves."

"Agreed. Now what?"

After a brief pause, an inexplicable twinkle of energy lit between the two mothers. That special gene that lay dormant until a woman reached a certain age of maturity and life experience sprang to life. In a shared heartbeat between friends, the plotting for their next project began. They smiled at each other and spoke as one.

"Grandbabies!"

* * * * *

Look for Julie Miller's
next Harlequin Intrigue,

THE DUKE'S COVERT MISSION,

part of the ongoing,
CARRADIGNE AMERICAN ROYALTY
series, in June 2002.

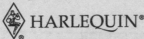

This Mother's Day
Give Your Mom
A Royal Treat

Win a fabulous one-week vacation in
Puerto Rico for you and your mother at
the luxurious Inter-Continental San Juan
Resort & Casino. The prize includes round
trip airfare for two, breakfast daily and a
mother and daughter day of beauty
at the beachfront hotel's spa.

INTER·CONTINENTAL
San Juan
RESORT & CASINO

Here's all you have to do:

Tell us in 100 words or less how your
mother helped with the romance in your
life. It may be a story about your engagement,
wedding or those boyfriends when you were
a teenager or any other romantic advice
from your mother. The entry will be judged
based on its originality, emotionally
compelling nature and sincerity.
See official rules on following page.

Send your entry to:
Mother's Day Contest

In Canada
P.O. Box 637
Fort Erie, Ontario
L2A 5X3

In U.S.A.
P.O. Box 9076
3010 Walden Ave.
Buffalo, NY
14269-9076

Or enter online at www.eHarlequin.com

PRROY

Two ways to enter:

• **Via The Internet:** Log on to the Harlequin romance website (www.eHarlequin.com) anytime beginning 12:01 a.m. E.S.T., January 1, 2002 through 11:59 p.m. E.S.T., April 1, 2002 and follow the directions displayed on-line to enter your name, address (including zip code), e-mail address and in 100 words or fewer, describe how your mother helped with the romance in your life.

• **Via Mail:** Handprint (or type) on an 8 1/2" x 11" plain piece of paper, your name, address (including zip code) and e-mail address (if you have one), and in 100 words or fewer, describe how your mother helped with the romance in your life. Mail your entry via first-class mail to: Harlequin Mother's Day Contest 2216, (in the U.S.) P.O. Box 9076, Buffalo, NY 14269-9076; (in Canada) P.O. Box 637, Fort Erie, Ontario, Canada L2A 5X3.

For eligibility, entries must be submitted either through a completed Internet transmission or postmarked no later than 11:59 p.m. E.S.T., April 1, 2002 (mail-in entries must be received by April 9, 2002). Limit one entry per person, household address and e-mail address. On-line and/or mailed entries received from persons residing in geographic areas in which entry is not permissible will be disqualified.

Entries will be judged by a panel of judges, consisting of members of the Harlequin editorial, marketing and public relations staff using the following criteria:
• Originality - 50%
• Emotional Appeal - 25%
• Sincerity - 25%

In the event of a tie, duplicate prizes will be awarded. Decisions of the judges are final.

Prize: A 6-night/7-day stay for two at the Inter-Continental San Juan Resort & Casino, including round-trip coach air transportation from gateway airport nearest winner's home (approximate retail value: $4,000). Prize includes breakfast daily and a mother and daughter day of beauty at the beachfront hotel's spa. Prize consists of only those items listed as part of the prize. Prize is valued in U.S. currency.

All entries become the property of Torstar Corp. and will not be returned. No responsibility is assumed for lost, late, illegible, incomplete, inaccurate, non-delivered or misdirected mail or misdirected e-mail, for technical, hardware or software failures of any kind, lost or unavailable network connections, or failed, incomplete, garbled or delayed computer transmission or any human error which may occur in the receipt or processing of the entries in this Contest.

Contest open only to residents of the U.S. (except Colorado) and Canada, who are 18 years of age or older and is void wherever prohibited by law; all applicable laws and regulations apply. Any litigation within the Province of Quebec respecting the conduct or organization of a publicity contest may be submitted to the Régie des alcools, des courses et des jeux for a ruling. Any litigation respecting the awarding of a prize may be submitted to the Régie des alcools, des courses et des jeux only for the purpose of helping the parties reach a settlement. Employees and immediate family members of Torstar Corp. and D.L. Blair, Inc., their affiliates, subsidiaries and all other agencies, entities and persons connected with the use, marketing or conduct of this Contest are not eligible to enter. Taxes on prize are the sole responsibility of winner. Acceptance of any prize offered constitutes permission to use winner's name, photograph or other likeness for the purposes of advertising, trade and promotion on behalf of Torstar Corp., its affiliates and subsidiaries without further compensation to the winner, unless prohibited by law.

Winner will be determined no later than April 15, 2002 and be notified by mail. Winner will be required to sign and return an Affidavit of Eligibility form within 15 days after winner notification. Non-compliance within that time period may result in disqualification and an alternate winner may be selected. Winner of trip must execute a Release of Liability prior to ticketing and must possess required travel documents (e.g. Passport, photo ID) where applicable. Travel must be completed within 12 months of selection and is subject to traveling companion completing and returning a Release of Liability prior to travel; and hotel and flight accommodations availability. Certain restrictions and blackout dates may apply. No substitution of prize permitted by winner. Torstar Corp. and D.L. Blair, Inc., their parents, affiliates, and subsidiaries are not responsible for errors in printing or electronic presentation of Contest, or entries. In the event of printing or other errors which may result in unintended prize values or duplication of prizes, all affected entries shall be null and void. If for any reason the Internet portion of the Contest is not capable of running as planned, including infection by computer virus, bugs, tampering, unauthorized intervention, fraud, technical failures, or any other causes beyond the control of Torstar Corp. which corrupt or affect the administration, secrecy, fairness, integrity or proper conduct of the Contest, Torstar Corp. reserves the right, at its sole discretion, to disqualify any individual who tampers with the entry process and to cancel, terminate, modify or suspend the Contest or the Internet portion thereof. In the event the Internet portion must be terminated a notice will be posted on the website and all entries received prior to termination will be judged in accordance with these rules. In the event of a dispute regarding an on-line entry, the entry will be deemed submitted by the authorized holder of the e-mail account submitted at the time of entry. Authorized account holder is defined as the natural person who is assigned to an e-mail address by an Internet access provider, on-line service provider or other organization that is responsible for arranging e-mail address for the domain associated with the submitted e-mail address. Torstar Corp. and/or D.L. Blair Inc. assumes no responsibility for any computer injury or damage related to or resulting from accessing and/or downloading any sweepstakes material. Rules are subject to any requirements/limitations imposed by the FCC. **Purchase or acceptance of a product offer does not improve your chances of winning.**

For winner's name (available after May 1, 2002), send a self-addressed, stamped envelope to: Harlequin Mother's Day Contest Winners 2216, P.O. Box 4200 Blair, NE 68009-4200 or you may access the eHarlequin.com Web site through June 3, 2002.

Contest sponsored by Torstar Corp., P.O. Box 9042, Buffalo, NY 14269-9042.